Night Cries

A Novel

Gary Copeland

Copyright © 2006 by Gary Copeland
Cover art and design by Fred Goldstein

ISBN: 1-4116-7706-4

All rights reserved. No part of this book may be reproduced or transmitted in any form or by any means, graphic, electronic, or mechanical, including photocopying, recording, taping, or by any information storage retrieval system known or yet to be invented, without the express written permission of the publisher, except by a reviewer who may quote brief passages in a review, magazine, newspaper, or broadcast.

For information address:
Gary Copeland at letters@garycopeland.ca

This is a work of fiction. Names, characters, events, places, corporations, and institutions in this novel are the product of the author's imagination, or, if real, are used fictitiously without any intent to describe their actual conduct. Any resemblance to actual events, locales or persons, living or dead, is entirely coincidental and not intended by the author.

Visit Gary Copeland on the World Wide Web at:
www.garycopeland.ca

Printed in the U.S.A.

Dedicated to my beautiful wife, Fiona, for her relentless belief and steadfast support in me during those long hours hammering away at the keyboard at a *blazing* 40 words per minute.

This book is for you.

I love you.

GC

NIGHT CRIES

1

WITH THE EXCEPTION of a van travelling several car lengths behind him, the canyon road was especially quiet. The drive to the top of Zion Point was usually a pleasant ten minutes, and Oliver Prescott was in no rush. He expected more traffic considering it was the fourth of July, and celebrations were already in full swing behind him in the small town of Paulo Brava. Just about any other night he would still be in his office at the Center, nursing a snifter of warm brandy, with Bach or Brahms playing softly in the background. But tonight was special. It was the celebration of his retirement: the end of the first chapter of his life, and the long awaited commencement of the next.

Elaine Prescott leaned across the passenger seat of the Porsche Carrera, nestling her head against her husband's shoulder. Oliver glanced out his window, taking in the beauty of the ocean, shimmering and glistening in the moonlight. He thought of his two beautiful daughters, Claire and Amanda. Claire would be out on the town tonight with her boyfriend, perhaps even watching the fiery display from Steve's boat in Paulo Brava harbor. How time flies, Oliver thought. Claire was already in her third year of university. A naturally gifted student, she'd made the dean's list two years in a row, determined to follow in her father's footsteps. Oliver knew several of her professors personally, and all agreed Claire was one of their brightest students. He thought of Amanda, and his heart pained. She had disappeared two years ago, without a trace, and despite the efforts of some of the finest law enforcement officers in the country, could not be found. She had simply vanished. For six long weeks the Prescott's once peaceful household had been transformed into a base camp for local and federal police agencies. Residential and business telephone lines had been tapped, background and association checks run on family, friends, professional acquaintances, and enemies. Sophisticated electronic equipment of various purposes had been set up to assist in every possible manner in an effort to monitor and track the progress of the search. A mobile command center had been posted at the entrance to the estate, manned around the clock. Only the Prescott family and those with on-premise security clearance were allowed access to and from the home. Both Oliver and Elaine knew the authorities had been excruciatingly thorough in their search for Amanda. Nothing, it seemed, had been overlooked, no stone left unturned. Yet, despite their best efforts, hours soon turned into days, days into weeks, and the many leads the investigators valiantly pursued into dead ends. Over time it became necessary to reduce the intensive manpower being exerted in the search, and the decision was made to pare down the investigation. The case, for all intent and purposes, had gone cold. Oliver could still recall the disappointed looks on the faces of the investigators who had been a part of their lives for weeks, now forced by their superiors to pack up their equipment and move on to other cases. They offered their prayers and apologies and wished them luck. As a family they had been drawn into an unending nightmare, relentless in its determination to test them beyond their limits, eventually forcing them to arrive at the unthinkable reality that for some unknown reason Amanda was gone, and in all probability, they would never see her again.

Waves charged into the shoreline, crashing violently over the rocks at the foot of the canyon, their rhythmic mantra barely audible above the soft whine of the Porsche and the occasional boom of the fireworks.

Elaine Prescott clutched the spoils of the night's affair in her arms. Oliver glanced at her in the mirror.

"Nice award," he said. "Care to read the inscription to me one more time?"

"Okay," Elaine replied. "If you insist."

"I do."

"The American Psychiatry Association Lifetime Achievement Award. Presented to Dr. Oliver Stanford Prescott in recognition of outstanding professional contribution to the field of Forensic Psychiatry." Elaine sighed. "Wow."

"That's all you have to say? *Wow?*" Oliver teased, putting his arm around her, watching the tight canyon road unwind before him, stealing a glance at her from the corner of his eye. He delighted in teasing her, leading her on, pretending he was serious when he was not. They had been married for twenty-six exhilarating years, and he still loved her with every ounce of his being.

Elaine turned in her seat. She had always been a beautiful woman, and the sparkle in her eyes told Oliver how much she still loved him.

"I'm so incredibly proud of you honey. I know how hard you've worked for this. All the hours you've put into building your practice, the sacrifices you've made."

"You mean *we've* made," Oliver said, weaving his fingers through her silky blond hair. "I couldn't have done it without your support. I hope you know that."

"I do," Elaine replied. "But this is your night, and I want you to enjoy every second of it. We should celebrate!"

"What did you have in mind?"

Elaine slipped her hand under his shirt. "I remember a time not so long ago when we would take a drive up this same canyon road and fool around until the sun came up."

"That was twenty-eight years and two kids ago, Elaine. And as I recall, The Amazing Mr. Winky and I were a little younger then."

"Really?" his wife said. "I have a feeling, given the proper motivation, Mr. Winky could probably be persuaded. Don't you?"

"Yes, if we don't end up in an accident before we get to the top," Oliver laughed. "Not that I necessarily *want* you to stop, you understand."

"Perfectly," Elaine said, loosening his tie.

The van slowly began to narrow its following distance. The driver turned on his high beams, and the powerful glare from the halogen lights reflecting in Oliver's rear view mirror illuminated the interior of the car with an incandescent pallor.

Oliver flipped the lever on the mirror to its night driving position, reducing the glare to a bright but manageable level.

"What's wrong?" Elaine said, sitting up in her seat.

"I'm not really sure. The van behind me suddenly accelerated and flashed on its high beams. To tell you the truth, I think its been following us since we left the awards ceremony."

"Can't you just pull over and let him pass?"

"Not here. This section of the road's too tight."

Oliver pressed down the accelerator. The Porsche responded immediately, speeding ahead towards the narrow turn to the top of Zion Point. Within seconds the van rounded the corner behind them, nosing closer still to the rear bumper, its powerful headlights bearing down like a wild beast stalking its prey. Oliver tapped his brake hard, then punched the accelerator. The front of the van nosed-dived, falling back. As though provoking a savage rage within the mechanical beast the van raced ahead, re-staking its claim on the tail of the Porsche. The driver pulled out, travelling alongside them, matching their speed, refusing to pass, narrowing the gap between the two vehicles, virtually touching Oliver's door.

"What the hell?" Oliver yelled, struggling with the steering wheel, desperately trying to maintain control of the car on the narrow gravel shoulder. In the distance, under the amber eye of a flashing caution light, orange crash pylons warned of the sharp turn ahead.

"I'm not going to make the turn! For God's sake Elaine, hold on!"

Oliver slammed his foot hard on the brake, and with a tremendous screech the Porsche screamed to a stop. The van sped past them up the canyon road, the glare from its high beams bouncing off the luminescent bands of the safety pylons, careening around the corner, tail lights peering back with malicious contempt, hugging the turn, tires squealing, disappearing from view.

"What in God's name was he thinking?" Oliver said. "That idiot could have gotten us both killed!" He slammed the car into gear. Loose sand and gravel spewed back from beneath squealing tires.

"Let it go Oliver," Elaine pleaded as Oliver raced up the canyon road after the van. "He could have had a thousand reasons for driving the way he did. Perhaps …"

"Damn it Elaine! He tried to run us off the road!"

"You don't know that for sure. Maybe his accelerator stuck, or he was distracted by a passenger and didn't realize what he was doing until it was too late, or …"

"Or maybe he's just a bloody fool. Either way, I'm going to find out."

Reaching the entrance to the parking area, the driver quickly reduced his speed, turning off his headlights. He drove to the end of the lot, parking the van adjacent to a service road at the foot of the town's radio broadcast tower, shutting off the engine. Quickly, he ran to the back of the vehicle, hurriedly opening the rear doors, retrieving a knapsack, slinging it over his shoulder. A gym bag lay in the corner of the van. He placed it on the ground by his feet. Slamming the doors shut, he picked up the gym bag, waiting, looking towards the entrance of the parking area. Within seconds the lights of the Porsche raced into view. He turned, jogging towards the entrance gate to the tower.

The gentle whine of the Porsche's engine trailed to a whisper as Oliver rounded the turn. In the commotion he managed to catch a glimpse of the fleeing vehicle: mottled gray, with reddish-brown or black trim. It bore no company logo, so it was likely a passenger van and not a commercial vehicle. Several cars were parked along the retaining wall of the canyon lookout. In the distance, exposed under the dim glow of a lamppost, stood the van.

Reaching the perimeter of the tower, the driver looked back along the path to be sure he had not been seen or followed. Satisfied, he dropped to his knees, opening the gym bag, removing a pair of heavy-duty bolt cutters. The surrounding fence was gated, protected against unauthorized access by heavy-gauge chain link wound around each post and secured with a padlock. Dispatching the heavy-duty lock, he unraveled the safety chains and slipped inside. Closing the gate behind him he replaced the chains so not to arouse the suspicion of a routine police patrol. He stayed in the shadows, running to the base of the tower. Looking up, he noticed the hatch leading to the main ladder was securely locked as well. He ascended the ladder and cut the lock, bracing the heavy metal door, lowering it slowly. With the knapsack

NIGHT CRIES

over his shoulder and the handles of the gym bag clenched in his teeth he ascended the narrow passageway to the transmission maintenance platform several hundred feet above. From the platform, an unobstructed sprawling view of Zion Canyon and Paulo Brava lay before him. Placing the bags on the serrated metal platform he opened the knapsack, removing a rifle stock fitted with a folding bipod, a reflection-resistant blue hued barrel, night scope, barrel silencer and two fully loaded clips. He could, if required, assemble the weapon in absolute darkness under any condition, recognizing the various components entirely by feel. However this talent would not be required tonight. This was not a professional operation.

This was personal.

Rummaging through the bag, he withdrew a cellular telephone and turned it on. The face of the phone cast an iridescent orange glow against the palm of his hand as it powered up. A single telephone number programmed into its memory flashed on the screen. Placing the phone at his feet he assembled the weapon, sliding the barrel into the rifle stock, inserting the clip, fitting the silencer and the night scope to the barrel, expanding the legs of the metal bipod from the stock. Intermittent bursts of brilliant color and spectacle unfolded before him in the night sky as he inspected the weapon. First, a thunderous crackle break, then a blue streak, then green glitter, then a red break, green again, then blue chrysanthemum, then another crackle break, and finally a multi-colored showering of red, white and blue. Looking down, he watched the Porsche back into a parking space on the opposite side of the lot from the van. Drawing back the rifle bolt, he chambered a round.

"I'm going to check out the van," Oliver said, turning off the car's headlights and ignition. Clicking open the glove box, he removed a cellular phone, programmed 9-1-1, and handed the phone to Elaine.

"If there's a problem, tell the police who you are. I've worked with every cop in town on one case or another over the years. Trust me, they won't waste any time getting here."

He removed his cell phone from his belt, checked to be sure it was on, then clipped it back in its plastic holster. "Sit tight. I'll be back in a few minutes."

"Don't go Oliver," Elaine pleaded. "This doesn't feel right." Before she finished speaking Oliver stepped out of the Porsche.

Oliver approached the van, tapping on the driver's window. No response. He thumped his fist twice against the door and stepped back. Still nothing. Cupping his hands against the window, he peered inside. Lamplight from above cast ghostly shadows within the interior, revealing several discarded coffee cups, empty packages of cigarettes scattered across the dashboard, a selection of CD's and a crushed sandwich wrapper. A folded map of the San Francisco Bay area lay open on the passenger seat. Oliver walked to the front of the van. The hood, still warm to the touch, crackled with the sound of hot metal cooling, contracting. The license plates, scratched and faded, were out of state - New Mexico.

The service road leading to the communications tower, flanked on either side by thickets of tall course grass, sloped up the hillside into the woods. Atop the structure a bright red light pulsed with metronomic precision, like the heartbeat of a monolithic metallic creature droning out a steady warning to the night, briefly illuminating the tree line every few seconds. Oliver walked halfway up the path, looking around. Whoever had been driving the van was long gone, he thought, and dismissed any further notion of locating the driver. Besides, Elaine was worried. The longer he thought about it the more he began to realize how foolish his actions must have seemed to her. Turning away, a glint of light caught his peripheral vision. A reflection. From somewhere on the tower? He looked up.

NIGHT CRIES

Saw nothing. He turned away from the tower and walked back to the Porsche.

From his perspective behind the lens Oliver's features took on a murky-green countenance. The gunman peered through the night vision scope, adjusting the weapons cheek piece, accounting for height, wind direction and pitch. The high-tech composite rifle had been custom designed, specifically modified to suit his individual shooting style, physical build and the most common posture he assumed when executing a hit. Removing the magazine from the weapon he inspected it for the third time. Satisfied, he locked it back in place and re-adjusted the scope, turning on the muzzle flash protection system to avoid any overlight which might otherwise impair accuracy. The tower itself presented another problem however, completely unexpected. Despite its heavy steel construction and deeply anchored concrete footings it swayed, perhaps by only three or four degrees - certainly not enough to affect a kill shot. When the opportunity presented itself this minor nuisance would be factored in. The scope, reliable to three hundred yards at starlight illumination or two hundred and fifty yards in absolute darkness would be perfect for target acquisition under the circumstances. It was equipped with a laser target module, which placed an infrared crosshair directly on the image tube surface of the scope. Brightness could be controlled with push buttons on its side. The gunman pressed the button *up*, and Oliver's features came into sharp fluorescent focus as he opened the car door.

"Well?"
"Nothing." Oliver placed the cellphone on the dashboard, glancing across the parking lot, surveying the broadcast tower and service road.

"Whoever was driving the van sure left it in a hurry. The engine's still hot."

"Maybe whoever owns it works up at the tower and was late for his shift. That's why they we're driving like mad. Just trying to get to work on time."

"Could be," Oliver replied, still preoccupied with the tower. "But I don't think anybody actually *works* there." He held his wife's hand. "I'm sorry if I frightened you honey."

"I really wish you hadn't done that Oliver," Elaine replied. "You scared me half to death! Who knows what could have happened to you? Whoever was driving that van may have had a gun, or been running from the police for all we know. Then where would we be? In a matter of seconds you'd be dead and I'd be a widow. I don't want that to happen to us Oliver. The world is full of dead heroes. I'd prefer you not be one of them."

"Of course. You're right," Oliver apologized. "From now on, I'll let the police chase the bad guys. Deal?"

"Promise?"

"Promise."

"Good," Elaine said, folding her arms, looking out the window. "Now please turn the car around. We can watch the rest of the fireworks from up here."

"I have a better idea," Oliver said, putting his arm around his wife, drawing her closer, kissing her gently on her forehead. "What do you say we head back home and set off a few fireworks of our own?"

Oliver's cellphone rang as he placed the key in the ignition.

"Dr. Prescott speaking."

"Beautiful night, isn't it Doctor? Sky's clear as a bell. Not a cloud for miles. And just look at those fireworks! Really something, aren't they? Bright and glittering... just exploding all over the place! It must cost a fortune to put on a show like that. What do you figure …

fifteen, twenty thousand bucks? I don't think I can recall a Fourth of July show quite as spectacular as this one for a long time. Can you?"

Oliver hesitated, struggling to place the caller's voice. "Who is this?"

"I'm not surprised you don't remember me. It's been a few years, but rest assured I've never forgotten you."

"Do you realize this is a private number?"

Elaine looked at him anxiously.

"Just listen to us, talking in circles," the caller continued, his voice jeering, contemptuous. "This is no way for old friends to get reacquainted."

"Old friends?"

"Perhaps skipping the formalities would be a good start. Yes, the more I think of it, addressing you professionally does seem a little too formal. How about Oliver? May I call you Oliver? I suppose we could get real familiar and I could call you Ollie, but that might be stepping over the line a little bit, don't you think? Before I forget, how are the wife and kids? What were their names again? Let me think for a minute. Oh yes. Now I remember. Your wife's name is Elaine, I believe. Quite a looker too, if you don't mind me saying. And there were two kids - both girls, right? Amanda and Claire. How are they doing? They must be just shooting right up there by now. Has Claire graduated from medical school yet?"

"Who the hell is this?"

The caller dismissed Oliver's angry tone. "I bet she's become quite a beauty too, just like her mother. Guess it's true what they say then. The proverbial apple never falls far from the tree. You're a pretty lucky guy Ollie. Gorgeous wife. Big house. Successful practice. Fancy-ass Porsche. And to top it off, another doctor in the family soon. You've just got life by the short and curlies, don't you? Pretty much everything a man could ask for." He paused. "Such a shame about Amanda though. Two years waiting, wondering. Is she alive? Is she dead? Not so much as a single phone call or a letter. But don't worry. She's quite alive. I've taken good care of her."

A sudden rush of adrenaline seized Oliver. His heart banged in his chest as though a thousand tiny scalpels were busily at work, cutting here, slicing there, leaving him gutted, speechless. Struggling to regain his senses, the callers words whirled in his mind.

"What did you just say?"

"Oh, Ollie *please!* No need to get yourself all worked up. Fair is fair, wouldn't you say? You stole my life. I took your daughter. Seems like a reasonable exchange to me. But don't worry. She's fine. Grown into a lovely young woman, actually. Hell of a lay, too."

"You son of a ..."

"Careful Ollie. Now you listen to me! You took me from *my* family. Had me locked away like an animal in a psychiatric hospital for five years. Five long, fucking years Ollie!"

Oliver's mind raced to recollect the voice on the end of the line. Conversations and faces from the past flashed lightening-quick through his mind as he struggled to identify the voice. In an instant, his memory became clear.

"Krebeck. Joseph Krebeck."

"Very good, Ollie. Nice to see you haven't lost your edge."

"I remember your case, but I thought you were dead. Killed in the hospital by another patient."

"It was an asylum, not a hospital. Let's be clear about that, shall we?"

"It was where you needed to be," Oliver said, recounting the details of Krebeck's case. "You murdered three hundred people Joseph. Every last one of them died at your hand, directly or indirectly. You had them bathe in gasoline and rub paraffin over their bodies, then gave them some poisoned concoction in the name of Holy

Communion and left them for dead. Then, while they lay writhing on the floor from the poison rushing through their bodies, *begging* you to help them, you left your church. You nailed the doors and windows shut and set the place on fire. Remember the trial, Joseph? The testimonies from the families of the victims who followed your prophecy? Your *failed* prophecy? You were not their saviour, Joseph. You were their murderer. Nothing more, nothing less. It was a callous slaughter of innocent and misguided souls, with you masquerading as Messiah."

"I didn't kill them. They gave themselves to a higher power. They sacrificed themselves … willingly."

"You lit the match."

"I *ascended* them!" Krebeck screamed. "They were desperate for spiritual sustenance, and I fed them. They were in a spiritual slumber, and I woke them."

"Where is Amanda, Joseph?"

Startled, Elaine looked at her husband. "What's going on?" she asked. "Who are you talking to? What's this about Amanda?"

Oliver motioned with his hand to quiet her. He couldn't speak now. He had to focus on Krebeck and the information he had about Amanda.

"Somewhere you'll never find her."

Oliver knew he had to keep Krebeck talking if he was to find out where the madman was hiding his daughter. Taking a deep breath, he steadied his voice.

"Give me back Amanda, Joseph. I'll give you anything you ask for. What is it you want? Money? Name your price and it's yours. I'm a very wealthy man. You know that. You have my word no one will ever know this conversation took place. Just bring my daughter back to me. Tonight. Back home where she belongs. If it's my professional help you need you have that too. But for God's sake let's talk about this. Face to face."

"You just don't get it, do you Ollie? You have absolutely nothing of value to offer me. But I have everything of value to you."

Time was running out. Every second ticked by like an eternity, each minute more precious than the last. He was losing ground. Krebeck had the control, had the power - had Amanda. Oliver felt as manipulated as a marionette under the control of a master puppeteer.

"Can't we talk about this? Come to an understanding? Where are you Joseph? Where are you now?"

"Watching you."

Oliver looked around the parking lot. A small crowd had gathered near the observation deck, watching the fireworks while their children played nearby. No one in the crowd was using a cellular phone, and the three telephone booths located at the entrance to the public washrooms lay vacant.

"What do you mean, watching me?"

"Look at your chest."

Oliver looked down. A red dot traveled slowly upward from his waist, tracing an invisible path, stopping over his heart. Though he had never seen an infrared beam from the scope of a high-powered rifle he knew intuitively what it was. He held his breath as the beam moved up his chest, then jumped to Elaine, inching up her neck, stopping in the middle of her forehead. She stared back, fixated on his conversation, innocently unaware of the bullet that lay between her and a single beam of light.

"Don't do this Joseph," Oliver pleaded. "Take me, not her. I'm begging you. For God's sake, please."

"For God's sake, Ollie? Just what the hell do you know about God?"

NIGHT CRIES

Got to keep him talking, distract him, Oliver thought. *A few seconds. That's all I need. Just give me a few more seconds!*

Keeping his body still, aware Krebeck was watching Elaine through the scope and not him, Oliver moved his hand to the ignition and turned the key. The engine started, thrumming quietly. He had only one option to save them both from certain death. Krebeck would kill Elaine. There was absolutely no doubt about that. In a matter of seconds he would pull the trigger, and Oliver would watch his wife's head explode before his very eyes.

"You asked me what I wanted Ollie," Krebeck said.

Placing his hand on the stick shift, Oliver slipped the car into gear, engaging the clutch.

"Yes, Joseph. Anything you want. It's yours."

"I want to see your expression."

"What expression would that be Joseph?" Bracing his foot over the gas pedal he stared at Elaine, watching the death dance of the tiny beam of light moving across her brow.

"I want to see the look on your face when I blow your wife's brains out."

Slamming the accelerator to the floor, the Porsche tore away from the parking spot as Krebeck fired, blowing out the passenger window.

"My face!" Elaine screamed.

"Get down!" Oliver yelled, throwing down the phone, grabbing her by the back of her neck, forcing her head down, trying to protect her from Krebeck's next bullet. Elaine brought her hand to her face. Drawing it back, she screamed. Blood covered her hands, running in rivulets from the bullet-torn gash. Her cheek hung open, split to the bone by the bullet.

"That explosion," Elaine cried. "I think I've been ... *shot!*"

"For God's sake, stay down!" Oliver yelled, wrestling with the steering wheel as parents ran for their children, pulling them from the path of the speeding car. The Porsche raced out of the parking lot, hurtling down the canyon road.

Cursing the sudden, unexpected sway of the tower, Krebeck refocused the nightscope on the spectral-green image rounding the turn. From his station on the tower his view was clear, unimpeded. Sharpening the focus of the scope, he zeroed in on the left rear tire and concentrated. This time there would be no opportunity for error. He had become one with the gentle sway of the tower, the momentum of the car, the balance of the weapon, and the firestorm seething within.

All factors were completely under control now.

Wind.

Trajectory.

Target acquisition.

Range.

Rage.

Two cars were on their way up the canyon road, which he approximated to be at least ten seconds away from the Porsche. Squeezing off a second round, the bullet found its mark, shredding the rear left tire. Through the scope he watched the car swerve violently to the left, then right, back to the left, to the right again, finally breaking through the wooden guardrail, launching off the cliff into the air, disappearing from view. Seconds later a spectacular orange fireball exploded up the side of the cliff from the shoreline below. Offertory tendrils of acrid gray smoke swirled skyward in silent, ritualistic procession, a stark contrast to the welcome glitter-dance of green, yellow, pink, red and white raining down from the sky.

The cars rounding the corner skidded to a stop as the Porsche broke through the barrier ahead of them. Panicked drivers and passengers leaped from their vehicles, swarming to the broken barricade in a vain

NIGHT CRIES

attempt to help the victims below, only to be pushed back by the rancid smoke pouring up from the twisted, burning wreckage.

No one would have heard a sound, Krebeck thought, unscrewing the silencer from the barrel, disassembling the weapon, returning each section to the knapsack. Turning off the phone, he placed it in the gymbag and picked up his belongings.

Descending the tower, he stopped periodically, careful not to draw attention to himself. Both the fireworks display and the commotion over the horrific crash provided substantial cover for his exit. Reaching the base of the tower, he walked down the service road to the van, threw the bags at the foot of the passenger seat, and drove out of the parking lot. Rounding the corner, he saw the frenzied commotion at the fractured barrier half a mile down the hill. Reaching the site of the crash he stopped, rolled down his window, and motioned to a young man with spiky hair and tattered jeans standing at the side of the road, his girlfriend beside him. The youth walked over to the van.

"What's going on?"

"You didn't see it? Geez! Some dude in a Porsche just did a half-pike off the cliff. Totally did himself in."

"Is anybody alive down there? Have the police been called?"

"Yeah, some guy called it in on his cell phone. No point though. Ain't no way anybody could have survived that drop. Gotta be almost three hundred feet to the bottom." The kid sighed. "Man, what a way to go."

"Yeah. Guess you never know when your ticket's gonna get punched."

"Damn straight."

In the distance, the faint sirens of emergency vehicles.

Krebeck rolled up his window, glancing in his mirror as he drove away, watching the smoke pour up the cliff. Continuing down the canyon road, he stopped on the narrow shoulder, giving the police cars and fire trucks plenty of room to pass.

Turning on the radio, he tuned in a jazz station and turned up the volume. Trumpets blared to the classic sound of Glen Miller's *'In the Mood'*.

He strummed his fingers to the beat. "Goodnight, Dr. Prescott," he said quietly. "Sweet dreams."

Reaching the foot of the canyon road he rounded the corner, disappearing into the night.

2

FIVE YEARS LATER

AT SEVENTEEN MINUTES past six, Claire closed the door behind her last patient of the night, Walter Pennimore. An accused child molester now living a life of seclusion, he had been released despite Claire's written objections to the parole board and granted his freedom. His reporting process required two sessions be spent weekly with Claire, during which time she delved into the most perverse corners of his mind, attempting to exorcise the demons that troubled him. Claire knew that they were not demons at all, but an irrational hunger that needed to be sated. The deliberate actions of a man-wolf, released into a wilderness of naïve prey.

Leaving the clinic after finishing a session with Walter always left Claire feeling uneasy. The underground parking lot, three levels deep, was accessible from the main elevator. High-tech security cameras monitored her every step from the lobby to the parking area. Claire's car was parked on Level Three, the lowest level. The security guards at the gated entrance to the lot always kept a faithful eye on the monitors, which added to her sense of protection, but the knowledge that Claire harbored about patients like Walter Pennimore and their unpredictable states of mind made her acutely aware of the monsters within the men. And all the video cameras and security guards in the world would be of no use to her if one of them should snap.

Watching the bright green numbers on the elevator display panel change as it descended to the third floor, Claire jingled her car keys nervously, twirling them in her hand, interlacing them between her fingers. As the elevator halted abruptly, her silver-brushed reflection dissolved with the separation of the doors.

The third floor was a restricted area, reserved for clinicians and doctors. Though well lit and electronically monitored, Claire was nevertheless afraid to be there alone. It bothered her that a building as secure as the Mendelson Clinic had never installed a key card system restricting access to the floor, despite her repeated requests. Anyone had simply to get on the main elevator, press the third floor button, and have immediate access to the staff parking area. Like Claire, many of the doctors working at Mendelson were psychiatrists dealing with high-risk patients. Though no doctor had ever been attacked at the clinic, Claire certainly did not want to be the first. She approached her car, disarming the alarm by pressing the remote control on her keychain. From the short distance a loud *chirp-chirp* sounded..

"Doctor Prescott?"

Startled, Claire wheeled around. Walter Pennimore stepped out from behind a black Lexus parked in the space adjacent to the elevator doors. At six feet, four inches he was a large man, with thin, slicked-back salt and pepper hair, thick black-rimmed glasses and a quiet but unsettling presence. Looming in front her, the bottle-thick lenses of his glasses did little to help his myopic condition. He squinted at Claire, his abnormally pale complexion jaundiced under the hard glow of the mustard-yellow ceiling lights. He held his crumpled jacket in his hands, fidgeting with it as he walked towards her. Claire gasped, stepping back, dropping her keys to the floor.

"Walter, what are you doing here? This area is off limits to patients."

"I know. I'm sorry if I startled you Doctor Prescott. I just wanted to tell you how thankful I am – you know, for spending so much time with me and all."

"That's alright Walter," Claire replied, trying not to let her welling inner fear speak for her. "I'm just doing my job, as your parole officer and the state board have asked me to do."

Claire looked past Pennimore to the panic alarm mounted on the wall beside the entrance to the elevator.

"I know that," Walter continued, shuffling closer. "But you're the only one I've ever been able to really talk to. All these years, the state kept sending me to different prison doctors. They'd just give me some more pills and send me on my way. Or I'd sit with a bunch of other guys in some room and listen to everybody else say how much better they're getting. Not me though. I just kept thinking about … getting out."

Claire kneeled down, picking up her keys, stepping cautiously to her left as she rose in an effort to create an escape route past Walter and to the security alarm.

"That's good Walter. Very good! You shouldn't be concerned about anyone else. Their situation is always going to be different than yours. What do *you* want to do Walter, now that you've been given the opportunity to live on your own again? Are you going to take personal responsibility for getting your life in order? You know I can only help you so far. The rest is up to you."

"I know. That's why I had to see you. I wasn't entirely honest with you tonight," Pennimore said, moving in front of Claire, blocking her path. He paced back and forth, agitated, wanting to speak, holding back.

"What do you mean?"

"I mean the demons – they're back."

"We've talked about this Walter. You know that's not true. There are no such thing as demons."

Walter grabbed his head violently with his hands. Shocked, Claire stepped back, dropping her keys for the second time.

"But there *are!*" he screamed, dropping his jacket to the floor. "They made me do those terrible things to those children." From his waistband protruded the handle of a handgun. Jesus! How did he get that into the building? He pulled out the weapon, pointing it to his head. "You've helped me so much Doctor Prescott…"

"Oh God, Walter. No!" Claire cried.

Sobbing, Pennimore fell to his knees, rocking back and forth like a child, the gun barrel rammed under his chin, thumbs squarely on the trigger.

"I can't take this anymore," he cried, tears washing down his face. "Every night I hear them. Taunting me. Telling me to find someone new. Someone for them."

Behind Pennimore the elevator door opened, and a security guard stepped out. Seeing his profile reflected in the rear window of the Lexus he drew his gun, leveling it at Walter.

"Drop the weapon!" he yelled nervously. "Put down the gun. *Now!*"

"I'm sorry Doctor Prescott," Walter continued, oblivious to the armed guard behind him, his attention fixed on Claire. "You're the only one who ever believed in me. I'll always be thankful for that."

"Of course I believe in you Walter," Claire replied. "I've always believed in you. But right now you need to do what the man says. Put down the gun. Talk to me."

NIGHT CRIES

The guard pressed the panic button beside the elevator door. A shrill alarm wailed throughout the parking garage.

"Are you deaf or just plain stupid?" the guard screamed. "Drop your weapon! Put your hands on top of your head!"

"I needed to see you Doctor Prescott," Walter cried. "One last time. There's something you need to know."

"What Walter? What do I need to know?"

Walter tried to speak, choking on his tears. "When I was in prison, I found out who you are."

"What do you mean Walter, who *I* am?"

"Your father was a doctor too, right? I heard he was the best. He was supposed to treat me, to make me better, but I got transferred to a halfway house instead. That's when I overheard the other guys talking. I know what really happened to him. I know about the accident."

"What do you mean Walter, what really happened?"

The security guard slowly moved forward, inching towards Walter. From the corner of his eye Pennimore watched him approach. Rising to his feet, he turned, firing twice. Claire screamed in horror as the guard reeled backward from the gunshots, slamming against the elevator, sliding down, his body slumping helplessly against the door, weapon in hand. Dark rivers ran from his shoulder and the center of his chest, streaming in ever-widening pools at his sides. His sunken eyes stared blindly at Claire, his body motionless.

"God Walter. What have you done? You've killed him!"

Pennimore turned back to her, placing the gun to his head.

"Your parents car crash wasn't an accident, Doctor Prescott. It was deliberate. They were murdered, and I know who did it."

Claire stared in numbed silence, speechless.

"I know it's none of my concern, but like I said before, you've been good to me - maybe the only person in this godforsaken world who ever has. And for that you should know the truth. I met a guy during my transfer. He told me what happened, about the accident - the car going over the cliff and all. Said he knew the guy who did it. That it was no accident. He told me his name. It's…"

The shots came from behind. Walter's mouth widened as the first bullet struck him in the leg, dropping him to the floor. The second found its mark in the middle of his back, crumpling him to the ground. Claire screamed, looking toward the elevator door. In his outstretched hand the security guard held his gun. His arm fell limply to the ground as his head lolled to the side. Drawing a final breath, he died.

Walter Pennimore lay face down on the floor of the garage, gagging, choking on the blood filling his lungs, crimson rivers trickling from the corners of his mouth.

Claire ran to him. "I'm so sorry Walter," she cried, holding him in her arms.

"His name…"

"Y-Yes Walter. His name. Tell me his name."

"*Kre..*"

"Kre … Kre what? I need to know. Tell me his name Walter … *please!*"

Too late, Walter rolled his head to the side and died in Claire's arms.

The security guards body slipped backward into the lift in a gentle arc as heavily armed emergency task force police officers burst through the elevator doors, rushing to Claire as she sat on the floor, Pennimore's dead body cradled in her arms.

Within minutes, the parking garage was filled with emergency personnel. Duty officers cordoned off the perimeter with ribbons of black and yellow tape which read, **CRIME SCENE DO NOT CROSS.** Police photographers snapped pictures of the parking lot from every possible angle. Investigators took notes as paramedics tended to Claire. The bodies of the two dead men were placed in black nylon bags, zipped closed, loaded onto stretchers, and wheeled to a waiting coroners van.

"Are you hurt, Doctor Prescott?" a voice said, kneeling beside her, draping a warm, comforting blanket around Claire.

"No. I'm fine, I think" Claire replied, pulling the wrap tightly around her neck.

"Are you sure you're okay?" the officer asked, helping her to her feet.

"A little shaky, but yes, I think so."

"I'm glad. My name is Maddox. If you don't mind I have some questions I'll need to ask you as soon as you feel up to answering them. You've been through quite a traumatic experience tonight. I'd rather you not leave here on your own. Perhaps one of my men could drive you home, unless of course there's someone you'd like us to call."

"Yes, please. Kelly ... Kelly Patterson?"

"Who is Kelly Patterson, Doctor Prescott?"

"My roommate. Yes ... I think I'd prefer Kelly take me home."

"No problem. Just give me her number and sit back. We'll locate her right away. If there's anything you need, just ask. My men will take care of it for you."

"Thank you."

As Maddox walked away he paused, then turned back to Claire. "I just wanted you to know I knew your father," he said. "I worked with him on a number of cases over the years when I was a detective coming up in the department. He was a good man. I reviewed the tape from the monitoring station in the lobby. This could have turned out a lot worse than it did. One of the guards saw what was happening and called it in. You kept your wits about you under very difficult circumstances, and that probably saved your life. If it helps to say, I think your father would be very proud of how you handled yourself here tonight."

"Thank you," Claire said.

The policeman withdrew a business card from his jacket pocket.

"If you ever need my help, don't hesitate to call."

"Thank you." Claire read the name on the card. "Inspector, are you aware my parents were killed several years ago?"

"Yes," Maddox answered. "A car crash, as I remember. I'm terribly sorry."

"Walter Pennimore spoke to me before he died," Claire continued. "He told me my parents death wasn't an accident. He said they were murdered, and that he knew who was responsible. Does the name 'Kre' mean anything to you?"

"*Kre?*"

"Yes. Walter died before giving me the full name. If my parents death wasn't an accident, as he claims, then I need to find out who is responsible .... who this *Kre* is. Will you help me do that?"

"Of course."

The paramedic returned with a wheelchair for Claire.

"Good. Then I'll call you tomorrow Inspector."

"That will be fine. Rest up tonight. Do your best to try to put this out of your mind, if you can."

NIGHT CRIES

3

CLAIRE TOSSED RESTLESSLY in her sleep, haunted once again by the dream.

The day of the accident. Languishing in the warm breeze of a midday summer sun, 'Pretty Lady' breaking through crests of gently rolling ocean swells. Swimming in the inviting Pacific waters. Charting a course back down the coastline to the Paulo Brava Yacht Club. The winding drive up Zion Canyon Road to watch the Fourth of July fireworks celebration from the top of the Point. Her boyfriend, Steve, recognizing the personalized licence plate of her parents Porsche, 'Dr. P', rounding the turn toward them from the top of the canyon road. Watching in numbed terror as the Porsche suddenly veers out of control, taking flight off the cliff. Disbelief giving way to unconsciously surrendered screams. Running to the broken guardrail, only to be thrown to the ground by the concussion and heat from the fiery explosion. Smoke and fire gorging up from the burning wreckage, belching plumes of putrid melting rubber, liquefied plastic and roasted metal high atop the side of the cliff. Police cars, fire trucks and ambulances racing up the canyon road, sirens blaring, lights flashing, screaming to a halt at the site of the splintered barrier. *Officers rushing to control the scene, busily cordoning off the area, keeping curious onlookers at bay. A second fireball exploding, raging up the side of the cliff from the inferno below. Paramedics who had begun to rappel over the crest of the cliff scrambling back for their own safety. A voice bellowing through fire engine loudspeakers. The incident commander, demanding all emergency personnel let the fire burn out before attempting another rescue. The frightening reality that below her parents lay dead or dying. She screams out in desperation as Steve holds her back. She breaks free, trying to climb down the jagged cliff face as Steve runs after her, grabbing her by the collar of her blouse, fighting to pull her back up the cliff before she should lose her footing and fall, but to no avail. Arms flailing, straining defiantly against his weakening grip, single-mindedly determined to save her parents, she tears free, particles of sand and gravel giving way beneath her. She is sliding down the broken slope now, out of control, riding a pebbled carpet of broken clay and tarmacadam, gaining speed with each passing second, her screams mute against the roar of the burning wreckage. Ahead, a slit at the edge of the cliff widens as though she is being drawn into the mouth of a malevolent demon, angrily awakened from its dormant state by the crash below. The precipice rushing toward her, opening its mouth to feed. She slides, faster still, to the edge of the cliff, scratching and clawing at the ground, rolling side to side, trying desperately to dig in, slow her descent, until at last she slides over the edge. A malevolent, hissing creature, born of roiling smoke and flickering flame welcomes her, then writhes in torment. Through smoke and fire the ethereal images of her mother and father rise, arms wide and welcoming, and she is no longer filled with terror but with serenity, tranquility. Catching her as she falls, they carry her on the air, soaring high above the burning wreckage, placing her gently on the edge of the cliff, their ghostly countenance vanishing as she looks towards the heavens. The smoke-serpent-fire thing rises above her once more, reborn from a thickening pool of fire and ash, looming over her, transformed into a greater, darker manifestation of its former self, as though denouncing the presence of the angels and the life forces in its midst. It attacks, engulfing her...*

Then, as always, she is awakened by the strain of the scream catching in her throat.

Claire bolted upright in bed, clutching the bedcovers with white-knuckled fists, her body shaking, bedsheets saturated with cold sweat, gasping for breath. Though five years had passed since her parents untimely death, the events of that evening remained as hauntingly vivid as though they had happened only yesterday.

Sitting on the edge of her bed in the darkness, she waited for her thundering heartbeat to slow. She picked up her housecoat from the chair by her bed, wrapping it tightly around her, and stared out the bedroom window. The bright glow of the moon had drawn a gossamer blanket over the sleeping inhabitants of the small town. In the distance, a silver ocean sighed and waned. She pondered the dream and its meaning. Over the years that had passed she sought the answer to the simplest question: *Why?* Why did her parents have to die so horrible a death, and why had she been commanded by fate to be there, at that specific moment in time? Had she been drawn to bear witness to her parents death by forces too powerful for her to comprehend? Was there a greater, higher purpose? So many years later the answers still eluded her.

Closing the window she returned to bed, tried to fall back to sleep, couldn't. On her nightstand the fluorescent-orange numbers on the face of the clock radio read two forty-five. Closing her eyes, she drew several deep breaths, exhaling slowly, calming herself.

It's only a dream, she told herself. *Just a dream.*

Minutes later, cocooned in the comforting warmth of her housecoat, she fell into a deep slumber.

The glaring numbers on the clock radio hung on her retina as she closed her eyes.

In her subconscious, they peered at her.

Eyes of fire ...

Rising through a column of smoke and ash.

* * *

The early morning aroma of fresh-brewed coffee filled Claire's bedroom. Her first waking thought was of the previous night's events, and of Walter Pennimore's frightening revelation.

That her parents death had *not* been an accident.

That most likely their killer was still out there.

And now he had a name …

"*Kre.*"

Kelly Patterson sat next to her, coffee cup in hand, waiting for her to awaken.

"How are you feeling kiddo?" she asked, placing the steaming cup on the bedside table.

Claire loosened the sheets around her and sat up. Kelly propped her pillows to make her more comfortable.

"Okay. What time is it?"

"8:25." She sighed. "Ever thought maybe you should have picked a safer profession, say bomb squad expert or something?"

"What do you mean?"

"At least you can look at the timer on a bomb and see when it's going to explode. People, on the other hand, are a whole different matter. Like this Pennimore guy."

Kelly handed Claire the morning paper. "Feel like breakfast?"

NIGHT CRIES

"Sure."

"Be ready in fifteen. There's a full pot of coffee downstairs if you want more. By the way, you made the headlines."

Claire opened the paper. The cover story recounted the events of the previous evening at the Mendelson Clinic. The reporter that had interviewed Inspector Maddox at the scene had written about the murder of the security guard at the hands of Walter Pennimore, as well as Maddox's account of Claire's heroic attempt to 'talk down the troubled man, at great risk to her own personal safety.' The photograph accompanying the story showed the draped body of Walter Pennimore being wheeled into the coroner's van. Three smaller pictures were inserted at the bottom of the main photograph: Walter Pennimore, Claire, and the murdered security guard, Clarence Demmings. Claire studied Demmings picture and bio. Married. Two small children; a girl eight, a boy ten. He had worked evenings at Mendelson for the last three months. His wife was pregnant with their third child, and his family needed the extra income to get by. Now she was alone, soon with three small children to care for. Clarence Demmings had given his life in an effort to save hers, yet she had known him only well enough to say hello and goodbye. Opening the drawer to her bedstand, she removed a small pair of sewing scissors and cut Clarence Demmings picture out of the newspaper. The picture was a standard photo-identification shot taken of Clarence in his security guard uniform. He was good-looking, black, in his mid-thirties, with kind eyes and a smile that belonged to a man satisfied with life. She placed the clipping beside the silver-framed photograph of her family. She had missed the opportunity to know Clarence Demmings in his lifetime. Now, she wanted to be sure she never forgot him.

The telephone rang, and Kelly answered the call. In her work as a literary agent she represented many authors, and the last few weeks had been extremely hectic. One of her authors, Martin Belgrade, had recently released a new book that was quickly climbing the charts.

Claire walked into the kitchen and sat at the table, nursing her coffee, listening to the one-sided conversation.

"Yes Martin, I'm very excited too. It's going to be quite a night. How many? We're expecting about one hundred, mostly industry types. I'll be sending a limousine to pick you up around 7:30. You don't have to worry about a thing. That's my job. Just have fun and be yourself. I'll see you around 8:00. Take care Martin. Bye for now."

Kelly hung up the phone.

"Sounds like you've got a busy night planned," Claire said.

"Yep. That was Martin Belgrade. My latest success story and one of the finest authors I've ever represented," Kelly replied proudly. "Plus, he's a genuinely nice guy. To tell you the absolute truth, if I wasn't representing him, you wouldn't be able to pry me off him with a crowbar. The man is totally hunkalicious."

"Single?"

"Oh yeah, and a *major* hottie. Tall. Blue eyes. Muscular. The athletic type. Wears a suit like a GQ model. And he's got big feet."

"Big feet?"

"Yeah, and you know what they say about guys with big feet."

"I hate to ask" Claire replied coyly.

"They wear big shoes, of course. What were *you* thinking?"

"Pervert."

Kelly laughed. "Hey, got any plans for tonight?"

"Not particularly. What did you have in mind?"

"Martin's book is going national tomorrow, so the publishing company is hosting an invitation-only party tonight. They're pulling out all the stops – first class all the way. It's at the Ambassador Room of the Harbor Plaza Hotel at 8:00. Very posh, very snooty. The full red-carpet treatment. Wine ... champagne ... caviar. The press will be covering the event. You wanna come?"

"I don't know ..."

"C'mon, Claire!" Kelly pleaded. "We both need a break. You and I work way too much. Besides, the dating scene of late has, as they say, rather sucked."

"I take it things didn't work out with Tom?"

"Tom Thornton? Absolute dweebsville. The only thing more exciting than being on a date with Tom is polishing my silverware. Besides, he lacks the main criteria I look for in a man."

"Big feet?"

"A pulse."

Claire laughed. "Alright, I'll go, but on one condition. If I feel like leaving early I will. No hassles. Okay?"

"No problem. I know you'll have a great time. Besides, Martin is a wonderful guy." Kelly smiled mischievously. "I'm sure the two of you will hit it off."

"Kelly Patterson! You're not trying to play matchmaker, are you?"

"Moi?" Kelly replied innocently.

"Yes, you!" Claire said. "I can get my own dates, thank you very much."

"Oh, please! Face it honey, the only guys you get to meet with any degree of regularity are through your work, and they're usually psychopaths. You might want to give some thought to raising the ol' expectations bar up a notch or two."

"I suppose you're right."

"Of course I'm right! I'm always right, dammit," Kelly chided. "That's why I get paid the big bucks. And I'm right about tonight too. You're going to come home from work early, get that gorgeous self of yours all dolled up, and come out with me for a night on the town. Who knows, you might even get lucky!"

"Kelly!"

"Okay then. *I* might even get lucky."

"You're incorrigible."

"Cute too. Don't forget cute."

Kelly gave Claire a light kiss on the cheek. "I gotta go. I'm already running late. I just wanted to wait until you woke up to be sure you were okay. I'm meeting with my assistant in an hour to review tonight's agenda. Are you going to the clinic today?"

"I haven't decided yet. I wanted to call police headquarters and speak to Inspector Maddox first."

"The cop from last night?"

"Yes."

"He told me you already gave him your statement."

"I did. But we have other matters to discuss relative to Walter Pennimore."

Kelly turned back as she headed out the door. "You *sure* you're gonna be okay?"

"Yes, I will. Thank you. You fuss over me way too much you know."

"Of course I do. That's what friends are for."

"You're the best," Claire said.

"You bet your ass I am!" Kelly laughed, bounding down the front steps to her car. "I'll see you later tonight."

Claire smiled. "I'll be there."

Upstairs in her bedroom, Claire retrieved Inspector Maddox's business card from her purse and called the number.

"Homicide. Maddox speaking."

"Inspector Maddox, this is Claire Prescott."

"I didn't expect to hear from you until later in the day, Dr. Prescott," Maddox replied. "I figured you'd need a lot of rest after last night."

NIGHT CRIES

"I appreciate your concern Inspector, but I need to see you. This morning, if possible."

"Sounds urgent."

"It is."

"If this is about last night, there's really no need for you to come down. Our investigation is pretty much wrapped up. The security cameras at the clinic caught the whole thing on tape."

"Do those cameras record audio as well as video?" Claire asked.

"No. Strictly video. Why?"

"Last night, before Pennimore was shot, he made a confession to me ... of sorts."

"Yes," Maddox replied. " I remember what you told me. Pennimore said your parents death wasn't an accident after all. That they were killed ... murdered." Maddox was silent for a moment, then spoke. "Look, Dr. Prescott, I know you're an expert in the field of forensic psychiatry, so I won't for one minute profess to have the same degree of knowledge or expertise on how the criminal mind works that you do. But from my experience, I do know this much. Walter Pennimore was, by all accounts, a very sick man. He'd been incarcerated or institutionalized most of his adult life. It stands to reason he may have wanted to shock you into believing something that simply was not true."

"Perhaps, but I don't think so Inspector. You said to me last night that you knew my father and that you respected his work."

"That's true. You won't find a senior officer in this department who didn't have the utmost respect for him."

"Then I'm asking you for a personal favor. In his memory, if you will."

"What do you want me to do?"

"Re-open the investigation into my parents death. Only this time, approach it as a homicide."

Maddox answered apprehensively. "That's quite a leap you're asking me to take Dr. Prescott - from accidental death to murder."

"I know, and I'd prefer to go over the details with you in person Inspector. Say, 11:00 am?"

"Under the circumstances, 11:00 would be fine."

4

BY TEN O'CLOCK Claire had showered, dressed, downed her third cup of coffee, put away the breakfast dishes and called her secretary to cancel her appointments. There would be no point in seeing patients today.

Though free of the fitful dreams that had haunted her throughout the night, she remained too preoccupied to concentrate on work. After her phone call to Inspector Maddox, she read and reread the newspaper article about the incident at Mendelson. With each additional reading, the compulsion to know the truth became the obsession of every thought, every waking moment. Soon, she found it difficult to concentrate on anything else.

In the remaining minutes of his tortured existence, Walter Pennimore's confession had succeeded in annihilating all that Claire had come to believe and accept about her parents death. The honesty in his voice as he spoke his dying words presented her with the possibility of a more frightening reality. One that drove a cold stake of torment through to the very marrow of her being.

Inspector Maddox had left specific instructions with his secretary to announce Claire as soon as she arrived. By eleven-thirty they had spent half an hour elaborating on Walter Pennimore, reviewing the man's case history for Maddox's report.

"I kept thinking about the name you gave me last night, '*Kre*', trying to make a connection for you Doctor. Unfortunately, it's just not ringing any bells. I'll tell you what I can do for you though. I'll run it through our computer and see if we get a hit, either as a partial or a full name. I can't promise you anything, but at least we can give it a try. If I find something I'll let you know. That's about the best I can do for now."

"I'd appreciate that Inspector."

"I gotta be honest with you though," Maddox continued. "If you believe Pennimore was telling you the truth, then it's not me you should be talking too. This is a case for the FBI. Their technology is much more sophisticated for searching this kind of information than what is available to us. Our search will be statewide. That's about it. But the boys at the Bureau can search federally. The problem is, I don't have an active investigation to work from - only speculation. And I'll bet my badge the Feds aren't about to invest their time and resources on a hunch, especially when they realize the only lead is coming from a guy who was under your care as a psych patient. Let's just say Pennimore's credibility would be somewhat ... suspect."

"I understand perfectly," Claire said, "but I'd appreciate it if you'd check it out for me nonetheless. Any information you find would be better than nothing."

"No problem. I'll do my best. But we're backlogged around here, and I've got a basket full of paperwork to get through first. Give me a few days. I'll make some inquiries and see what turns up. I wouldn't get my hopes up just yet. These things can take time."

"Thank you Inspector."

Maddox hesitated. "You're welcome."

NIGHT CRIES

Claire didn't need to rely on her professional abilities to see Maddox was trying to suppress his displeasure at the prospect of re-opening the investigation.

"You seem troubled Inspector. What's wrong?"

Maddox turned uncomfortably in his chair. "I took the liberty of pulling the jacket on your parents accident before you got here, and…"

"Yes?"

"Well, you may find the eyewitness statements made to police on the scene to be rather … unsettling."

"I don't understand."

Picking up the manila folder from his desk, he removed a copy of the occurrence report, handing it to Claire.

"It seems everyone we interviewed commented on the rapid speed at which your father left Zion Point. He was clearly not in control of the car. The general consensus has him swerving and driving recklessly as he left the parking lot, apparently engaged in an altercation of some sort with your mother. He almost struck one of the witnesses. Based upon these statements, it seems your parents may have been arguing, and when your father tore out of the parking area he lost the ability to control the car at high speed, after which the accident ensued."

Claire knew this behavior was entirely out of character for her father. She also knew he had far more self-control than to ever have put her mother in such peril. He would have pulled the car over to the side of the road and they would have talked if there had been a disagreement. More likely, he wouldn't have left the parking lot until the disagreement had been resolved.

"Investigators on the scene had been at a loss to explain mechanical failure as the reason for the accident," Maddox continued. "As you know, the car was winched from the bottom of the cliff and taken to the vehicular investigation center where it was examined by a team of police *and* insurance investigators. The braking, steering and acceleration mechanisms – what was left of them anyway – checked out. The skid marks where the car left the road served as a vulcanized fingerprint, indicating it jerked suddenly, violently, as if avoiding something in its path. Perhaps a small animal darted in front of the car, and your father took his eyes off the road for a split second. Maybe he looked up at that very moment and tried to avoid hitting the creature, pre-occupied with the argument, too late to correct the vehicle before it went off the cliff. Fragments of tire debris were found both on the road and in the gravel shoulder near the top of the cliff. The insurance investigators matched it to the melted rubber on the tires of the Porsche. An animal in the road is just one theory. The accident could also have been caused by something as simple as the car running over a nail or any sharp object which could have pierced the tire, causing a blow out and sending it over the cliff. Tragic? Yes ma'am. Unfortunate? Absolutely. But an accident nonetheless."

Claire passed the report back to Maddox. "I'd still appreciate you're keeping an open mind Inspector. At least until we can find out if your computers can tell us more than we know right now."

"As you wish."

"Thank you Inspector. I'll be in touch."

At one o'clock Kelly called to check in and tell Claire her name had been placed on the guest list for the party later that evening.

"Wear your black dress. You'll knock 'em dead," Kelly insisted.

Her excitement over the coming nights festivities was infectious, and Claire began to look forward to the party.

"You sure it's not too dressy?"

"Honey, if I had a body like yours, I'd be wearing that dress seven days a week."

NIGHT CRIES

Even before Kelly's phone call, Claire had tried on several dresses she thought suitable for the evening. Kelly's choice had also been her favorite. A full-length black gown, side-slit with a deep plunging neckline and spaghetti shoulder straps. The dress fell gracefully over her delicate frame, accentuating her long shapely legs and the fullness of her breasts. It had been one of Steve's favorites, and whenever she wore it he had always told her how beautiful she looked.

"Okay, you've convinced me," Claire said. "One black evening gown coming up. By the way, where will I meet you tonight?"

"I'll be in the lobby of the Ambassador Room around seven forty-five. Your VIP pass is in my name. I'll have to sign you in, so meet me there. God, I'm looking forward to this. We're gonna have an absolute blast! Just think about it – You, me, and a room full of the most eligible testosterone in town. What more could a girl ask for?"

"You're something else," Claire laughed. "You really are."

By seven o'clock Claire left her apartment for the Harbor Plaza. She had, for the time being, managed to put Walter Pennimore out of her mind.

Backing out of the driveway, she drove to the end of the quiet street, turning left at the intersection. Local boys were playing an intense game of basketball under dusky street lamps, while their girlfriends chatted on the sidelines. Claire remembered how she and Amanda passed countless hours in a similar playground on the other side of town where, as children, they played hopscotch or softball or little league soccer while their parents watched, cheering them on from the bleachers. The evening was beautiful, and the ocean breeze wafting in from the Pacific possessed a serenity Claire found relaxing and purifying. The muddy-gray storm clouds that had threatened rain in late afternoon had long since dissipated. Twilight now dressed the sky with the radiant black hue of fine Japanese silk, while wisps of silver cloud stirred delicately, as though born on the breath of angels.

The Harbor Plaza Hotel was awash in glamour when Claire arrived promptly at seven-thirty. Police officers on point duty directed traffic. Stretch limousines lined both sides of the street. Parking valets, attired in black tie and white glove, greeted guests as they reached the main entrance. Lovely young models in formal dress escorted VIP's to the front door of the hotel. Miniature lights adorned each tree and shrub, glittering and sparkling. Commercial spotlights were stationed on the boulevard, their lanterns swinging randomly. Pillars of brilliant white light mingled in the night sky, dancing playfully across the heavens.

Upon Claire's arrival, a handsome young man opened her door, extending a gloved hand.

"Welcome to the Harbor Plaza ma'am. May I escort you inside?"

"Yes. Thank you," Claire replied.

Walking through the hotel lobby, he handed her keys to the concierge. "Just give the front desk this ticket before you leave," the attendant said courteously, handing her a slip of paper. "My staff will have your car brought around for you. Enjoy your evening."

"Thank you," Claire replied. "Perhaps you can help me. I'm meeting a friend in the Ambassador Room."

"The Janus Publishing party," the young man said, pointing to his left. "Straight down the hallway, past the boutiques. When you reach the fountain, turn right. The Ambassador Room is straight ahead." He winked. "Believe me, you won't miss it."

The concierge was right. As Claire approached the fountain and turned the corner the receiving area of the Ambassador Room was ablaze in camera flashes. The entire wing of the hotel had been themed to the night's event. Large gold-framed portraits of Janus' most successful authors and their biographies hung from the walls,

NIGHT CRIES

running the length of the reception hall. A gift table bearing copies of their latest releases stood outside the main entrance to the room. Reporters busily conducted interviews with several of the more familiar faces. Janus was a heavy promoter, and the best-sellers in their talent pool were fortunate enough to receive national radio, print and trade exposure, even television appearances on Oprah, The Tonight Show, CNN and Larry King Live. Hotel serving staff gingerly eased their way through the guests, deftly balancing flutes of champagne and plates of caviar on silver platters. A classical string quartet played softly in the corner, barely audible amidst the cacophony of conversation surrounding them.

"Hey, Claire!" Kelly's unmistakable voice climbed above the boisterous chatter of the room as she skillfully negotiated her way through the crowd, champagne glass hoisted high above her head. "Glad you could make it, kiddo!"

"Me too. But are you *sure* it's okay for me to be here? I feel a little out of place, not being in the publishing industry."

Giving her a welcoming hug, Kelly took her by the hand. "Don't be silly. You're here as my guest. And let's not forget, I represent half the people in this room." In a snooty, aristocratic voice she said, "Truth be told, I'm quite the little powerhouse in this biz." She handed Claire her guest pass. "Listen, hon. I've got to do a little business - schmooze, say hello to a few old friends, press some flesh - that sort of thing. Just show your pass at the door. We're seated near the stage - table two I think. Old man Janus wants to make a few formal presentations before dinner. You know, the usual corporate stuff. After that… we *par-tay!* In the meantime, relax. Have a drink or three. Mingle. Meet a few normal people for a change! They won't bite. At least not most of them. I'll meet you inside soon – say, twenty minutes?"

"Sounds good." Claire said, glancing around the room. "Is Martin here yet?"

"Uh-huh," Kelly replied, sipping her champagne. "His limo dropped him off ten minutes ago. I'll introduce you to him the first chance I get, but for now, shoo! Have fun! I'll talk to you in a bit."

"Kelly... oh Kel-ly." Kelly turned around to the singsong call of her name. A beautiful, buxom blonde in her mid-fifties was walking toward them from across the room, a white miniature poodle sporting a red diamond-studded collar cradled in her arms. Kelly smiled and waved. She turned back to Claire.

"That's Penelope Nash and her dog, Ladybug. Nasty little thing'll bite your hand off. The dog, I mean. She wrote a diet and exercise book called *'Fifty and STILL Fabulous!'* I represented her for the deal. Good thing I did. Turned out to be a national best seller. Made her gazillions."

Penelope Nash sauntered through the crowd, turning heads in her red stiletto heels and skin-tight white latex bodysuit.

"Damn! Looks like someone bought new toys for the poolboy. Look at the size of those hooters!" Kelly winked. "Probably should have called the book, *'Thanks for the Mammories!'*" Claire laughed. "Penelope darling! Ladybug!" Kelly said as she turned away. "So nice to see you!"

Claire accepted a glass of champagne from a passing hostess and wandered back to the reception area, casually reading the biographies below the pictures of the authors and special guests. Finally, she came to Martin Belgrade's photo. Unlike the glamour shots many of the celebrities opted for, Martin's picture had not been re-touched. It was a simple shot. Sitting on the grass, wearing a blue denim shirt, beige cable-knit sweater and blue jeans. Beside him lay a beautiful golden retriever. Claire read the bio below the photograph aloud. "Martin Belgrade is the author of several award-winning novels, including *The*

NIGHT CRIES

Devil's Wrath, Soul Takers, and *An Unholy Path.* His latest novel, *Heaven on Earth,* is a New York Times bestseller. Mr. Belgrade resides in Santa Clara, California with his best friend and lifelong companion, Maggy (as pictured)."

The photograph brought a smile to her face. Martin Belgrade did not seem the least bit influenced by the trappings of his celebrity. In fact, there appeared to be nothing pretentious about him. He was handsome. His most compelling feature was his eyes – striking, ice blue eyes that seemed not to look at her, but through her. His face was strong, modelesque, his hair wavy, sandy blond. He was young, athletic-looking, in his mid thirties, and exuded a calm demeanor which transcended the lens. With his arm draped over the dog and his warm smile, he and Maggy appeared to be perfect company for each other. There was obviously much more to Martin Belgrade than she could gather from a mere photograph, yet there was something about him that intrigued her, made her want to know more. She would meet him later, as Kelly had said. Then she would know for certain if he were anything like the man that she had spent the last few minutes analyzing.

"Not exactly a centerfold pin-up, is he? But the dog has all kinds of potential. Wouldn't you agree?"

Startled, Claire turned. Several feet behind her stood a distinguished looking gentleman in a black tuxedo, hands folded neatly in front of him.

"Perhaps," Claire replied, catching her breath. "But that's a purely subjective opinion, isn't it?"

"Meaning?"

"That beauty is in the eye of the beholder."

"Just my luck, you *are* referring to the dog. Hi, I'm Martin Belgrade. The photogenic one in the picture is Maggy."

"Claire Prescott. It's a pleasure to meet you, Mr. Belgrade."

"Please, call me Martin."

Claire smiled. Kelly was right, she thought. *He's even better looking in person.*

"So, Ms. Prescott. What brings you here?"

"A friend of mine, and by association, a friend of yours. Kelly Patterson. Your agent, my roommate."

"How did you know Kelly was my agent?" Martin asked.

"She talks about you all the time. She thinks very highly of your work."

"Of *my* work?" Martin joked. "You sure we're talking about the same Kelly Patterson?" he said, raising his hand shoulder-high. "Five-foot nothing? Kind of ballistic personality? Reddish-blonde hair? *That* Kelly Patterson?"

"The one and only," Claire laughed.

"I'll have to thank her for the compliment when I see her later." Martin paused. "Incidentally, I guess I should apologize for kind of sneaking up on you like that. I'm really sorry if I startled you."

"That's alright," Claire replied. "I was reading your bio and daydreaming. I guess you caught me off guard."

"I'm that interesting, huh? Kind of explains why the main girl in my life is a dog, doesn't it?"

Claire laughed. "I didn't mean it *that* way. Actually, I found it rather intriguing."

"Really? How so?"

"The titles for your books, for example. *The Devil's Wrath, Soul Takers, An Unholy Path, Heaven on Earth.* They all sound similar. What exactly do you write about?"

"Cults, mostly. Or more specifically, the nature of them."

"As in demonic cults? Satan worshippers, that sort of thing?"

"In some instances, yes," Martin replied. "But mostly I research and write about doomsday cults, and the hold their leaders can have on their followers. In many cases, a hold strong enough to make them kill for the cult, or be killed defending it."

"Sounds frightening."

"It can be. But hey ... mind if I change the subject, just for a minute? First things first. Are you planning on staying for the evening?"

"Truthfully, I wasn't sure if I should. I kind of feel a little out of place here. I don't know anyone besides Kelly."

"Well then, I guess we've solved that problem."

"How so?"

"Now you know me! Truthfully, I was going to bring Maggy, but she looks terrible in a dress. Exceptionally hairy legs, and her table manners are truly embarrassing."

"Is that so?" Claire laughed.

"Swear to God," Martin nodded, crossing his heart. "So, if you're not here with anyone, perhaps you would consider doing me the honor of joining me at my table for dinner this evening?"

Say yes, you idiot! This guy is gorgeous and obviously wants to get to know you better. So take your foot out of your mouth and speak already!

"Thank you Martin," she replied. "I think I'd like that very much."

"Wonderful!" Martin said, taking her arm in his. "What do you say we get this party started?"

The Ambassador Room was truly stunning. It had been decorated like a fantasy dreamland, themed after one of Janus' most successful romance novels. Claire was awestruck. Massive ice sculptures, some six and eight feet tall, adorned heavy crystal pedestals throughout the room. A horse-drawn carriage on one. A prancing unicorn on another. A beautiful fairy-tale princess on a third. A gentle rolling fog generated by dry ice misters swirled at their feet as they crossed the room. The subdued lighting lent a mysterious glow to the mist, complimenting the total effect. In the center of the room an immense tree appeared to be growing out of the floor and through the ceiling, its trunk, limbs and branches painted metallic silver, each leaf gold brushed. Blue and white sashes of entwined silk had been draped together and hung from the ceiling, creating a sky of brilliant color. The serving staff wore costumes, representing many of the characters from the book.

"Wow," Claire said. "This is absolutely the most beautiful room I've ever seen."

"Me too," Martin said. "Looks like old man Janus really outdid himself this time."

"Are all your company parties as elaborate as this?"

"Truthfully, yes. But I have to say this one really takes the cake."

A shining knight walked past, a rack of bells in his arms, chiming them slowly in succession. *Ding! Dang! Dong!* "Hear ye, hear ye, lords and ladies," the knight announced diplomatically. "Dinner is now served." Slowly, the guests made their way to their tables.

Walking across the room, Martin said, "Claire, would you mind if I paid you a compliment?"

"No Martin, of course not."

"If you will allow me to say so, you are definitely *the* most beautiful woman in this room tonight."

Claire blushed. "What a sweet thing to say. I'm flattered."

"I wouldn't say it if I didn't mean it," Martin replied, pulling back her chair.

As the evening progressed they enjoyed a wonderful meal and even better conversation. Martin received a standing ovation and accepted an award for the success of *Heaven on Earth,* his fourth consecutive bestseller. After the speeches, Kelly stopped by to congratulate Martin

NIGHT CRIES

personally, though Claire knew her underlying motive was really to find out how the two of them were getting along.

"Well Martin, I see you've met the good doctor. Guess that saves me the trouble of making the introductions."

"Actually, I didn't know Claire was a doctor," Martin replied. "She hadn't told me."

"Second generation, as a matter of fact," Kelly bragged.

"Then I'd say you've been holding out on me."

"How's that?"

"You never told me your roommate was a doctor, and a beautiful one at that."

"What? Kelly sighed. "And have your affections distracted from me? Why would I do a foolish thing like that? Besides, I know you lay awake at night, dreaming up steamy fantasies about me."

Claire laughed. "Maybe I should leave you two alone."

"God, no!" Martin said. "I wouldn't be safe for a second. Besides, I suspect she just wants me for my body."

"Who wouldn't!" Kelly teased. "Anytime, anywhere. Actually, right now's pretty good for me. Your room or mine?"

"Very funny" Claire said.

"Okay, okay," Kelly quipped. "I can tell when it's my cue to split. I'll leave you two alone to get better acquainted." She leaned between them, whispering in Martin's ear loud enough for Claire to hear. "Suite 1422. I'll leave the key under the mat. See you around 11:00?"

"*Goodnight, Kelly!*" Claire teased.

"Goodnight kiddo," she laughed. "I'll see you later."

Martin turned to Claire. "I have an idea. It's a beautiful night. Why don't we take a stroll along the boardwalk?"

"Sounds marvelous. But wait a second. I have to go to the lobby. I'll be right back, okay?"

"Okay ... I think," Martin said, puzzled.

Claire returned, holding a copy of Martin's book in her hand.

"Mr. Belgrade, sir" she smiled. "Would you autograph my book for me. *Please?*"

"Sure," Martin laughed. "But it'll cost you."

"*Cost me?* ... How much?"

"Once along the boardwalk, and twice around the block."

Martin signed Claire's book. She read the inscription and laughed:

For Claire, who's table manners are definitely better than Maggy's.
Martin Belgrade

Below his name, he had written his phone number.

Away from the harsh lights of the hotel, the evening sky teemed with a canopy of bright stars as they walked to the symphony of the surf along the boardwalk. At its end, a fishing pier jutted out over the water. A single yellow lamp cast a phosphorescent glow upon the water. They strolled to the end of the dock, staring out over the glistening waters of Paulo Brava Bay, watching the evening tide roll in.

"Martin," Claire said.

"Yes?"

"When we first met earlier tonight I was asking you about your books. You mentioned you write about cults."

"Yes, I do. Why?"

"Of all the things to write about, why such a fascination with cults? Especially ... how did you put it, destructive cults."

"It's a long story actually," Martin replied. "Cults are sort of an obsession with me. For all the wrong reasons, I'm afraid. Five years ago, I lost my wife and daughter to a cult."

NIGHT CRIES

"Lost? How?"

"Before I became a writer, I was a university professor. So was my wife, Anne. I taught English literature, and Anne's area of expertise was religious studies. We were doing well. We had stable jobs, a decent income and a big house in the country ... living the all-American dream, you might say. After a couple of years we had a daughter, Melanie. My wife had been teaching longer than I, so we decided she would take a sabbatical. I would continue to work and she would stay home with Melanie. Money wasn't a problem for us. We could afford it. Anne's father passed away several years before Melanie came along and left her a sizable inheritance, which we had invested well. But after Melanie was born Anne began to change, gradually at first. She wasn't the sweet Anne that I had fallen in love with anymore. She became distant, non-communicative."

"What did you do?"

"I tried to get her to open up and tell me what was wrong, but she wouldn't. Said it was none of my business, and that I probably wouldn't understand anyway. She began spending more and more time away from the house with people from the university she explained away as friends. I thought I knew all her friends, because they were *my* friends too. But I'd never seen these people before. I began to get worried. A few of them gave me the creeps. They'd speak to Anne but never to me. One day I came home early from work, and a van I hadn't seen before was parked in the lane near the back of our house. Melanie was two and a half at the time, and when I walked inside I found her sitting alone on the kitchen floor. I was shocked. Anne never let Melanie out of her sight - not for a second. I looked upstairs and down, but she was nowhere to be found. The window was open in the kitchen. That's when I heard voices coming from the barn where we kept a couple of trail horses. It sounded like singing, only softer. I picked Mellie up in my arms and we went outside. The closer I got to the barn I realized it wasn't singing that I was hearing at all. It was chanting. I slid the barn door open and there was Anne and her friends, sitting in a circle. Four men, five women. They were wearing black robes, and the women wore veils. They were praying or reciting a mantra - something like that. When I walked in they stopped what they were doing immediately, stood up, and left. They didn't even acknowledge my presence. Neither did Anne. She walked past me like I was a ghost. Like I wasn't even there. I remember her eyes – distant, vacant. I ran after her, but she just kept walking. I grabbed her by the arm and turned her around to face me. Next thing I knew, it was lights out. Someone struck me from behind, and I went down for the count. When I finally came around they were gone. And they had taken Melanie with them."

"I assume you called the police?"

"Yeah, for what good it did me. They said there was *nothing* they could do. Technically, Melanie was with her mother. And since there was no order of protection placed against her by me, and since we weren't in a custody battle, and because I didn't see who hit me there was no one to press charges against. All the cops said was I should give it some time. That they'd probably turn up in a few hours. I was on my own. I had no choice but to try and find them myself."

"Where did you go?" Claire asked. "What did you do?"

"At first I didn't know where to begin to look for them. Then I thought of the university. I figured if that's where Anne met these people there was a chance that's where she might be. I looked everywhere. I scoured the campus. I talked to some of her fellow professors, but they claimed they hadn't seen her since she took her leave." Martin took a deep breath, letting it out slowly. "That was the last time I saw my wife and daughter."

"So you believe Anne and the people who were with her were part of a cult?"

"I found out two months later she was. She turned up in Uganda, of all places."

"Uganda? What was she doing there?"

"Maybe I should re-phrase that. Her dental records showed up in Uganda."

"I don't understand."

"It seems she fled the country, probably the same day I last saw her. It turns out the people she was with were part of a Christian doomsday cult known as, *"The Movement For The Restoration Of The Ten Commandments Of God."* Over one thousand people died in a fire that gutted their church in Kanungu, a small town about two hundred and twenty miles southwest of Kampala. Anne was one of them. The local police found over three hundred skulls, including the remains of seventy children. There was no way to tell how many actually died. The Ugandan government estimated the count at closer to fourteen hundred. Almost all had been burned beyond recognition. Most of the bodies had been reduced to ash due to the duration of the blaze and the intensity of the heat. Dental impressions from those remains salvageable for autopsy were taken and entered into a database. One of their hits turned out to be a match for Anne."

"What about Melanie? Was she with her mother? Did she survive the fire?"

"I don't know. Melanie just ... disappeared."

"Disappeared?"

"Yes. I've been trying to find her for the last eight years. Melanie's picture and vital statistics are registered with the National Center for Missing and Exploited Children. I've traveled to Uganda twice looking for her, hired private investigators, posted a web page and filed missing person's reports everywhere I can think of. There's not a day that goes by that I don't curse myself for not listening to my gut instinct about Anne - that she was involved in something way over her head. If I could have stopped her she would never have had the opportunity to take Melanie, and we'd still be together today, like the family we were meant to be."

With his last words, Martin's voice cracked.

They stood in silence, looking out over the waters of the moonlit bay, connected in their thoughts. Claire took Martin's hand and squeezed it reassuringly.

"You're a good person Martin. I sense that in you. You'll find your daughter someday. You have too. It's that simple."

"I hope so Claire. More than you could possibly know."

* * *

When Claire walked in the door at one-thirty in the morning her answering machine message indicator light was blinking. Inspector Maddox had called to tell her he had run a preliminary search on the partial name but had not been able to turn up any leads. He had, however, promised to make a few calls on her behalf the following day.

Changing for bed but not tired enough to sleep, Claire went to the kitchen and prepared a cup of hot chamomile tea with honey and lemon. She sat at the kitchen table, thinking of Martin. The past experiences they shared were eerily coincidental – the loss of his wife and daughter, she of her parents and sister - both under mysterious circumstances. Before tonight, she knew very little of Martin Belgrade. Now, it seemed, their lives had become inextricably entwined.

Slowly the tea began to produce its desired effect, and Claire headed up to bed. She noticed Martin's book on the front entrance table where she had dropped it as she retrieved her phone message.

NIGHT CRIES

She picked it up and walked upstairs. Maybe a little light reading would help her drift off to sleep.

Turning on her nightlight, she propped her pillows and made herself comfortable. She re-read the inscription and smiled.

She flipped through the pages of the book, concentrating on nothing in particular, randomly reading a few paragraphs here and there, until one chapter caught her attention. Suddenly, her blood ran cold.

The chapter dealt with a lesser-known faction of the cult Martin's wife had been involved with. The group was called *The Brethren* and the picture, though grainy, showed members of the cult farming a field.

A girl, rake in hand, stood facing the camera, wiping the sweat from her brow. Beside her was a man at least twenty years her senior.

Claire read the caption below the photo, then sat up in bed, heart pounding, eyes glued to the girl in the photograph:

> 'Members of *The Brethren* and their leader,
> Joseph Krebeck'.

"It's not Kre…" Claire gasped, recalling the words of Walter Pennimore. "It's *Krebeck*!"

She drew the book closer, staring intently at the picture of the girl.

The pretty girl, with shoulder length hair, slender build and porcelain-fine features ...

Grabbing a framed photograph from her bedstand, she compared it to the picture in Martin's book.

There was no denying it.

"*Amanda*," she cried. "It *is* you. *You're alive!*"

GARY COPELAND

5

"CALM DOWN, CLAIRE! You're not making any sense!"

Picking up his watch from the bedside table, Martin pressed the nightlight and checked the time.

2:20 a.m.

"Take a deep breath, then tell me what's wrong."

"It's my sister, Amanda," Claire said, her voice trembling. "I saw her picture in your book! I know it's her, Martin. It's got to be!"

"You've lost me. What are you talking about? What significance does your sister have to my book?"

It was then that Claire remembered she had not told Martin about Amanda or her disappearance. He had talked about the loss of his wife and daughter, but she had not shared with him the loss of her parents and sister.

"I'm sorry to be calling you at such a crazy hour Martin," Claire said, regaining her composure.

"I know we talked about your family tonight, but what I didn't tell you is what happened to mine. Many years ago, my sister Amanda disappeared. The police tried to find her but couldn't, and there were no ransom demands. I'm telling you this because I saw a picture in your book of a young girl who is part of a group called 'The Brethren', and I think … no, I know, that girl is Amanda. I need to find out who took that picture and where it was taken. This could be my connection to finding her. You have to help me Martin. Please."

Martin drew a deep breath. "Of course I'll help you Claire. But there's nothing either of us can do right now. Come to my place around nine-thirty. We'll pay a visit to some associates of mine who help me with the research I do for my books. One of them is a retired FBI agent. They'll know who took the photo you're talking about, and if they don't, I'll have them find out who did."

"Thank you Martin. Give me your address. I'll be there at nine-thirty. I know how bizarre this must sound to you, but I'm telling you the truth. It *is* Amanda."

"I have no reason not to believe you, Claire. If you say you saw a picture of your sister in my book, then that's good enough for me. One way or another, we're going to find out if it is your sister. Okay?"

The relief in Claire's voice was evident. "Okay. I'll see you in a few hours. Sleep well."

"You too. And Claire?"

"Yes?"

"I'm glad you called."

"Me too."

The following morning Claire met Martin at his home in Santa Clara. Together with Maggy they drove for the next two hours up the California coastline. Claire slept for most of the trip, exhausted from the emotional roller coaster she had ridden until morning light. Occasionally, Martin stole a glance at her seated beside him. He had known this woman less than twenty-four hours, yet knew without a doubt that something unmistakable was happening to him. His every instinct told him that her life, her very well being, had somehow become his responsibility. He had begun to care for her, and he welcomed the opportunity with an exhilaration he hadn't felt in years.

Slow down, Marty, he thought. *You don't even know for sure if this girl really likes you or not. Maybe she was just being kind to you last night because you were the man of the hour. Maybe she has a boyfriend, or worse, a fiancée. Then how would you feel? Better to just let it take its course. See where it leads.*

Claire sighed, turning in her seat.

Martin glanced in his rearview mirror at Maggy, her nose out the open window, busily taking in the sights and smells along the way. "So, Maggs?" he whispered. "Think this one's a keeper?"

Maggy stirred in her seat to the sound of her master's voice, chuffing quietly. She leaned forward, nuzzling her muzzle into Martin's ear, licking his face. Martin smiled, scratching her behind her ears, smoothing the side of her head. "Guess I'll take that as a yes."

Minutes later, Claire awakened with a yawn and a stretch. Maggy took the opportunity to say hello to her newfound friend, moving between the seats and licking Claire's face until she started to laugh.

"Good morning, sleepyhead."

"Good morning," Claire laughed, unsuccessful in her attempt to evade a sudden onslaught of slobbery, wet, canine kisses.

"If you haven't already taken the hint, Maggy *really* likes you."

"I think you may be right!" Claire took the retrievers lolling head in her hands, nuzzling her nose. "I like you too, Maggy. Yes I do, you beautiful girl!" Claire continued to dote on the dog as Maggy's overzealous tail wagged repeatedly, whacking Martin on the side of his face.

"Hey! Can't you two see I'm trying to drive over here?"

"Oops! Sorry," Claire laughed. "It's her fault, not mine."

NIGHT CRIES

Martin looked at Maggy. "Maybe you forgot, fur face, you're supposed to be *man's* best friend."

Maggy chuffed, licked Martin once, then went straight back to smothering Claire with a plethora of doggy affection.

"Traitor," he teased.

The rumble in Martin's stomach reminded him he hadn't eaten since he had gotten up. "You hungry?" he asked.

"Absolutely famished."

"There's a great spot I know of just before the Hayward exit called Belinda's. I can personally guarantee they'll make you the best breakfast you've ever tasted, bar none."

"Sounds perfect."

Arriving at Belinda's, a wide smile and friendly voice greeted them in the form of a pleasant-faced Hispanic woman, whose nametag proclaimed her to be Rosa.

"Martin!" Rosa said, welcoming him with open arms and a kiss on each cheek. "Cómo esta? So nice to see you again! What brings you here?"

"Muy bien, gracias," Martin said. "We're on our way up to Sacramento to see some business associates of mine. Rosa, I'd like you to meet a friend, Dr. Claire Prescott."

"Mucho gusto Doctor," Rosa said, shaking her hand. "Very pleased to meet you." The warmth of her smile never waned, as though it were a permanent fixture on her kind face. "Entrar! Come in! Make yourselves at home."

Rosa escorted Martin and Claire to a quiet table by the window and took their order.

"You sit with your beautiful lady friend and be comfortable. I'll be back before you know it." Within minutes Rosa had returned to their table and they were enjoying a delicious breakfast of blueberry waffles with maple syrup, hickory-smoked bacon, home fries and a carafe of freshly brewed coffee.

"You and Rosa seem to know each other quite well," Claire said.

"I've known Rosa and her husband, Miguel, practically all my life," Martin replied. "They worked for my parents while I was growing up in San Mateo and lived in our guest house on the property. Rosa was our maid, Miguel our cook. I'm very close to both of them. My parents were both professionals and traveled a lot. Rosa practically raised me. When my parents retired, they sold the estate and moved to Switzerland. They wanted to find an appropriate way to thank them for their many years of dedicated service and for always taking such good care of me when I was young. They offered to set them up in a business of their own, just in case the new owners might decide against keeping them on as staff at the estate. They accepted their offer and opened this diner, naming it after my mother. Rosa seems very happy. I'm glad to see they're doing well. I know how hard they've worked for it."

"That was a very kind gesture on your parents behalf."

"That's the way they are. They're good people."

"Do you see them often?"

"As often as I can. My writing keeps me pretty busy, as well as my work with Mark, Justin and Cynthia, whom you'll meet shortly when we get to Sacramento. But we try to get together as much as possible."

"That's nice." Claire paused. "God, you're lucky. I miss my family so much."

"Speaking of family, would you mind if I ask you a few questions about yours?"

"No, not at all. What do you want to know?"

"You said Amanda ... disappeared."

"Yes."

"That you believed she was abducted."

"That's right."

"But you don't have any actual proof of that, do you?"

"No," Claire replied. "But everyone who knew Amanda would tell you she simply wasn't the type to just walk away from her life. Quite frankly, until I read your book, I had resigned myself to believing she was dead. Now, after seeing her picture, I just don't know what to think anymore."

Martin stirred his coffee as Claire spoke, twirling his spoon in slow, thoughtful circles.

"In your experiences as a psychiatrist, have you ever dealt with patients who had been affected by a condition known as Stockholm Syndrome?"

"I'm familiar with it. But no, I haven't. Why?"

"I've come across it many times in my work dealing with cults and the people who have become involved with them. When a person is taken against their will and held for long periods of time in an environment where escape is all but impossible, such as in the case of a kidnapping or hostage taking, they begin to manifest a wide range of obsessive emotional connections toward their captors, especially if acts of kindness are extended to them contrary to the degree of treatment they would have expected to receive under such circumstances. For example, they may begin to sympathize with their abductor, believing they brought the situation upon themselves, when of course nothing could be further from the truth. Some victims have actually fallen in love with their captors. It's a psychological form of self-defense that kicks in at a certain point in the relationship, sort of the same way the fight or flight principle works. In one particular case we dealt with, the victim physically resisted the rescue attempt by the extraction team. They barely got out alive."

"So what you're implying is if Amanda was taken years ago by members of The Brethren, she could conceivably have made a conscious decision to *avoid* being found?"

"That's exactly right."

Claire sat back in her chair, contemplating Martin's words. "I never considered that."

"Most people wouldn't. The psychological control of these groups is much stronger than you or I as sound-minded individuals could ever possibly imagine, and to an impressionable young girl like Amanda probably was at the time she disappeared, well ... who knows? I can practically guarantee you this much though. If The Brethren were responsible for Amanda's disappearance, we're going to need some very professional help. Tracking them to a specific location will be a tough job, which is probably why the police had such a hard time getting any leads on her."

"Dear God! What has Amanda gotten herself into?"

"Nothing we can't get her out of Claire," Martin said, reaching across the table, holding her hand. His touch was warm, calming. "Don't be scared. I'm not going anywhere. I agreed to help you, which means I'm in this for the long haul – for as long as it takes. But, if this is as serious as I think it may be, I suggest you call your office as soon as we leave. You're going to need to clear your schedule for the next couple of days, maybe longer. Can you do that?"

"Of course. Amanda is my main priority right now. I'll advise the clinic to put my cases on hold until I get back, whenever that may be."

"Good. Then let's get going. I don't want to be late for our meeting."

Rosa came to their table as they prepared to leave, a yellow rose in her hand.

"For you, Doctor. A little thank you for your visit."

Claire accepted the gift. "How sweet of you Rosa. Thank you."

"De nada, Señora," Rosa said. "It's nothing. You are always welcome at Belinda's. Just be sure to bring my Martin with you when you come again. I don't get to see as much of him as I'd like to these days."

"I'll do my best."

Martin kissed Rosa on the cheek. "Adiós abuela," he said. "Give my best to Miguel."

Claire smelled the rose, appreciating its rich, aromatic fragrance, as gentle as the woman who gave it to her.

How interesting that Rosa should give her a yellow rose.

Yellow, Claire thought.

The color of hope.

Maggy greeted them at the Navigator with a hearty *Woof!*

"I know, I know. Geez! Be patient, will ya?" Martin said, pulling a serviette out of his pocket into which a strip of bacon had been carefully wrapped. He gave Maggy her treat, which she promptly devoured.

"See what I mean? No table manners whatsoever. The dog's a canine vacuum cleaner. She doesn't eat her food – she inhales it. But she is great company. Aren't you, bacon-breath?"

Licking her mouth, Maggy panted an eager smile from the back seat.

Claire laughed, removing her cell phone from her purse. "Guess I better make that call."

They drove towards Sacramento, leaving Hayward, San Leandro, Oakland and Berkeley behind. The mid-morning traffic was lighter than usual, and Maggy decided it was a good time to settle in for a nice long snooze. Snoring lightly, she barked playfully in her sleep, likely dreaming of a world filled with two-hour walks in the park, an endless supply of bacon-flavored treats, and all the frisbees she could catch.

To the west of Vallejo off Interstate 80 San Pablo Bay glittered and danced in the morning sun. Sailboats, power yachts and windsurfers skimmed along the turquoise waves, while beachside the water teemed with families splashing and playing together.

"Martin," Claire said, looking out the window at the bay, "tell me about the people we'll be meeting with."

"Sure. The organization is called The Reformers," Martin replied. "It's run by a fellow by the name of Mark Oyama, together with his two associates, Justin Dale and Cynthia Rowe. Mark is a retired special agent of the FBI's Domestic Terrorism unit. Justin and Cynthia are professional de-programmers and field agents. They specialize in gathering covert intelligence on extremist groups who pose a threat to public safety, such as neo-nazi movements, paramilitary separatists, white supremacists and religious cults. They're also trained to conduct rescue missions, or extractions."

"And you think they can help us find Amanda?"

"Trust me. If anyone can, Mark's team can. They've successfully extracted many individuals from cults at the request of their families. Afterward, they undergo de-programming sessions with Justin and Cynthia to help rid them of all the crap that's running around in their head. Eventually, they're able to integrate back into society and lead contributing, productive lives once again."

"What state are they in when they've been rescued?"

"You name it," Martin said. "Depressed, suicidal, angry, confused. Some spend weeks at a time not knowing what to believe, simply because their concept of right and wrong has been thrown into a tailspin. Think about it. For as long as they've been with the cult, all their decisions have been made for them - what to eat, what to read, what to say, what to believe. Their sensory stimuli have been carefully controlled for the benefit of the cult and its leaders, not for them as individuals. They've basically surrendered their will, so reestablishing their identity as individuals, with the right to freedom of expression and self-governance, is extremely difficult. They feel tremendously alienated from their families, and they're scared to death of not living in accordance with the rules and constructs they've become accustomed to. It's a difficult period of adjustment for everyone, especially their families. But once they're into the deprogramming process, the walls of resistance come tumbling down. Eventually, you get that person back, whole again. It's a wonderful feeling."

"What do you think motivates them to get involved with the cult in the first place?"

"Could be any number of reasons. Some are street kids looking for anywhere to call home, and the cult is only too pleased to welcome them. Others come from extremely wealthy families, or are college or university students introduced to recruiters on campus by their friends. But it's mainly the doctrine of the group that seems to be the primary reason they get involved, and when they're in it's pretty much impossible to get out. Abusive cults immediately set about the task of isolating them from their family and friends, encouraging them to find the answers to their questions and problems from within the group itself. They begin to hammer their ideologies and beliefs into their mind, and pretty soon they're brainwashed into believing they can't say or do anything without the approval of an elder or group leader. To do otherwise would risk disapproval, punishment, excommunication ... possibly even death."

"It's hard to believe that one individual could be so charismatic as to hold such extreme influence over so many."

"Not when you're desperate for love and attention. If the people you call family demonstrate their paternal affection for you by beating you senseless on a routine basis, it soon becomes pretty easy to see how a person could eagerly attach themselves to any individual or group willing to show them a little sympathy and respect. When you're at your weakest and meet people who *want* to believe in, understand, and care for you, you won't just walk to them; you'll run to them - arms wide open. It's only after you're in that the pressure to conform, the isolation, the inter-dependence and the mind games begin. That's when they have you. By that time, you'll do whatever they tell you to do for continued acceptance. Just look at what happened to my wife, Anne. She was a very intelligent, well-educated woman. But when they got inside her head and began pushing the right buttons, she didn't have a chance. And she paid for it with her life." Martin paused. "Believe me Claire, there's no way in hell we're going to let that happen to Amanda."

Forty-five minutes later the city of Sacramento came into view, at once disappearing then re-appearing in rhythmic intervals as the swish-swish of the windshield wipers swept away the last remnants of a brief sun-shower. Rainbows bled across the windshield in ethereal hues with each pass of rubber over glass, vaporizing in mosaic swirls with the on-coming wind rush. Silver mirages floated on the road ahead in the distant lanes of traffic, swallowing parcels of rain-slicked blacktop as they shape-shifted, appearing then disappearing from view. Indeed, the city ahead had not drowned, had not been swallowed up, but rather appeared to be thriving, as though the sudden, unexpected needles of rain had managed to vaccinate it, lancing the city of pent-up impurities.

"Well, here we are," Martin said, bringing the SUV to a stop in front of the gates of a stunning turn of the century Victorian home.

"This is it?"

"Not exactly what you had in mind, is it?"

"Well, I …"

"You were expecting a little more brass and glass perhaps?"

"Yes, I suppose I was."

"Well, as they say, looks can be deceiving. This is not just any house. It's a safe house. No one gets in here without their identity being authenticated first."

Martin drew Claire's attention to one of several forty-foot high metal poles, atop which long white rectangular boxes angled downward, turning slowly left then right, panning the grounds.

"This place is as technologically advanced as it gets, from intruder-sensing perimeter security devices buried beneath the ground throughout the property, to those day and night-vision cameras you see scanning us as we speak. As soon as I entered the driveway from the road and began to approach the gates, that camera was zooming in on my license plate, running it through the DMV. The staff inside have identified to whom this vehicle belongs even before I've come to a full stop."

An eight-foot wall of wrought-iron fencing surrounded the property. To Martin's left a camera whined, turning in his direction. A speaker mounted in a stone column crackled to life. "Good afternoon, Mr. Belgrade." The voice was courteous, the tone professional, yet undoubtedly all business. "Please speak into the microphone for voice print verification and identify your passenger."

"Belgrade, Martin K. Security clearance GWB122903. My passenger is Dr. Claire Prescott. Mark Oyama is expecting us."

"Thank you. Please wait," the voice said. Seconds later, the massive, wheel-mounted security gates in front of them clicked open, slowly rolling back, allowing them access to the grounds.

"Please proceed," the voice said.

Martin drove through the gate and down the winding driveway. The lawns were perfectly manicured, lush and green, as though excruciating attention had been paid to each individual blade of grass. Tall trees lined the driveway like century-old sentinels. Landscaped flowerbeds adorned the lawn in tiered, scalloped rows. The house reminded Claire of a stately mansion, wedding-white in color with gingerbread molding and hourglass curtains, the windows flanked by rich-black hurricane shutters. A deep, white-picket verandah surrounded the main floor. Martin parked in front of the entrance and opened the side door of the Navigator. Maggy bounded out, barking and running playfully across the lawn. The screen door opened.

"Good to see you again Martin. This must be the young lady you spoke of on the phone."

"Indeed she is," Martin replied. "Dr. Claire Prescott, I'd like you to meet Mark Oyama, a good friend of mine, and one of the finest special agents the FBI was ever unfortunate enough to lose to early retirement."

"It's a pleasure to meet you, Agent Oyama."

"Likewise. But call me Mark. I left the title behind when I left the Bureau, though it still comes in handy if I need to throw a little weight around once in a while."

Maggy woofed and came running to the porch, tail wagging madly.

"Hey Maggs!" Mark said, kneeling to greet her. "How's my girl?" Maggy pressed tightly against him, nudging her head under his hand. Mark smoothed her coat, scratching behind her ears. It was only a matter of seconds before the retriever lay sprawled on her back at his feet, having successfully negotiated her way into receiving a first-rate belly rub.

"Looks like somebody missed you," Martin said.

"You think so?"

Maggy lifted her head and licked his face. "I think you might be right about that," Mark laughed. "Okay ... Come on girl. Let's go inside." Maggy shuffled to her feet, prancing to the door, pawing at the screen.

"I bet I know what you want," Mark said, opening the door. "Okay. Away you go. Justin's downstairs. He'll give you one of your treats." Maggy barked happily and ran inside, following a direct course for the downstairs offices.

Mark held the door as Martin and Claire walked into the house.

"My goodness," Claire said, impressed by the period décor of the elaborately appointed home. "This is beautiful."

"Thank you, or I suppose I should say, thank you *Martin*. Without his endowment, this place would never have been possible."

Claire turned to Martin. "Your endowment?"

"Well," Martin replied casually, "I guess I helped out a little."

"A *little*?" Mark said. "Let me put this in perspective for you, Dr. Prescott, since Martin is obviously too humble to admit it. This place, our organization itself, would never have been possible without his philanthropic assistance. Everyone who has ever been helped by us owes a direct debt of gratitude to our friend Mr. Belgrade here. The non-profit foundation he established pays the bills and all of our expenses. But knowing Martin as I do, he probably forgot to mention that little tidbit of information, didn't he?"

"Only one-hundred percent of what you just told me."

"He's a pretty quiet guy," Mark joked. "He doesn't like to call a lot of attention to himself."

"Author, philanthropist ... any other surprises I should know about?" Claire teased. "You don't perhaps run a small country in your spare time?"

"Very funny," Martin replied. "Thankfully, I'm in a position to help out, so I do. It's really that simple."

"And we appreciate the help very much," Mark said, gesturing them inside to the comfort of the dining room. They seated themselves around a mahogany table so heavily polished Claire could see her face in its surface as clearly as if she were looking into a mirror. "Now that you're here, what can we do for you?"

Martin placed his briefcase on the table, clicked open the latches, and removed a copy of his book *Heaven on Earth*, opening it to the picture taken in the farming field. "I need to know a few things about this picture."

"Sure. Like what?"

"Like who took it, and when and where it was taken."

"That shouldn't be too difficult to find out. We'll have the information on file, either in hard copy or on our database. I'll have Justin look it up for you right away. But somehow I get the feeling you didn't drive all the way from Santa Clara just to talk about this picture. I have a copy of this book in my study. You could have asked me for that information over the phone just as easily."

"You're right," Martin replied. "It's the girl in the picture we're concerned about. She may be a missing person. Claire believes it may be her sister, Amanda. We need to confirm if that's true."

"What do you want us to do?"

"Did you bring along a picture of Amanda with you Claire?" Martin asked.

"Of course," Claire replied, reaching into her purse for the framed picture. In her haste she hadn't taken the time to remove it from its frame.

NIGHT CRIES

Martin removed the picture and handed it to Mark. "Do we have the technology to compare my picture against Claire's?"

"You bet," Mark replied. "Justin can run a probability analysis on both photographs to verify or deny the similarities. We use the same software forensics labs do to perform modeling analysis. By inputting both pictures into the computer, we'll be able to tell if these individuals are, in fact, one in the same person."

"Even with the age difference? There's several years between the appearance of the girls in these pictures." Martin tapped the picture with his finger. "There's also some suspicion that this guy, Joseph Krebeck, may in some way be responsible for Amanda and Claire's parents death."

Mark leaned forward in his chair. "What makes you suspect that?"

"One of my patients told me." Claire interjected.

"Then let's not sit around here wasting anymore time," Mark replied. "Let's go to the lab and check it out."

The period charm of the home, true to its century old heritage, ended abruptly at the bottom of the stairs. The computer facility was a startling contrast of high technology, outfitted with the latest in computer systems and scientific instrumentation. On the far wall of the room glossy photographs were tacked to a large corkboard.

"Who are all these people?" Claire asked.

"Surveillance subjects," an unseen voice announced. Across the room a young man stood up, sliding his chair out from behind a workstation at the back of the room. He walked over, introducing himself.

"I'm Justin Dale, Mark's partner in crime. These are pictures of people we're in the process of building intelligence profiles and databases on. Some of them we know a little about already, but most of these faces are new."

"How did you get them?" Claire asked.

"By various means," Justin explained. "Some are taken by our field operatives. Others we download when LEWIS tells us it's found a match."

"LEWIS?"

"Law Enforcement Web-based Internet Surveillance," Justin explained. "It's a computer program that scans all major media and newswire services around the world for information based on keywords we specify in our search criteria. When we get a hit, our computers transfer that information to a master database, and a message flag comes up on my screen. We compare the new information to what we have on file and update our records as applicable. It helps us keep on top of key people or groups internationally, while assisting with our current investigations."

Mark interjected. "At any given time we have the ability to track the last known whereabouts of anyone in our database. There are over one hundred field operatives in our organization whose job it is to monitor the activities of anti-government and political dissident groups in specific geographic regions, all over the world. They feed us reports on a weekly basis."

"Amazing," Claire replied. "How do they get their information?"

"Covertly. They operate in deep cover, which means they've gained the confidence of key people in the group and infiltrated it, then report back to us on the group's activities when it's safe to do so. We share that information with federal and international authorities in return for their assistance when we need it."

"So, you're sort of a spy agency."

"I suppose you could call us that."

"This group that Amanda appears to be associated with, The Brethren. How much do you know about them?"

NIGHT CRIES

"Not much actually," Justin said. "Most cults establish a base of operations, but these guys are what we refer to as a gypsy cult - in one place one day, gone the next. Truthfully, they're pretty tough to keep tabs on."

"But you can find them, can't you?"

"It won't be easy, but yes, we can track them down."

Mark handed Justin the photograph of Amanda that Claire had given him. "I need you to run a biometric comparison on these two pictures. We need to confirm if they're the same person."

"Duck soup. The computer will run an analysis on both pictures," Justin began, explaining the identification process to Claire as he walked to a nearby computer station. "Each image will be compared for similarities, like the width of the face, distance between the eyes, plus any general anomalies like scarring, birth marks, and so on. Depending on how good the photographs are that we have to work with, the system will try to find verification matches on as many as seven hundred and fifty random points of reference."

While the computer scanned both photographs, the word **PROCESSING** flashed repeatedly in the bottom corner of the screen. Within seconds, the words **ANALYSIS COMPLETE** glared back at them. A laser printer next to the computer terminal whined, and a sheet of paper fell from the machine into the receiving tray.

Justin examined the report. "Based on the photographs provided, and factoring in computerized enhancements to compensate for the age differences, the probability of the girl in Martin's photograph and your picture to be one in the same person would be accurate to 99.956 percent."

"Then I'm right. It is Amanda!" Claire exclaimed.

"There's no denying it," Justin replied, patting the hard drive. "The software under the hood of this puppy doesn't lie. The girl in this photograph standing beside Joseph Krebeck can be one person and one person only. It is your sister. It is Amanda Prescott."

NIGHT CRIES

6

VIRGIL LUTT WAS a simple man who yearned for a simple life. His aspirations never included gratifying an insatiable need to unravel the mysteries of the human genome or to design supercomputers capable of mapping distant regions of the galaxy. All Virgil Lutt and his wife Sky ever wanted was to be left in peace. To live life on their own terms. And to raise their only child, Blessing, in an environment where love, honesty, mutual respect and an unfailing belief in the existence of a higher power were as accepted as the sun's unfailing commitment to rise each day. To Virgil, the outside world was corrupt, its inhabitants populous lesions occupying a host body which had been permitted to fester and decay despite of being tested time after time, yet never given to the common-sense understanding that such repeated acts of collective faithlessness cannot forever go unpunished. That those actions would, one day, bring about consequences of unimaginable proportion. And that time was running out.

With the wick of mankind's pre-eminent destruction burning steadily to the quick, Virgil and his family had traveled across the country in search of a new Eden. Now, in the waning hours of the afternoon, attaching the stretcher unit to the last of the wooden line posts, slowly tightening and nailing the final yard of barbed wire securely in place, Virgil knew in his heart he was finally home.

He stood back, surveying the last half-mile of finished barricade with great pleasure.

"Go ahead," Fallon said. "You do the honors."

Virgil stepped forward, affixing a painted wooden plank that read POSITIVELY NO TRESPASSING to the top wire, patiently adjusting the sign until it hung perfectly centered between the posts.

"Hard to believe, isn't it?" Virgil said, the contemplation of his words weighing heavily in his voice. He leaned back, propping one foot against the fence, surveying the rolling hillside, watching it melt away as twilight crept up from the foot of the rugged mountain valley. Basking in the dying breath of daylight, Mount Horning stood red-faced in the distance, its quiet majesty guarded by the echoing cries of a lone hawk spiraling above, lifted higher and higher on unseen thermal updrafts.

"How's that?" Fallon replied, picking up a loose rock from the ground, lobbing it up and down, testing its heft. Aiming for the trunk of a distant tree, he threw it. The stone found its mark with a muffled *thump*.

"Look around you," Virgil said. "For years I only dreamed about this. I never thought I'd see the day my family and I would live in a place like this, with all this land to call our own."

"I suppose," Fallon replied matter-of-factly, running a hand through his wiry black hair. "Personally, I never had any doubt we'd end up here. It was only a matter of time before Prophet found what he was looking for. He's true to his word. Always has been. And I've known him a long, long time."

NIGHT CRIES

Malignant-gray clouds grumbled in baritone timbre from the peak of Mount Horning. The hawk cried again, circling in one last long arc, then rushed against the face of the mountain, diving down, opening its wings and flapping to rest in its crag nest, invisible from sight. A flash of lightning vaulted across the tortured sky, serrating the tops of the clouds with a parry of electricity as erratic and unpredictable as the thrust of a madman's dagger.

"We'd best be heading back," Fallon said, looking up as the mountaintop disappeared beneath the irritated clouds. "Looks like it's going to pour."

A fat droplet of rainwater christened the back of Virgil's neck as he leaned over. "You grab the rifles," he said. "I can manage the tools by myself." He slipped his hammer into his belt and lifted the metal wire stretcher to one shoulder, the sledgehammer to the other. Together they walked up the hill. In the distance they could see the others preparing to seek shelter from the coming thunderstorm. Blessing was playing hide-and-seek among billowing sails of shirts, pants and linens as her mother pulled the clothes and bedding off the laundry line, struggling against the roiling wind and splattering raindrops.

"*Boo!*" Sky teased, pulling down a bed sheet. Blessing laughed with glee every time she was discovered, running further down the clothesline only to be enveloped in another wind-shorn hiding place. With the last sheet pulled down and the game finally over, Virgil heard Blessing cry out.

"Mommy, look! Daddy's home!"

Tossing the tools to the ground, Virgil dropped to his knees and spread his arms.

"*Three ... two ... one ...*"

Running as fast as her little legs could carry her, Blessing threw herself into her father's arms in a revelry of high-pitched laughter.

"Gotcha!" Virgil laughed. "Hi baby. How's my angel?"

"I'm fine Daddy. I helped Mommy take in the laundry."

"Really? It looked to me like Mommy was doing all the work out there."

"I was supersizing."

"You were what?"

"Supersizing."

"You mean super*vising*."

"That's what I said. Supersizing."

Virgil laughed. "Come on baby. Let's get you inside before it starts to rain. What do you say … King of the Mountain?"

"Okay!"

"Alright then. Climb aboard!"

Virgil leaned over as Blessing squirmed her legs around her father's neck and laced her fingers under his chin.

"Ready?"

"*Ready!*"

"Okay. Away we go!"

Virgil picked up the tools by his feet and wrapped his arms around his daughter's legs, balancing her on his shoulders as he stood.

"Prophet wants to have a meeting tonight," Fallon said as they walked toward the compound. "Says he has some important news we need to hear."

"Did he say what it was about?"

"Nope. Just that it was important, and that we all needed to be there."

"What time?"

"Around nine. In Communion Hall, after supper."

"Alright. I'll tell Sky." Virgil motioned to their Brethren brothers and sisters still tending the fields despite the ominous thunderhead rumbling above. "Perhaps you can tell the others."

NIGHT CRIES

Grunting his acknowledgement, Fallon walked off in the direction of the fields. They had said more to each other in the last ten minutes than they had all day, which in truth was just fine with Virgil. Something about Fallon always made him uneasy. He was not of overwhelming physical size, nor did he possess an intimidating presence. Actually, quite the opposite was true. Fallon was weak in appearance, with a jaundice complexion that made every effort to stretch itself over a frame of skin and bones. But it was his eyes Virgil found most unsettling - cold, irradiant eyes. Earlier, while Fallon held the fence post in place for him to stretch and staple the last section of wire, Virgil had to break his gaze. Not because he felt intimidated or challenged, but because looking into his eyes was like staring into a soulless entity, darkly gifted, absent of emotion, somehow capable of fulfilling the blackest of intentions.

As Virgil dropped his tools outside the doors to the supply room, Blessing scrambled down from her father's shoulders and ran to her mother.

"Did you finish the fence?" Sky said, setting down the clothesbasket, tying her long blond hair into a ponytail.

"Yep. Every last inch of it."

"I suppose Fallon was his usual mix of effervescent personality and irresistible charm?"

Virgil nodded. "If the man was capable of breaking a smile I swear he'd shatter into a million pieces."

Sky wrapped her arms around her husband. "Be careful around him, okay? Don't ask me why, but I don't trust him. Not at all."

"I know what you mean," Virgil replied. "We were out there since sunrise, and the only time he spoke to me was when I spoke to him first. That's just plain strange." Virgil shrugged. "Maybe it's just me. Prophet doesn't seem to have a problem with him, so I guess he's alright."

"Now that you mention Prophet, has he seemed a little different to you recently?"

"What do you mean?"

"It's just that for the last two weeks, other than leading us in prayer at supper, he hasn't so much as left his room."

"So?"

"That doesn't strike you as a little odd?"

"What Prophet chooses to do with his time is up to him, Sky. He doesn't owe us any explanation."

"I suppose you're right. I'm probably just overreacting."

"You have a habit of that you know," Virgil teased.

"Very funny."

As the brewing storm grumbled a last minute warning, fierce raindrops hammered down around them, each droplet drumming off the ground harder and louder than the last. Virgil and Sky watched the others run for shelter to the adjoining buildings while Fallon walked through the field behind them, a rifle slung over each shoulder, one meandering step after the next, as though the rain would dare not be bold enough to soak him to the skin. Or perhaps, Virgil thought, the concept of expending unnecessary energy to run for cover from the now torrential downpour was an utterly foreign concept to him.

Set a mile and a half in from the main road, the Brethren compound was comprised of six large buildings spread over several acres, three of which served as sleeping quarters for the eight families, though they could easily have accommodated eighty. The fourth building was used to house supplies, mostly farm implements and general-purpose tools. It had been decided by Fallon, and agreed to by all, that the fifth building would be for Prophet's exclusive use: a token of thanks for his guidance and leadership. The last and largest of the buildings, with its forty or so floor-to-ceiling windows, many of which still suffered broken panes of glass, had been named

NIGHT CRIES

Communion Hall. It was here that they would gather with their families for breakfast in the morning and dinner in the evening. Pack lunches were prepared at breakfast to ensure a more productive day, and as daily work assignments were given out after breakfast so too were lunches: a simple fare of fruit, raw vegetables, a sandwich or two, a bottle of water. Breakfast was served promptly at six o'clock in the morning and dinner at eight in the evening, with thirty minutes of prayer following each meal. The process of restoring the buildings and cleaning up the property was proving to be a long and arduous task. Virgil often thought the decrepit buildings should simply have been torn down and rebuilt. Instead, he and the others endured the drafty windows and boarded up doors, preferring to look upon their new home as a work in progress, knowing whatever they needed to do to make it livable they would, because they would do it *together,* unlike the outside world, where nothing was done for the good of the many, but only for the selfish benefit of the few. Amid amber wisps of trampled grass and wildflowers a broken artery of crumbled asphalt wound through the grounds, connecting the buildings. It too would eventually be repaired, but was not a current priority. They could put up with broken roads, broken windowpanes and boarded up doors for the time being. They had discovered the true value of the land was not in the buildings, but in the earth upon which they stood. The soil had proven to be a rich and fertile tract, perfect for growing crops of grain and vegetables. Selling part of their harvest in town at the farmers market, they used their profits to pay for whatever supplies were needed, including purchasing the building materials required to make the necessary repairs to the property. Yard goods and farming implements were acquired from a nearby Quaker community who understood their need for self-reliance, offering them whatever they required in exchange for their crops. With a little instruction from the Quakers, some of the women came to realize a previously undiscovered talent for knitting and sewing, and would spend days each week perfecting their skills, making simple clothes, quilts and bed linens. Their abundant crop yields also bought lumber from the local mill. When the fields were not being tended to the men turned planks of wood, studs, doweling and nails into bunk beds, window and door frames, banquet tables, chairs, furniture, shelves and storage cabinets. Lacking electricity, kerosene lamps were abundantly mounted on walls and placed on tables in the common rooms of each building. The responsibility for the lighting of the lamps at dusk and the extinguishing of their flames in the evening was a duty assigned on a rotating basis. This week that duty fell to Virgil.

Sky had taken Blessing inside to bathe and change her as Virgil made his rounds between the buildings, lighting each lamp as he went, setting their wicks to a warm, radiant glow. One by one, dimmed points of light flickered to life. Soon, each of the buildings was aglow in the orange-yellow cast of welcoming lamplight.

His task completed, Virgil left Communion Hall and walked back to his building. The waning chroma of the harvest moon painted the wet asphalt a glimmering topaz. The day had been long and hard, and Virgil was thinking only of spending the remainder of the evening with his wife and daughter. Walking past the building that served as Prophet's residence, angry voices fell through the cracked glass pane in the second story window. Ghostly silhouettes cast formless figures against the walls and ceiling, gliding about the room. Virgil stepped into the shadows at the foot of the window, listening to the conversation. Others were in the room with Prophet, and for reasons unknown, their presence made him uneasy. With the first indication that Prophet may be in danger, Virgil knew that from his vantage point he could be through the doors and up the stairs into Prophets room in seconds, prepared to take any action necessary to protect his spiritual leader from harm. He waited and listened. The voices had become clearer now, and he recognized them immediately.

The first voice, the familiar voice, was that of Fallon. The second was Prophets wife, Cassandra.

"What *about* the girl?" Prophet said.

"She's an unnecessary risk!" Fallon yelled. "Can't you understand that?"

"Not any more," Prophet replied calmly. "Her past life means nothing to her. *This* is the life she knows now. I see no reason for you to concern yourself with her."

Virgil looked up. Lamp-cast shadows swirled about the room. Floorboards creaked under the weight of phantom footfalls.

Cassandra spoke. "Think about what Fallon is telling you Joseph. Maybe he has a point."

Joseph. Only his wife was permitted to address Prophet by his given name. It had been so long since he had heard it, he had nearly forgotten.

"No, he doesn't."

"For God's sake Cassandra," Fallon yelled. "You better talk some sense into him, because it's obvious as hell that I can't!"

"Calm down, both of you!" Cassandra said firmly.

Having retreated to neutral corners, the shadows stopped moving. A hush fell over the room. Virgil pressed his body closer to the wall, as though the sudden infusion of silence had the traitorous power to pour out of the crack in the window above, trickle down the side of the building and manifest itself into a pool of brilliant light, trapping him against the night, exposing his duplicity, revealing his presence.

Cassandra continued her mediation.

"I understand how you feel Joseph. If I had been through what you had, I might well have done the same thing myself."

"She poses no threat to us now. None at all," Prophet reaffirmed angrily.

"You don't know that for certain," Fallon countered.

"We have nothing to fear from her, Fallon. If we did, I'd know it. You're getting yourself worked up over nothing."

"Is that so? Then how do you explain this?"

A dull thud. Something falling to the floor. Virgil couldn't see into the room. He could only hear the dampened sounds and muted voices emanating from the animated shadows.

Prophet picked up the half-folded section of newspaper from the table beneath the window where Fallon had tossed it.

"What is it?" Cassandra said.

"Just a picture," Prophet replied with feigned disinterest, passing the newspaper to his wife, "taken at the University campus."

Cassandra opened the paper and examined the photograph, puzzled. "So? A reporter took a picture of us handing out a few pieces of paper," she said. "What's so harmful about that? No one has been named, and no one spoke to the press."

"It's who they photographed that's important, not what they said," Fallon replied.

"What do you mean?"

Fallon grabbed the newspaper out of Cassandra's hands, stabbing an accusing finger at the picture, pointing to a girl in the background handing a leaflet to a passing student.

"That's Amanda! Damn it Prophet! I thought we agreed she would never participate in recruiting missions. We've had a hard enough time concealing her identity. As far as I'm concerned, you should have killed her after you killed her parents. If the police or the FBI recognize her picture we're in for a world of hurt. And trust me, it's all going to fall on you. They'll start looking for her again. Only this time they won't stop until they find her, because they'll know for certain she's alive. And they *will* find her. That means they'll find us, and I'm not about to stand around waiting for that to happen."

Voices coming from the distance.

On the approach.

Closer now...

Virgil looked up to the window before moving, cloaked in the shadows, trying desperately to remain calm, not panic and run. The side of the building around him was bare, altogether devoid of shrubs or trees, offering no place to hide. Pressing tightly against the building and remaining statue-still would do nothing to hide his presence. He had to take a chance - to step out of the shadows and into the moonlight. Surely they would recognize him, and naturally they would want to strike up a conversation. What if they did so within earshot of Prophets window? Virgil knew if he had been able to hear the dimmed conversation through the cracked window, they would be able to hear him as well. What if Prophet or Fallon, worried their words had been overheard, came to the window? They would want to know who was outside and how long they had been there. They would suspect their secret was no longer safe. It wasn't, of course. Virgil would have to tell Sky what he had overheard tonight. He needed her rational mind to help him think this through, to make sense of it all. Where Virgil's decisions in life were unreliably dictated by emotion, Sky's were thankfully ruled according to the calm, collected tenets of unbiased logic.

Virgil chose his steps carefully, tracing his way along the wall to the back of the building, challenged by the near absence of light and the unaccustomed terrain beneath his feet. Reaching the back wall, he stopped, and peered around the corner.

No one in sight.

With a quick sprint he knew he could make it to Communion Hall, sight unseen. He would let himself in through the unlocked back door, come out the front, and no one would be the wiser. He could still hear the voices, though fainter now, on the road in front of Prophet's. Their arrival was well timed, and would provide him the misdirection he needed to make good his escape.

He wanted to run, to take advantage of the marginal window of opportunity that had presented itself. Instead, his legs felt rooted to the soil, metastasized by fear, as though the wish he had asked for mere seconds ago - to be one with the building in an effort to avoid detection - had been granted at this precise, ill-timed moment, anchoring him helplessly to the ground.

Movement within the building again.

The resumed creaking of floorboards.

Descending.

Someone was coming down the back stairs.

Virgil ran, tearing free of the emotional snare rooting him in place, racing across the grounds to Communion Hall.

Thirty yards ...

Lamplight from the window of the back door of Prophets building streamed out at his feet. He picked up his pace, trying to outrun the light, desperate to remain cloaked in the darkness, an ally of the night.

Fifteen yards ...

Closing on Communion Hall, he heard the creaking of un-oiled hinges behind him as Prophets door pushed open.

Mere feet away ...

Racing around the corner of Communion Hall, suddenly blinded by the black wall of night, he tripped, tumbling over a pile of discarded lumber stacked carelessly at the back of the building. Searing pain gripped his left leg mid flight, exploding from his shin, as though it had been severed at the knee. Crashing to the ground, he drew his wounded leg tightly to his chest, twice rolling on his side, his back at last meeting the safe refuge of the wall. Biting down, grinding his teeth until he thought they would turn to diamonds, he tried to displace the writhing pain racking his body. Releasing the pressure of his hand against the wound, he rolled up the leg of his jeans and examined the cleave in his skin. The gash was narrow and deep but appeared to be a clean cut. If he could get back to his room quickly before the bleeding began, Sky could treat it with a basic first aid kit, even stitch the wound if necessary. Right now, however, keeping out of sight was his main priority. He had fallen hard over the woodpile, his wounded leg evidence of that, and no doubt the clattering of the falling woodpile would have been heard. As his eyes slowly adjusted to the limited light of the moon, he noticed a thin strip of plastic lying on the landing near the woodpile, used to hold the stacks of wooden planks together during transport from the mill. He wiped the band with his shirt and fashioned a crude tourniquet, placing the plastic strip above the wound, tying it tightly until he could no longer feel the pain in his leg. Struggling to his feet, using the wall for support, he tested the ability of his bad leg to support him. Slowly, he transferred his weight from his right foot to his left and took a trial step forward. His gimp leg buckled at the knee and he clawed at the building as he fell, clutching a rusted metal downspout for support. He slumped to his side as a second wave of pain erupted from the wound. He pulled up his pant leg, assessing the damage. The plastic band he had tied securely in place to reduce the circulation of blood to the wound had shifted as he lost his balance, sliding down his leg, lodging itself in the open gash. Blood poured freely now, its warm sticky ooze coating the narrow plastic strip. He tried to grip the plastic and manipulate it free of the wound. Instead, it slipped in his wet fingers, cutting deeper still. The makeshift tourniquet had proven useless after all. Virgil grimaced as pulses of hot pain radiated from the wound as he untied the plastic strip and threw it aside.

"Who's there?" Fallon's voice boomed from the rear of Prophets building.

Stiffly, Virgil lifted himself to his feet.

"Is anybody out there? Answer me!"

Lamplight. Swaying in undulating waves across the ground.

Brighter ... dimmer ... brighter ... dimmer ...

Limping to the side of the building, Virgil peered around the corner, watching Fallon approach, the lantern in his hand swinging back and forth. He had heard the noise when Virgil fell over the woodpile and was coming to investigate the source of the mysterious sound.

He had to get inside Communion Hall before Fallon found him hiding in the shadows. Eyes now accustomed to the near absent light of the moon, he could, at the very least, avoid falling over any other debris that might be scattered around the back of the building. Looking over his shoulder, he saw the entrance, no more than thirty feet away. Fallon would find him soon if he didn't quickly get out of sight. Relying on the wall for support, he kept low, hobbling along the side of the building, limping beneath rows of dust-filmed windows until he reached the door. Turning the knob, he slipped inside.

Saved from total darkness by the dim moonlight pressing at the windows, Virgil quickly surveyed the room. The primary function of the old storeroom was that of a woodworking shop. Stacks of newly crafted wooden chairs stood floor to ceiling against one wall, and bolts of fabric lined the shelves of another. Furnishings of every description in various stages of completion covered the floor – a partially finished dining table, end tables, bed frames - propped and stacked against one another. Sawdust and wood shavings covered the floor under a patina of swirling footprints.

Negotiating his way through the nearly lightless room, careful not to accidentally strike his inflamed leg, Virgil wound his way through the wooden obstacle course, reaching the far wall of stored fabrics. He tore a strip of linen from of one of the bolts and draped it around his neck. He would need the cloth later, to dress the wound. But first, he needed to hide.

Eerie shadows of lamplight rose and fell about the room as Fallon's ghostly visage floated silently outside the moon-stained wall of windows.

Slipping behind an upturned picnic table, Virgil peered between the slats, watching Fallon's phantom form search the grounds at the back of the building, investigating the pile of tumbled wood. He held the lantern above his head, studying the area. As the glow from its flame flashed about the room, Virgil was able to get a brief look at his surroundings. The service door leading into Communion Hall was to his left, perhaps ten feet from his hiding place behind the table. He wanted to scramble for the door and disappear inside before Fallon had the chance to investigate the room. Perhaps, he thought, with his curiosity satisfied after exhaustively searching the area and finding nothing, Fallon would dismiss the incident without further consideration. Virgil watched and waited.

Outside, Fallon lowered the lantern to the level of the ground, plunging the storeroom into darkness.

Taking advantage of a final flash of lamplight, Virgil committed to memory the location of the tables and chairs that lay scattered between his hiding place and the door leading into Communion Hall. With his escape route transfixed in his mind, he focused on the zigzag path he would need to take to get to the door and safely inside. Crawling out from between the legs of the table, his damaged leg flared to life once more, as though fire smoldered white-hot beneath the broken surface of the skin. He had no choice but to move. With Fallon lurking outside he had to make himself mobile *now*, which meant forcing his crippled leg to bear the unwanted trauma if he were to successfully escape the room without being detected. Unraveling the length of linen he had torn from the fabric bolt, he wrapped it several times around his leg, maintaining a tight, even pressure, tucking the remaining fabric snugly into the top and bottom of the improvised truss. Needles of pain shot through his leg as he tested it with his full weight.

The amber glow of Fallon's lamp floated up from the ground, peering in through the bank of windows, as though it were not mere light but rather a formidable energy source of extra-sensory intelligence, aware of Virgil's presence, capable of revealing him at will.

Trapped in the gaze of this all-knowing, all-seeing oracle, Virgil felt his way around the obstacles in his path, keenly aware that the eye that watched his every move from outside might close without warning and plunge him back into total darkness. Sliding his hands along the tops of the furniture he moved slowly, each predetermined step a calculated risk, careful not to lose his way and find himself an open target should Fallon suddenly come crashing through the door, led to him under the powerful influence of the psychic oracle-lamp.

Negotiating the first ten feet was relatively easy. Only two turns remained: the first around several stacks of wooden chairs, the second past a set of bookcases. As Virgil reached the second turn the eye beyond the windows blinked, narrowing its focus, following him, matching him step for step, floating past the bank of windows, accusingly aware of every step he took. Once more the room was brought to life. Ethereal shadows danced across the floor, crept up the walls, and slithered back and forth between the ceiling beams. The bookcase ahead of him moved in the faint light, stepping in his way, growing wider and taller, blocking his path to the door. The bookcase hadn't actually moved, of course, not physically at least, but its shadow had, as did those of the rest of the objects in the room, shape-

NIGHT CRIES

shifting in otherworldly unison as the transient luminescent glare of the oracle-eye fell upon them.

The form that was Fallon was on the move again, turning in the direction of the doorway. Substituting heightened tactile senses for much preferred night vision, Virgil felt his way around the monolithic shadow of the bookcase, past wooden crates and packing boxes, until at last his hand slipped around the welcome brass door handle, as well hidden in the dark as the nested hawk high atop Mount Horning.

Cracking open the door leading into Communion Hall, he listened. Voices carried from the kitchen and the adjoining dining room above where dinner preparations were underway, but outside the service corridor lay empty. Virgil slipped out of the room and into the corridor, closing the door. Through a crack in the doorframe he watched the room behind him explode with light. Too late, the oracle had found his hiding place, bringing Fallon with it. His pursuer stood in the doorway, bathed in the soft glow of the lamp.

Glancing the lantern side to side and up and down, searching for signs of the intruder, anticipating a confrontation, Fallon listened for a creak, a squeak, a rattle - anything that would deceive his quarry into surrendering their presence. Other than the voices emanating from the kitchen area above, the room lay perfectly silent. Nothing appeared out of place. He surveyed the room a second time with the lantern. Empty. There was no place to hide in a room such as this. Several stacks of chairs here and there, several tables angled against the far wall.

Perhaps it was all in his mind.

Creatures of the night.

And yet every instinct told him he was *not* wrong.

If someone had been in the room, they had already made good their escape.

Taking a last look around he opened the door, stepping out into the shadow of the silver moon. Perhaps a quick inspection of the grounds was necessary. If an intruder had infiltrated the compound they would be found and dealt with - swiftly, permanently.

The outside world was not welcome here.

Fallon walked back and forth, inspecting the fallen woodpile. Soaked from the downpour that had hammered the grounds earlier, it occurred to him that perhaps the rain-slicked stack had simply collapsed under its own weight, a result of the logs being precariously placed atop one another. He nudged the side of the remaining pile with his shoe, testing his theory. As if by cue they fell, scattering at his feet. A field mouse fled the bottom of the woodpile, scurrying for safety from the sudden earthquake that had condemned it to homelessness.

Creatures of the night, after all.

Placing the lantern on the ground, Fallon watched the clouds glide across the peak of Mount Horning, thinking about the time he had just wasted. It was almost funny.

He reached down and picked up the lantern.

A glint of lamplight bounced off a shiny metallic object at the bottom of the toppled woodpile. He knelt down, placed the lantern on the ground, and lifted several pieces of wood from the pile, casting them aside, freeing the object.

Just a thin strip of plastic with a silver metal crimp - the kind used to bind lumber.

Twisting the length of wet plastic in his fingers he tossed it aside, wiped his hand on his jeans, and picked up the lantern. Rising to his feet, he noticed a smear on his jeans where he had wiped his fingers.

Drawing the lantern against his pant leg for a closer inspection, he checked his fingers in the bright light. Frantically, he began to search for the strip of plastic he had carelessly discarded, and found it laying several feet from the pile of fallen wood.

He drew the band closer to the lantern, carefully examining it in the light of the lamp.

The binding was not rain-soaked as he had assumed.

It was covered in blood.

He crumpled the plastic strip in his hand and shoved it into his pocket

Confidence overwhelmed him. An intruder *was* on the grounds, only now he would have an easier time of finding him. The blood on the binding was fresh, still tacky to the touch, and past experience had taught him that wounded prey was always the easiest to track.

And to dispatch.

7

WITH A MUG of hot coffee in each hand, Martin shouldered open the front door of the house and stepped onto the porch, delicately balancing the steaming liquid. Maggy lay at Claire's feet, heartily chewing on the rawhide Justin had given her when she arrived. As Martin stepped through the door Maggy sat up, sniffing the air. Recognizing the familiar smell was not on her list of allowable treats she lay back down, and reassumed the task of devouring the rawhide.

"Thought you could use a little pick-me-up. Black with two sugars, right?"

"Yes. Thanks."

Mark Oyama walked through the door behind Martin and settled into a knotty pine swayback chair across from Claire. He noticed the yellow file folder resting on her lap.

"Case file?" Mark asked, sipping his coffee.

"A patient file," Claire replied. "I thought it might prove useful."

"How so?"

"Remember earlier, before we examined the photographs, Martin mentioned I had reason to suspect someone killed my parents?"

NIGHT CRIES

"Yes. You believed it was Joseph Krebeck."

"Right," Claire said. She opened the file folder and removed the case photo of Walter Pennimore. "This man was one of my patients. With his dying words he told me Krebeck had something to do with their death."

"What would a guy like Krebeck want with your parents? What's the connection?"

"I don't know," Claire replied. "That's what I'm trying to find out."

"Mind if I take a look?" Mark asked. "Sometimes a fresh perspective helps."

She handed Oyama the file. "If your professional eye can find something in here that I missed, something that will help me figure out how Krebeck is involved with my parents death, then go for it."

Mark flipped through the thick pages of Pennimore's patient history. "How long had you been treating him?" he asked.

"Twice a week for a little over a year, at the request of the parole board."

"That seems unusual. Board's don't generally specify the treating physician, do they?"

"Not usually. But this case is different. They learned about the success I was having applying a series of psychoanalytical procedures my father had developed before he died. The results were nothing short of amazing."

"Your father was a psychiatrist as well?"

"One of the best in the country. He'd made significant gains in research over the course of his career, but the results he'd attained with patients through the application of these specific methodologies were nothing short of spectacular. During my first couple of years in university he was testing these new approaches, applying them in practice on a select group of high-risk patients."

"What was the nature of his research?" Martin asked, "Did he create a new drug or something?"

"The opposite, actually. He created a psychological model that, when applied in a state of deep hypnosis, enabled patients to affect immediate behavioral changes: a paradigm shift at the sub-conscious level, if you will. By working with the patient and introducing a behavior modification skillset that resulted in permanent attitudinal change, my father was able to treat the patient's problem at its root cause, without having to resort to the more traditional means of therapy you mentioned, such as prescribing anti-psychotic medications. His success rate over several months with neurologically healthy patients was almost one hundred percent."

"Sounds to me like this was a major breakthrough," Mark said, "and I assume one of immense proprietary and monetary value as well."

"Without question. Remember Mark, my father was *curing* patients. "They weren't going through life reliant on their meds anymore, ready to snap or kill somebody just because the prescription ran out. This was a total and complete pain and pharmaceutical-free rehabilitation process, of significant benefit to both psychiatric medicine and mankind. There was talk that with further research and greater refinement of his techniques my father may likely have been nominated for a Nobel prize."

Martin leaned forward. "I know that look, Mark. What's going through your mind?"

Pensive, fingers steepled, elbows resting on the arms of his chair, Oyama's body language was as subtle as a train wreck.

"It seems to me that if Claire's father's research is as valuable as it appears to be, then it's possible someone would be willing to kill for it. Professional jealousy, perhaps. Claire, did your father have any enemies you're aware of, or have a falling out with a past colleague or research associate?"

"Many doctors were envious of his work and reputation," Claire replied, "but I can't think of one that would be willing to resort to murder."

"You'd be surprised," Mark replied. "Not that you need a life-lesson, but trust me, the human animal is as unpredictable as any you'll ever find. Experience has taught me to start with all the possibilities, then rule them out as I go along, one by one. Sometimes the answers to the most difficult questions are found in the most obvious places. So, let's start with your father. I take it he kept a daily diary of some sort to track his progress?"

"Yes," Claire said. "My father was an exhaustive records keeper. He kept meticulous notes, assessing each step of his research, from the day he began the project to the day he died."

"Where are those records now?"

"Locked in my safe at home," Claire replied.

"Does anyone else have access to that safe besides yourself?"

"No, just me."

"Good. We may want to have a look at those files. Maybe there's something in your father's records that can tell us more about this Joseph Krebeck character. Have you spoken to anyone else besides Martin and I about this?"

"Yes. Inspector Chris Maddox. He's with the Paulo Brava police department. He was also a friend of my father."

"What did you discuss?"

"I told him what Walter told me – that my parents death wasn't an accident. He made some inquiries but never came up with anything significant. Seeing Amanda's picture in Martin's book and recognizing Krebeck's name is how I made the connection to the partial name Pennimore had given me."

"Just the same, I think I'd like to talk to Inspector Maddox and compare notes. He may know more about the case than he realizes. Do you have his number?"

"Yes, I do. I'll get you his card."

Claire got up from her chair and stepped inside, Maggy following closely at her heels, still chewing on her treat. Martin walked over to Mark and sat on the wooden porch rail.

"What do you think?"

Oyama shook his head. "This is going to be a tough one, Martin. Think about it for a second. First, the daughter of a prominent doctor and scientific researcher disappears. Shortly after that, her parents are killed. Then the same daughter pops up again, years later, having successfully sidestepped what I would imagine to have been a pretty extensive investigation by both local and federal law enforcement. To make matters worse, when she's finally located, she's photographed in the company of her parents suspected murderer."

"What are you driving at?"

Oyama's face bore an experience-hardened look, but it was the glint of revelation in his eyes that Martin found most unsettling.

"I'm just examining the facts as I see them, Martin. Evaluating them at face value. Putting the square peg in the square hole, so to speak."

Martin stared at the agent. "Wait a minute," he said. "I'm getting it now. You think Claire's sister may somehow have been *involved* in her parents death."

"It's too soon to tell if that's true or not, but considering the facts as we know them right now, it's a distinct possibility."

"Jesus! If you're right about this, Claire's going to be devastated. Her sister is the only family she has left."

"I realize that, and I empathize. But you know better than anyone we don't always like what we find in these matters. The evidence and the facts never lie."

"I just hope for Claire's sake you're wrong on this one."

The screen door to the porch opened, and Maggy and Claire returned.

"Found it," Claire said, handing Mark the business card. "I'm sure the Inspector will give you all the information you need."

"Thank you," Mark said, taking the card from her hand. "I'll phone him first thing in the morning. But right now, if you'll excuse me, I still have a few reports to review before I can call it a day. Are you planning on staying over Martin?"

"Yes," Martin replied. "I want to review our files on The Brethren with Justin in the morning."

"Good idea. We'll need to gather as much intel on this group as we can. Tell Justin to concentrate on this Krebeck fellow and to search for any links he may have to other groups besides The Brethren."

"What can I do to help?" Claire asked.

"I'd like you to work with Martin and Justin," Mark said. "Review the information they come up with on Krebeck. See if anything catches your attention. I'd also like to borrow your file on Pennimore and study it tonight, if that would be alright."

"No problem."

"Excellent," Mark said. "It's going to be a busy day tomorrow. I suggest you both get a good night's sleep."

"Goodnight Mark," Martin said. "You get on with your reports. I'll show Claire to her room."

"Thank you Mark," Claire said.

"Don't mention it," Mark replied, taking his leave. Martin and Claire sat alone on the veranda in the pale moonlight. A symphony of cicadas shrilled harmoniously among the cyprus trees.

"Mark seems like quite a guy," Claire said.

"He's the best."

"Have you known him very long?"

"About ten years now."

"How did you two come to meet?"

"Mark was my case officer during the investigation into Anne and Melanie's disappearance."

"He strikes me as a man very dedicated to his work."

"Believe me - Mark *is* the Bureau, through and through. Never before have I met anyone with such conviction for helping people. Mark is doing exactly what he was born to do, and he does it very well. I don't think there's anything else he could do even if he wanted to. When I came up with the idea for this place, I immediately knew who I wanted to run it."

"So he quit the FBI to come here?"

"In a manner of speaking. Mark was still with the Bureau, but he was eligible for early retirement. Like many other organizations, they were going through a period of *right-sizing*. They wanted young blood, fresh ideas, less grey hair. Mark and I met for lunch one day. He told me they'd made him a lucrative offer to accept an early retirement package. The only catch was it was a limited time offer. He had two weeks to make his decision. Either take the package and retire comfortably with full benefits, or take a pass and take his chances on being laid off within in a few years."

"Doesn't sound like much of a choice."

"It wasn't. Mark's a proud man, and a total professional. He wasn't about to have a successful career end with a don't-let-the-door-smack-you-in-the-ass-on-your-way-out conversation in the Directors office the third week after turning down the offer. I offered him the position as director of this center, and he accepted."

NIGHT CRIES

"Still, it must have been a difficult transition," Claire said. "To go from the FBI to working in the private sector."

"Yes, and no. Over the years the Bureau had taken its toll. Mark was special agent in charge of Domestic Terrorism for four years before he packed it in. He'd seen a lot in that time. It's not an easy job. You're privy to a world of secret information most of us wouldn't even want to know about. When the country goes to bed at night, they don't worry about going to work the next day and becoming innocent victims of a poisonous gas attack in a subway station, or being blown to bits minutes after they arrive at their office by some whackjob. It was Mark's job to be sure the fanatics behind that way of thinking never got the chance to make their point. Yet things can still go wrong, even with all the intelligence gathering and resources the Bureau has available to them. Unfortunately, in Mark's particular case, all hell broke loose one morning in Oklahoma City."

"My God," Claire said. "The bombing of the Federal Building?"

"That's right. Mark was supposed to have been there that morning to attend a seminar, but his wife had been admitted to hospital with a ruptured appendix, so he was excused. Everyone who was in that seminar room at 9:02 a.m. was killed when Timothy McVeigh drove a van packed with fertilizer and fuel oil to the front of the building and detonated it. Emergency services pulled one hundred and sixty nine bodies from the rubble that day, even children from the daycare center inside the building. Hundreds more were injured in the blast."

"But Mark can't blame himself for their deaths," Claire said. "He had no way of knowing what was going to happen."

"You're right. He shouldn't feel responsible, but he does. It goes deeper than that. Let me explain. Go back two years, before the bombing in Oklahoma. Do you remember what happened in Waco, Texas?"

"The FBI raided some kind of religious group, right?"

"It was a compound for an anti-government sect that called themselves the Branch Davidians. Their leader was a fanatic named David Koresh. I wrote about them in my last book, *An Unholy Path*. Mark was in charge of that raid. His team was supposed to have executed a no-knock warrant with the assistance of the ATF who had reason to believe the group was stockpiling weapons. Right out of the gate they met with armed resistance. Shots were fired, and from that moment things went from bad to worse. The result was a standoff that lasted for the next fifty-one days. When Mark finally decided it was time to put an end to the ordeal he ordered in HRT, the Bureau's Hostage Rescue Team, and together with ATF agents they stormed the grounds. By the time it was over, the Branch Davidian compound had been burned to the ground, and four ATF agents were dead. Eighty other men, women and children trapped inside the buildings within the compound died as well, either during the assault or from the fire, including Koresh. Because Mark was the agent in charge of the HRT assault, the Office of Professional Responsibility, which is the FBI's internal affairs department, took him to the mat for his actions taken that day."

"What happened?"

"Eventually, nothing. Mark was cleared of any improper conduct, but the OPR investigation was extremely hard on him. A committee had been set up to investigate the incident, and they tried to tag him with use of excessive force and not following the FBI's rules of engagement. Some of the higher-ups blamed Mark personally for the deaths of those agents, which of course was crap. But that was just the beginning. They really put his feet to the fire when it came out that the bombing in Oklahoma City two years later had been sanctioned by the Branch Davidians. Turns out it was payback for Waco. The brass believed if Mark had handled things differently at Waco, Oklahoma might never have happened."

NIGHT CRIES

"So that's when he decided to leave the FBI?"

"Yes. That's when I told him about my plans to start this organization. By then he'd had enough of the bureaucracy of the Bureau and had been giving thought to retiring anyway. I guess the timing was right. He took the package and my offer the same day. It's been six years, and we haven't looked back since."

"You both should be very proud of yourselves. You're making a difference, helping people. That's an admirable way to live your life."

"Thanks, but if we didn't do it somebody else would. In truth, Mark and I both have our independent motivations. In my case, I want to help the families of the Anne's out there whose lives have been ripped to pieces by people like Krebeck. And though it's not for me to say, I think Mark does this for the people who died at Waco, and for those that perished in Oklahoma City. He may seem like a strong guy on the outside, everything always under control, but I know the inner torture he deals with every day. In the bottom drawer of his desk he keeps a folder filled with pictures and newspaper articles about the incidents at Waco and Oklahoma. I came across it by accident when he asked me to get a file for him. I never mentioned anything to him about it, didn't even bring it up. The fact he keeps it close at hand tells me it's there for a reason."

"He's internalized the responsibility for their deaths. He never wants to allow himself to forget what happened."

"That sounds like Mark. Carrying the burden of the world on his shoulders."

"It's more than that," Claire said. "It's not healthy for him, or you, to assume that degree of guilt. You both need to put what happened behind you and move on with your lives."

"We both know that's a lot easier said than done."

"I agree. But you need to take consolation from the fact you're doing all you can. To accept any less is simply unfair. Look around you Martin. This organization you've created, the people who work for it, the many lives you've saved, the families you've reunited … these are the successes you and Mark need to celebrate every day. It's *that* file of memories Mark needs to keep stored in his desk drawer, not of lives lost for reasons beyond his control. Those positive events should be the motivators that drive you and give meaning to what you do and why you do it, not the negative events of the past. The past is valuable to us for one reason only. It gives us a baseline to measure how we're going to deal with today. That's all."

"I suppose you're right," Martin said thoughtfully. "I guess our natural tendency is to dwell on the bad things that happen to us and not the good. It's easier to accept our failures than our successes."

"That's a reflection of the competitive world we're living in. And when you've chosen a career that focuses on mastering an acute understanding of the worst in people, like Mark has, it's easy to become jaded, to see the darkness in others instead of the light, including yourself."

"Has anyone ever told you you're a very, *very* smart lady, Dr. Prescott?"

Stunned by Martin's sudden compliment, Claire found she could only smile. She wanted to respond, but the look in Martin's eyes captivated her, stealing her words. For the first time in many years, she could have sworn she felt her heart skip a beat.

"Has anyone also told you how incredibly beautiful you are?"

Those eyes. God, he could melt her with those eyes! Here she was, a grown woman, staring into the eyes of a man she had known for less than twenty-four hours, as speechless and weak-kneed as a teenager on her first date. There was an undeniable quality about him that mesmerized her. She had seen it in his picture the night before at the gala. Martin had the unique ability to communicate his thoughts and emotions with the cast of his gaze. Now, on the receiving end of this sudden wave of emotion, she knew his heart was speaking directly to hers. He closed his eyes and leaned forward, pressing his lips softly to hers. She felt his hand in the small of her back, cradling her, drawing her closer. She sighed involuntarily, feeling her arms slowly rise from her sides, finding their place around his back as naturally as if they had been doing so for a lifetime. The warmth of his touch and gentle embrace carried Claire to heights of emotion she had not felt in years. When he finally released her she stood breathless before him.

"I've been wanting to do that since I first laid eyes on you," Martin confessed. "But now, I have to admit, I'm scared to death to know what you're thinking."

Claire clasped Martin's hands, bringing them to her chest. She smiled.

"I'm glad you did."

#

Mark Oyama's chair sighed as he sat down. Propping his leather cowboy boots up on the corner of his desk, he unscrewed the cap from a bottle of spring water he had taken from the kitchen on his way to his office. He took steady swigs of the cold water, and before he had stopped drinking he had consumed half the bottle. Sliding the phone across the desk, he removed the business card Claire had given him from his pocket and dialed the number. The call picked up on the first ring.

"Homicide. Maddox speaking."

"Inspector, my name is FBI Special Agent Retired Mark Oyama. I'm calling from Sacramento on behalf of Dr. Claire Prescott. Do you have a few minutes to speak with me?"

"Certainly, Agent Oyama. You say you're calling from Sacramento. Is everything okay with Dr. Prescott?"

"She's fine," Mark replied. "I'm working with her on a missing persons search. I told her I wanted to touch base with you on matters which may be of importance to my investigation. Mind if I ask you a few questions?"

"Fire when ready."

"According to Dr. Prescott, you were the primary on the Mendelson incident. Is that correct?"

"I was."

"What can you tell me about Joseph Krebeck?"

Maddox sounded puzzled. "*Krebeck?* No one by that name was involved with the Mendelson situation, Agent Oyama. Just Clarence Demmings, the security guard who saved her life, and Dr. Prescott's patient, Walter Pennimore. But no Krebeck, I'm afraid." The inspector paused for a moment. "Wait a minute. The day after the attack at Mendelson Dr. Prescott did mention to me that Pennimore told her some cockamamie story about her parents being killed. Murdered, actually."

"Go on."

"According to Pennimore, some guy named *'Kre'* was responsible for their death. I ran the partial through our computers: first name, last name, known aliases – the usual drill. I came up empty, as I expected I would. Personally, I think the good doctor was taking this Pennimore guy way too seriously. He was a psych patient and a child molester - a real waste of skin."

"That doesn't mean he wasn't telling the truth," Mark interjected.

"True enough," Maddox agreed. "But my understanding of Pennimore from the interviews conducted with clinicians and staff led me to believe he was prone to some pretty heavy-duty shit. Voices in his head, hallucinations - that sort of stuff. Besides, we scoured the accident scene where Dr. Prescott's parents were killed. It was a car crash, in case you weren't aware. Dr. Prescott's father lost control of his vehicle, launched it off a cliff, and had a serious disagreement with the rocks below. He and his wife were killed on impact. Eyewitness reports taken at the scene confirm our findings. It was an accident - case closed. Dr. Prescott was there. She witnessed the whole thing. It's all in my report. I can Fed-Ex you a copy in the morning if you want to review it."

"Whoa, back up a second!" Oyama remarked. "You said Dr. Prescott was there? She *saw* the crash?"

"Not the actual crash, no. But she witnessed the car go off the cliff and the explosion that followed. Like I said, it's all in the report."

"I think reviewing your report might be helpful after all," Mark said. "But let's go back to Krebeck for a minute. You turned up nothing on him?"

"Not in our database. I told Dr. Prescott I'd make a few additional inquiries though and call some friends in the Bureau as a courtesy to her. Looks like she beat me to it."

"Sounds to me like you've done all you can, Inspector. If I need to check back with you ... "

"Don't even hesitate to call," Maddox finished. "My office will be more than happy to assist you with your investigation. I'll have that file sent off to you in the morning."

"I'd appreciate that. Thanks."

Mark gave the inspector his address and hung up the phone. He thumbed through Pennimore's file, page after page, looking for something that might jump out at him - a clue in the body of the report, an overlooked notation.

"What is it you know that I don't, Walter?" he said aloud, flipping through the pages at random. Pennimore's picture had been stapled to the inside of the file folder. He pulled it off and stared into the dead man's eyes. A lifetime of professional experience had bestowed upon him a master's degree in intuition. The longer he stared at

Pennimore's photo the louder the little bell inside his head rang, telling him something was not right. Pennimore's eyes spoke to him.

Oyama put the picture back into the file, closed the cover, took a final swig of water and tossed the empty bottle into the wastebasket. He sighed heavily.

"Accident, my ass," he muttered.

#

"Don't you *ever* leave this place?" Cynthia Rowe joked as she entered the computer lab, her short blonde hair bobbing up and down as she crossed the room. Her skin-tight leather pants accentuated every curve of her long shapely legs, and the suppleness of the leather crinkled with every step. Over her shoulder she carried a leather knapsack, which she tossed to the floor beside Justin's chair. She untied the long-sleeve yellow sweater she wore draped over her shoulders and wrapped it around her waist.

Justin barely looked up, tapping away on the computer keyboard, carefully watching the screen as he scrolled through an internet search. "That would require having a life," he replied. "Too busy trying to catch the bad guys, I guess. Anyway, what are you doing here? I thought you were working an intelligence op upstate."

"Wrapped it up this afternoon." Cynthia tapped the knapsack with her foot. "I've got three memory cards in here that need to be downloaded asap."

"Run away with me to the Caribbean and I'll have them ready for you in five minutes."

Cynthia smiled. "How about I buy you dinner instead. What do you say, boy genius? Fajitas and a pitcher?"

"A reasonable compromise," Justin replied, a hint of mock disappointment in his voice. "And stop calling me boy genius! I'm more than a brilliant mind you know. You really should re-think my Caribbean offer. Besides, you'd look totally hot in a …"

Cynthia gave him a friendly poke in the side, then mussed his hair with her fingers. "Throw some ice on it Romeo," she said, wrapping her arms around him in a friendly hug, pressing her cheek to his, looking over his shoulder at the computer screen. "What are you working on?"

Justin sighed and rolled his eyes. "Sure. Get me all hot and bothered. Just my luck! I finally meet the girl of my dreams, and she's *all* business."

"Speaking of business …"

"Okay, okay. A new client arrived today, Dr. Claire Prescott. She's a friend of Martin's. A real hottie too!"

"I'm festering with jealousy," Cynthia chided. "So, what's the doc's story?"

"Her sister disappeared years ago, but we think we've got a lead on her already. Seems she's mixed up with a cult called The Brethren. Ever heard of them?"

"Nope."

"I'm not surprised. They're pretty low key. The top man's got a rather nasty rep though."

"Namely?"

"Joseph Krebeck," Justin said, minimizing the internet search he was working on and pulling up the file picture of Joseph Krebeck and Amanda; the same photo that appeared in Martin's book. "Excuse the crappy photo. Looks like it was taken with a telephoto lens."

Cynthia stood up, her playful tone suddenly turning very matter-of-fact. She walked across the room to her desk, unlocked her filing cabinet and rummaged through a series of files, removing a photograph.

"What's the matter, Cyn?" Justin asked, surprised by her sudden turn of mood.

"Can you run a photo enhancement on the girl in your picture, maybe clean up the resolution a little and enlarge it?"

"Sure. Why? Something catch your eye?"

"Just do it, will you please?" The urgency in Cynthia's voice was disturbing.

"Geez woman, don't bust a seam on me! I'm working on it already! I did a comparative analysis earlier for Martin. Let me see now. Where did I put that file ... oh yeah, here it is."

Cynthia's concentration was fixed on the computer screen. "You say this is a file photo from Martin's book?"

"Yeah. So what?"

"And you've already made a preliminary match?"

"Yes. Dr. Prescott brought a family photo with her, which I compared to this one. It's a *definite* match. Now, would you mind telling me what's going on? Why are you so interested in this girl?"

"In a second." Cynthia handed Justin the photograph from her file. "Do you have the photograph from the doctor here?"

"Yeah. I scanned it into memory to compare it with Martin's photo."

"Can you scan in my photo and bring all three pictures up on the screen?

"P-lease," Justin said cynically. "Is the pope Catholic?"

Cynthia tweaked his ear. "Ouch!" he cried. "Man! Put the woman in a pair of leather pants and suddenly she's a dominatrix." He turned to Cynthia and winked. "By the way, did I ever tell you that's a quality I find extremely appealing in the women I date?"

Cynthia shook her head and smiled. "You never give up, do you?"

NIGHT CRIES

"Not while you can still wear *those* pants," he said, watching the screen as he typed the instructions into the computer. In seconds, the three pictures appeared side by side on the screen.

"Okay. Good," Cynthia said. "Now, young Einstein, can you cross-reference all three woman for similarities?"

"Sure. Just let me enter a few instructions and ... here we go."

Instantly, the images on the screen began to flash as dozens of lines criss-crossed the faces in the three photographs, extracting points of reference from each respective picture, creating three-dimensional profiles which rotated in circles left to right. The word **VERIFYING** blinked in the lower left corner of the screen.

"What's happening?" Cynthia asked.

"Magic, my dear," Justin replied. "Technological magic. A facial recognition program in the computer is scanning the images we input from each of the photos and is creating a biometric signature. After that, a mathematical algorithm normalizes the pictures, which is to say it re-configures each picture so that they are the same size, shape, perspective, resolution, and so on."

The images rotating on the screen came to a stop, and the profiles of each woman looked straight ahead from the screen. A matrix of inter-connecting lines began to flash over each picture. The word VERIFYING had now been replaced with **IDENTIFYING**.

"What you see happening now is the matcher program at work," Justin explained. "The program is trying to compare the normalized signature of your picture with the sub-set of the normalized signatures from the first two photographs already in memory. It's looking for characteristic similarities between the three photos, such as cranial structure, sameness in the eyes, nose, mouth and so on, especially any dominant abnormalities. Based on its findings, it'll give us a ranking."

"English, please?" Cynthia said.

"It will give us a final decision."

As though caught in the web of an electronic spider, the images on the screen waited for the matrix of intersecting lines to cease their searching pattern. Within seconds, the word **RANKING** flickered on screen, quickly followed by the word **MATCH**.

"There you go babe," Justin said, extending his hand to the screen in a greeting gesture. "Same girl as in the other two photographs. Cynthia Rowe, I'd like you to meet Amanda Prescott."

"Incredible." Cynthia said.

"Yes, I know," Justin said with a grin, "though you've got to give the computer *some* of the credit."

"Not you, smart ass." Cynthia tapped the computer screen with her finger. "I took this picture two weeks ago. And I spoke to *this* girl."

"You spoke to Amanda Prescott?"

"Yes."

"Where?"

"West of here. On the campus of Sonoma State University. In Rohnert Park."

"Jesus," Justin said. "That's too close for comfort. If we don't mobilize on this right away we could lose her, and then who knows when we'd pick up her trail again. You better let Mark know about this first thing in the morning."

"Screw the morning," Cynthia said. "He's got to know right now!"

#

"We need to talk," Cynthia said, bursting through Mark's door, waving the biometric printouts in her hand.

Mark lowered his feet from his desk. "Don't you believe in knocking? What's so important you need to break the door down to see me?"

"Sorry, but this is important. You know the UC I've been working on upstate?"

"The intelligence gathering at the University."

"Yes. Justin showed me the profile of the new client's sister, Amanda Prescott."

"So?"

Cynthia laid the copies of the printouts out on Mark's desk, tapping her finger on the first and second comparisons. "These are the profiles generated by the computer. I took the photo on the right two weeks ago at Sonoma State. See the girl standing beside the guy handing out the leaflets? That's Amanda Prescott. The computer confirms it."

Oyama picked up the printouts, examining them closely. "Jesus," he said. "You're right. Do we have identification on the other subjects in the photo?"

"Not yet. I'll have Justin get to work on it."

"Good. I want to know who these people are. Every last one of them."

"Yes sir," Cynthia said, collecting the papers off Mark's desk. She turned to leave the room.

"I also want you to put your other cases on hold," Mark added. "Since you've made peripheral contact with the subject your input could be invaluable. This case is high profile. Amanda Prescott had been all but given up for dead. Now that we've got a handle on who she's involved with I have no doubt we'll get the go ahead to proceed with a hard target extraction, and I'm going to need my best operatives on point when it goes down." Oyama leaned back in his chair, its springs heaving a tired sigh. "I'm calling a meeting in the morning. I want you to assist me in organizing the team. Just make sure Dan Raines and Karen Lassiter are on that list. They're ex-FBI like me. Dan commanded Los Angeles SWAT when we worked together at the Bureau. Nobody's more field qualified than he is, and Karen's an excellent negotiator and marksman. If they're on any other assignments tell them to be ready to be pulled at a moment's notice."

"Yes sir."

"Oh, one last thing."

"Sir?"

"That was great work. To be able to pull that photo out of memory considering your caseload is just about as damn professional as it gets. Go get some rest. You've earned it."

"Thank you sir," Cynthia said. "That's sounds like a pretty good idea."

NIGHT CRIES

8

PEERING THROUGH THE crack in the doorframe, Virgil watched the ghostly countenance of Fallon drift past the outside window as the light inside the storeroom faded to black. The hot air that had been trapped in his chest let go, and he breathed a sigh of relief. He was safe, but only for the moment. Voices echoed through the floorboards above, and the sound of purposeful footfalls increased in their intensity. The empty service corridor would only provide temporary refuge. Fallon was still out there, somewhere. Virgil knew him well enough to know he would not give up the search easily. He had to get back to his room and tell Sky. Could it be true? Could Prophet have murdered Amanda's parents? No. That was simply impossible. He was a disciple of God, entrusted with the lives of those who needed him for spiritual guidance and leadership. Prophet had been chosen by God to seek a better life, devoid of the chaos and evil the outside world read about every day in their newspapers and watched on the six o'clock news. He had come into their lives to show them they had been called to serve a higher purpose, and Virgil believed him without reservation, until now. For the moment, he was unsure what to believe. Sky would know. He had to get to back to his wife and daughter. Most importantly, he needed to tend to the gash in his leg and rejoin the others quickly before his absence arose suspicion.

The room behind remained bathed in darkness, and Virgil wondered if perhaps he should return the same way he had come. Fallon had gone, and he had not been detected. He thought about the maze of wooden chairs and tables he had successfully negotiated moments ago in the last flicker of light from Fallon's lantern. He could do it again - re-trace his steps, follow the route he had taken through the room, out the door and into the night. He could slip around the corner, avoiding the woodpile this time, and follow the stone path, staying in the shadows of the buildings, keeping a watchful eye open for Fallon. Opening the door, Virgil slipped back into the storeroom. His damaged leg flared to life, as though the devil himself had grabbed him by the wound with a hand of fire, intent on holding him long enough to alert Fallon to his attempted escape. His leg buckled beneath him, and he grabbed the brass handle of the door for support. The temporary compress of torn linen wrapped around his leg was wet to the touch and slipped from side to side, grating against the wound as he tried to walk. Suddenly, the task ahead took on a greater, more troublesome perspective. He wouldn't get far in his present state. The quick building-to-building sprint that had been his plan was quickly diminishing with each passing second. With his range of mobility reduced to a mere hobble, Virgil forced himself to come to terms with the inevitable.

He was trapped.

#

As Fallon walked away from Communion Hall, the back door to Prophets residence creaked open. Prophet stepped onto the landing.

NIGHT CRIES

"I heard you calling out a minute ago. What's wrong?"

"We have an intruder on the grounds," Fallon replied, removing the bloodstained plastic strip from the pocket of his jeans, re-examining it in the pale yellow light of the lantern. "I found this under the woodpile at the back of Communion Hall." He smoothed the darkened ooze between his fingers. "That's blood. Fresh blood. Someone has infiltrated the compound."

Prophet took the strip from Fallon's hand and turned it over, examining the metal crimp in the moonlight, testing the tacky surface of the plastic.

"How do you know its not animal blood?" Prophet said. "A fox maybe. Could have gotten tangled up in it, chewed its way free. Foxes are always roaming around here at night. The mountain is thick with them."

"It's not a fox, Joseph. It's probably another damn reporter. Those leeches never know when to leave well enough alone. And I bet I know why he's here."

"I'm sure you're going to tell me, whether I want to hear it or not," Prophet replied coolly.

"You know why as well as I do. The picture in the paper. Someone recognized Amanda. Now they've come looking for her, looking for proof. And if they find it, if they find *her*, it's all over." Fallon paused momentarily. "If it is a reporter, we may have an even bigger problem to deal with."

"What do you mean?"

"We don't know if our conversation was overheard. If it was, we can't take any chances. They'd know for certain she's here."

"*Shit*," Prophet cursed, looking around, searching the shadows that fell from the adjoining buildings for signs of unusual movement. "Okay," he said. "Let's assume for the moment you're right, even though I don't think you are. Where do you think he could be?"

"Anywhere," Fallon replied. "That's the problem. There's too much area for me to cover on my own. We need to work the grounds together. You take the east side, I'll take the west. We'll meet up full-circle. But for now, wait here." Fallon turned and walked away, heading back in the direction of Communion Hall.

"Where are you going?" Prophet asked.

"The storeroom," Fallon answered without looking back. "I'm going to get the rifles."

#

Unwrapping the makeshift dressing, Virgil examined the wound, lightly tracing his finger around the outside of the gash. The bleeding had stopped, at least for the moment. If he could make it across the room in the darkness he could reach the stack of fabric bolts and re-dress the wound. He would make the compress tighter this time, restrict the blood flow. His eyes were accustomed to the darkness now, and the pale moonlight filtering through the windows provided shadowy dimension to the objects cluttering the room. Cautiously, he began to navigate his way between the wooden furnishings, focusing his attention on the wall containing the many shelves of fabric bolts. Once he had re-dressed the wound he would regain his mobility, or at least a portion of it. He might even be able to manage a crippled sprint for short distances from building to building, and be back to the security of his room in a matter of minutes. Once there, he would clean up the wound, change clothes and join the others in Communion Hall. No one would be the wiser. Muffled voices came from outside the storeroom as the others made their way to the dining area. The acoustics of the room made the voices indistinguishable, spiriting them off the walls and ceiling. Still, he found himself strangely grateful for their company. Reaching the middle of the room, he stopped suddenly, frozen mid-step. Waves of familiar lamplight rose and fell against the bank of windows, breaking against the glass barricade as if by command, attacking and retreating in dutiful service. Quickly, their intensity illuminated the room once more, chasing the shadows that had become his allies back to their corners in reluctant submission. Fallon was returning! Perhaps he had been seen after all, or maybe Fallon had smelled fear in the air and was tracking him now, like a wolf tracking its prey. With no time to spare, Virgil scurried around the obstacles in his path, slipping into a narrow space between the storehouse wall and the rack of fabric bolts, as dust-rich beams of lamplight infused the storeroom. Several fabric bolts stood against the wall beside him, too tall to have been laid lengthwise in the rack. Virgil angled the loose bolts in front of him, pressing his back to the wall. As the lamplight charged in from outside he peered out from behind his hiding place, examining the sawdust-covered floor. Footprints, *his* footprints, traced a distinct path around the tables and chairs to where he stood. Thankfully, no blood had dripped from his leg to the floor, at least none that he could see from his limited perspective. Not that it would have mattered. To this point he knew he had been lucky, but now he had the distinct feeling his luck was running out. Only a distance of twenty feet separated him from the door, and as it swung open he turned his body against the fabric rack, as though he might somehow be able to slip behind it further still. Fallon stood in the doorway, surveying the room with a careful eye, sweeping it with the light of the lantern. He looked directly at Virgil, and he felt his stomach drop. Fallon walked into the room. Standing statue-still behind the fabric bolts Virgil calculated his options should he be discovered. If Fallon got within several feet he could charge him before being recognized, take him by surprise, push the fabric bolts on top of him, and knock him to the ground. He would be distracted, and Virgil would pull more bolts off the shelf and throw them on him too, perhaps ensnaring him long enough to make good his escape. But that solution wasn't practical. Fallon would fall to the ground, as would the lantern he held in his hand. It would smash to the floor in the melee, and a fire would inevitably ensue. The sawdust that covered the floor would accelerate the blaze, along with the many wooden furnishings, cans of paint and bolts of cloth. In truth, there was probably nothing Virgil would have liked more than to see Fallon collapse into a tomb of fire, a fate he would likely face on his day of reckoning if the conversation he had overheard was true. Besides, others were in the building, and they would become innocent victims. Virgil could not allow that to happen. He could not expose his friends and family to such a risk. He needed a better option. Perhaps he could step out from behind the security of his hiding place and confront Fallon face to face, telling him what he had heard, demanding an explanation for the murderous conspiracy. *One option or the other,* he thought as Fallon stepped further into the room. *Make up your mind now. You're not going to get a second chance.*

    Fallon placed the lantern on a chair and turned away, walking sharply across the room where he removed two rifles from a small closet. From behind the fabric bolts, Virgil watched as he placed the rifles and a handful of shells on an unfinished table, loading them one by one, first breaking the breach and inspecting the barrel for obstructions, then snapping the weapon closed. A single shell rolled across the surface of the table in a wandering arc, and fell to the floor. Fallon walked around the table to retrieve the elusive projectile that had disappeared among the fat mounds of sawdust. He picked up the lantern from the chair and placed it on the floor beside him, raking through the sawdust with the tips of his bony fingers in small, sweeping circles. Finding the errant casing, he shook the excess sawdust from his hand and slipped the shell into his pocket. The thin brass handle slipped in his grip as he lifted the lantern, and he caught it quickly before it fell to the floor. The handle felt slick, damp to the touch. He settled the lantern in place, examining his hand in the pale yellow light, brushing away the fine particles of sawdust from his fingers.

More blood.

Whoever he sought had been in this room.

Fallon remained motionless, listening intently to the sounds around him. He picked up the lantern, rising slowly to his feet. Were they still here? Watching him, even now? Lifting a rifle from the table he drew back the bolt, chambering a round.

Sounds from above echoed throughout the room. Towards the door, floorboards creaked.

Fallon swung around, raising the weapon to his shoulder, crossing the room in Virgil's direction. A weakened floorboard sighed underfoot as Virgil pressed his back to the wall, trying to disappear behind the veil of the cloth barricade. He couldn't watch Fallon approach. If he did he might panic, and react prematurely. Fallon had him dead in his sights. He would pull the trigger and ask questions later, assuming Virgil would still be alive to answer. But Virgil too had questions; many of them, and he wanted answers. He held his breath, waiting to be discovered. He thought of Sky and Blessing, and despite the grimness of his situation, realized he would still be better off alive than dead. His questions would be answered, in due course. But for now they would have to wait.

Another creak. This one more definite than the last. Outside the door.

Fallon turned his attention away from the rack of fabric bolts, zeroing in on the phantom sound. As the handle began to turn, a familiar calmness overtook him. Spotting a chair several feet away he moved into position, dropping quickly to one knee, slipping the barrel of the rifle through the chair slats, resting it on the cross-brace, focusing on an imaginary target above the door handle. In all likelihood the intruder was armed. He turned out the lantern, plunging the room into darkness.

Centre mass, he thought. *Never high or low. Without a scope a headshot is a waste of a perfectly good round. Drop the target on the first shot. The game is about shooting to kill, not to wound.*

His training had been invaluable.

Finger on the trigger, crouched behind the chair in the gloomy blackness of the room, he was all but invisible. The power to steal the final breath of a life he did not know filled him with tremendous confidence, and surged through him with such force it made him shiver. The raw power of the moment captivated him as he balanced the rifle, aligning the sight. His concentration was peaked. He felt as though he was no longer within the confines of the small room but rather kneeling amidst a maelstrom of writhing electrical currents, drawing them into him, harnessing their power to do his bidding, the rifle in his hands the conducting rod.

The silhouette in the doorway spoke. "Fallon? You in here?"

Fallon's finger flew back from the trigger. He lowered the butt of the rifle to the floor, angling the barrel away from the doorway. Slowly, he stood up from behind the chair.

"Why didn't you stay where you were?" Fallon said curtly, choosing not to share with Prophet how close he had just come to being shot and killed. "I told you I'd be back in a minute."

In the darkness he withdrew the barrel of the rifle from the chair slats.

"What do you think you're talking to? A fucking *puppy*?" Prophet yelled, shoving the door open, slamming it against the wall, "I *had* to find you! We're out of time. We'll search the grounds later. The others are assembling for dinner, and if we're not there on time they'll come looking for us. Put away the rifles and meet me in Communion

NIGHT CRIES

Hall in five minutes." With an air of disgust Prophet turned and walked away.

Fallon stood silently, staring at the empty doorway, Prophets words replaying in his mind. *If I hadn't been watching your back all these years you'd be a fucking puppy alright,* he thought. *More like somebody's bitch. Probably fetching slippers for some nasty piece of work named Alice in the state penitentiary right now, and getting your ass popped every other day for a pack of smokes and a Coke.*

Picking up the rifles, he returned them to the gun rack inside the closet and emptied his pockets of the shells. Uncomfortable with the idea of being unarmed with an intruder lurking on the grounds, he removed a semi-automatic handgun from its hiding place in an old cigar box beside the rifles. He inspected the clip and slipped it back into the weapon, locking it in place. Chambering a round, he put the gun in his waistband, covering it with his shirttail at the small of his back, and closed the closet door.

Walking across the room, he stopped once more at the table and knelt down, re-examining the sawdust-covered area where he had found the drops of blood. Cupping his hands, he scooped up a generous amount of the powdered wood, letting it sift through his fingers, examining it in the flickering lamplight. A sudden draft blew in through the open door, sending the sawdust surrounding him swirling about the room in violent wisps, like a sirocco racing across a miniature Sahara. Opening his hands, he shook the last of the fine particles from his fingers. Several small, dark clumps stuck to his skin. Smoothing them together, he opened his palms to the light of the lantern. Erratic streaks smeared his hands in a coagulated mosaic, confirming his suspicions. He pressed his palms together, testing for a sensation of tackiness as he pulled his hands apart. It was what he expected to find. In that second his decision was made. He would slip out of Communion Hall after dinner was underway and search the grounds alone. He knew his absence would not be missed. He preferred it that way. Relationships, other than those born of immediate convenience, only complicated matters. Attachments were for those who needed such crutches - like a blind man's reliance on his seeing-eye dog.

He picked up the lantern and walked out of the room, closing the door behind him. The sooner he joined the others the faster he could resume the hunt. Perhaps in the interim his quarry would assume he had simply given up the chase and grow bolder, inadvertently exposing themselves. Throughout his life he had enjoyed an unequaled reputation as an excellent tracker of men. It was his god-given gift, one he had learned to use well. His gut was telling him the intruder was an amateur. He would simply give him a little more time to expose himself. In the long run patience had always proven to be his ally, and this thought raised his spirits. As he rounded the corner of Communion Hall past the fallen woodpile that had initially piqued his curiosity, he thought about the emotional rush he felt seconds ago - harnessing the energy of the room, steeling himself for the kill shot. He could manage to wait another thirty minutes.

Virgil listened as Fallon's footsteps faded into silence, each creak on the landing at the back of the building more distant than the last. Rolling one of the tall linen bolts aside, he slipped out of his hiding place. He was safe once more, yet he could not help but feel strangely exposed, as though his every move was being watched. Had Fallon really given up the search? Perhaps he lay in wait around the corner, anticipating the opening of the door - an outstretched arm pressed against the wall of the building, steadying the handgun he had taken from the closet, lining up the shot. *Am I going to walk into a bullet the minute I step outside?* Virgil thought, drying his damp palms against his shirt. He recalled the anger in Prophets words before he left, ordering Fallon to meet up with the others for dinner. It was obvious now that Fallon was much more of a concern than he had originally thought him to be. He was willing to challenge Prophet, and that made him dangerous. He had to warn Sky and the others. If Fallon was losing control he could be capable of anything, including killing Prophet, and anyone else for that matter.

Virgil cautiously cracked open the back door. If Fallon was waiting for him to show himself perhaps he wouldn't take the shot after all. The gunfire would draw too much attention, and the others would come running. Fallon knew the consequences that would befall him from such an act. If he were to bring violence to them, especially the shooting and killing of one of their own, he would be disgraced and ex-communicated. There would be no police investigation, no formal charges. They were a family, and as such took care of their own. Fallon would be dead to them. Not that that mattered much, Virgil thought. He was already viewed as an outcast by many - a tannic personality steeped in mystery, shrouded in secrecy. Every prophet has his Judas, Virgil thought, some more deadly than others. Perhaps the real danger was not in their relationship, but what might come from the breaking of it.

A cool mist had swept down from the mountain, bringing with it patchy clouds of dense, moon-silvered fog which swirled at Virgil's feet as he cautiously opened the door and looked out at the wooden landing. The sudden, erratic creaking of the door startled him and he froze, swallowing hard, waiting for a bullet to find him. To his relief, the silence of the night remained unbroken, his body intact. Perhaps Fallon had given up the search, after all. Still, better to err on the side of caution, he thought. He had to know if Fallon was out there waiting for him - if he would draw fire the second he stepped outside. He needed a diversion. He could open the door fully and time his escape, dashing out into the night, cloaked from immediate view by the blanket of fog. But that would require two able legs to carry him a safe distance from the building until he could regain his bearings and make his way back to his room, and the pain in his leg quickly reminded him this was not an option. He resigned himself to the fact that the journey back to his room would have to be a slow, circuitous one, in light of his impeded mobility. Looking back into the room, he spied a discarded chair leg a few feet away. He tested the door, checking to see if the rusty hinges would squeal if challenged by an outside breeze, should he leave it ajar for a few seconds. Immediately the door failed the test, and he held it tightly again. But the chair leg had given him an idea. It was a gamble, at best, but one he would be willing to try. He gave the door another chance. This time it held, in silence. Virgil dropped to his hands and knees, crawling outside the open door. He picked up the chair leg and stood up, pressing his shoulder to the doorframe, listening for any telltale sounds that his attempt to move discreetly in and out of the storeroom had been discovered, and that Fallon was coming for him. The sounds of the night had fallen eerily silent. Either Fallon was not waiting for him after all and had gone to join the others or he was not to be fooled so easily, and was simply waiting for a suitable moment to make his presence known – most likely from the business end of his gun.

Virgil knew he had no options. He had to assume he was still a target.

Testing the weight of the chair leg in his hand, he stood in the shadow of the doorway and tossed the wooden shaft in the direction of the field with as much strength as he could muster, watching it disappear into the heavy fog. He listened as it thumped once, then twice more, toppling end over end across the hard-packed ground.

No reaction came from the outside of the storeroom. Virgil steeled himself, peering around the corner, testing the limits of his nerves, his warm breath softly glazing the night-dampened doorframe with layer upon layer of adrenaline. A cricket stirred, then another, and soon the cicadas resumed their melodic chirping. The night had accepted the interruption without concern.

Shuffle-stepping out of the storeroom, he waited for Fallon to appear out of the fog - gun trained, quarry trapped and wounded ...

Cornered.

But there was no sign of Fallon. Virgil quickly took advantage of his opportunity, stepping off the wooden landing, moving as quickly as he could across the grounds towards the perimeter of the fields. The thick fog had reduced his visibility to less than six feet, and with each step needles of pain seized his leg, encouraging him to stop and rest. But he could not stop. He had to garner as much distance from Fallon as he could and make it back to his room, to his family.

He had taken this route a dozen times before under better circumstances, his path made clear by the brilliant glow of the moon on clear, star-filled nights. Behind him, the voices from Communion Hall faded the further along the well-trodden path he traveled. He arrived at last at the broken asphalt road leading back to his building. He was not far now. Beyond the remaining several hundred yards of worn tarmac lay safety and security in the form of his wife and child, and Virgil stopped for a moment to rest. His leg ached up the side of his body from the source of the pain to his waist. He fought back the cramps that complicated his journey, gently massaging his thigh muscles, trying not to give in despite his desperate desire to sit and rest. If he stopped now he would never make it back to his room unseen. The cramping in his leg was getting worse. Against the wishes of every muscle in his body he struggled down the road, dragging gravel beneath the weight of his wounded leg. Brilliant flashes of pain and panic-stricken thoughts burst through his mind, blurring his vision, challenging his concentration. Perhaps Fallon *had* known it was him, *had* seen him hiding between the rolls of fabric when he examined the droplets of blood in the sawdust. Perhaps he was simply waiting for the right opportunity to make him pay for being in the worst place at the worst possible time. More starbursts of pain exploding from his leg. *My God*, Virgil thought, wincing away the blinding light show. *Maybe I'm not the target. That's why he never shot at me when I stepped out of the room. He's going after my family! He'll use them to get to me!*

   The shock of this revelation grew in his mind, and a newly formed strength rose deep from within. A wellspring of determination, the likes of which he never believed he could possess erupted through his body, like pent up lava bleeding through a fissure.

   Blessing ...

Like the hawk that instinctively knew which wind currents to take as they rose and fell, Virgil relied on intuition to lead him through the fog-blessed night.

   Sky ...

   Fallon would never get the chance to hurt his family. He would kill him first.

   Of that he was certain.

9

DRENCHED IN THE milk-white cast of the halogen security lights, Claire and Martin strolled through the gardens at the back of the estate. The sweet smell of bougainvillea blossoms gave fragrance to the still night, and Claire stopped to appreciate their aromatic gifts, raising a cluster of the brilliantly colored flowers in her hands, breathing their mellow perfume.

"The white ones were Melanie's favorite," Martin said. "They grew all over the place at our house. Once in a while I'd take her out back and we'd pick a big bouquet for Anne." He laughed. "She was too young to pronounce them by their proper name, so she called them *boogums*. Every time I go for a walk out here they remind me of her."

He reached out, smoothing the delicate petals Claire held in her hands, then released it back to its family of gentle blooms. "God, I miss that little girl so much."

"When we were young, maybe fifteen or sixteen," Claire replied in a smiling voice of quiet introspection, "Amanda and I would visit the Hampton Botanical Gardens almost every Saturday morning. She'd haul me out of bed before seven, and by the time I'd showered the sleep out of my eyes she'd have our lunches packed and be ready to go. She looked forward to that trip every weekend, like it was the most important thing in the world to her. Hampton's collection of plants and flowers was one of the largest I'd ever seen - orchids, lilies, rhododendron, sunflowers, desert cactus, ferns – you name it. And of course bougainvillea, like you have here - Barbara Karst, California Gold, Mary Palmer's Enchantment, Orange King, Manila Red. To Amanda, those gardens were like a candy store. It wouldn't have surprised me if one day she announced she wanted to become a botanist. Plants, especially flowers, intrigued her. When she was around them she was in her element. Her ability to appreciate the beauty in what so many of us take for granted never failed to amaze me. I'll always remember that about her, as long as I live."

"Don't speak about her in the past tense Claire," Martin said. "She's not gone, she's just … missing."

"I know. But it's been so long. So much time has passed, and we still have no idea exactly where she is."

"Give Mark and his team time to do their jobs. It's what they do best. In the meantime, try to have a little faith. Okay?"

"I want to have faith Martin. I want to believe you when you tell me they're as good as you say they are. But if they really are that good, then tell me something. With all the technical resources at their disposal, why haven't they found Melanie?"

Martin turned away. At the end of the yard, beyond the wary gaze of the sentinel towers of security lights stood a large wooden gazebo. Within it a low-back cedar glider stared at the moon, stirring lazily with each random breeze. Walking up the stairs, Martin sat in the glider with his back to Claire, pushing off with his feet against the pock-marked floorboards, swinging silently in the darkness, staring up at the night sky, watching the fingers of a prestigious cloud curl out and pocket the moon. How befitting, he thought, to observe this moment of celestial sleight of hand. Melanie had disappeared in a similar fashion. One second there, gone the next. Right before his eyes. In his mind the voice of his unseen attacker mocked him. *Now you see her ... now you don't! And there's not a thing you can do about it Martyboy ... not one damn thing.* The contemptuousness in the voice sickened him. *Just look at yourself, for God's sake. LOOK AT YOURSELF! Lying on the ground in a crumpled heap, like the pathetic sack of shit you are, while we take your wife and little girl away from you. By the time you come around we'll be far, far away. Where we're going you'll never think to look. You'll never find them. We'll see to that. Better to not even try Marty. Just in case you don't possess the gray matter to figure it out on your own, remember this: we* are their present and their future. So just lay there ... lay there and sleep it off…

Tendrils of silver-edged clouds appeared, giving up the stolen moon.

Consider yourself nothing but a faded memory… the voice taunted, drifting away from his consciousness.

"Oh God," Claire said, realizing her words had fallen hard on Martin. "I can't believe I just said that. I'm sorry Martin. I didn't mean to hurt you." Claire lay her hand gently on his shoulder. "Please, forgive me?"

"It's alright. Don't be sorry. I ask myself that same question every day. Sometimes I'm so angered by the fact that no one can give me an answer that I want to pull the plug on this whole damn thing. To say to hell with it, and just give up. But then another lead comes in, another case finds the break it needs, and another child goes home where they belong. It's like trying to find the cure for cancer. You know it's out there, and you know one day you'll find it. So you keep trying. You learn to take it one day at a time, one lead at a time, because you know that that son or daughter you're looking for *is* out there somewhere. No one can hide or be hidden forever. They may elude us, in some cases for a very long time. But eventually we find them, and that's when I'm reminded it is all worthwhile. That's also when the last flicker of hope that I thought had been extinguished forever within me finds the air it needs to burn again. So I take a deep breath and I fan that flame. I try to make it burn harder and brighter than it did before. Bright enough for Melanie to find her way home."

Claire sat beside Martin on the glider. "What will happen when you do find her? What then?"

"We'll get to know one another all over again. Starting from scratch, if that's what it takes."

"Aren't you scared?"

"Of what?"

"That Melanie will have forgotten you. These cults can do that. Isn't that what you said earlier? They force their followers to forget not only who they are but also all that mattered to them in the past?"

"Yes, but that's when we draw upon Cynthia and Justin for their expertise. Being professional de-programmers, it's their job to break down the doctrines and ideologies that have been imposed upon them by the cult, and help them regain their focus."

"How will it work with Amanda when we find her?" Claire asked. "How will she be de-programmed?"

"We'll bring her back here and make her as comfortable as possible, keeping in mind she may not be in the most cooperative of moods. It'll take some time before she settles down enough for us to begin the process. And one very important thing: Don't expect Amanda to be the same person you remember her to be. She won't revert back to her old self overnight."

"I can prepare myself for that."

"You'd better. Over the days or even weeks that follow, Cynthia and Justin will work up a psychological profile on her. We want to get into her brain - to map her psyche, so to speak. We want to know all we can about the activities the group has been involved in, how they work, how they recruit, and their leadership hierarchy. In this particular case, we have one very distinct advantage. We've identified Joseph Krebeck, and we know he's dangerous, so we have a better idea how to approach the extraction. I would also imagine the same could be said for the people who make up his inner circle. Leaders like Krebeck are usually well insulated. It's their underlings who carry out the dirty work. So you see the information Amanda provides us is critical. What she has to tell us could be enough for law enforcement to move in and arrest the leaders of the group. Depending upon the severity of the acts they've committed, they could be going to prison for a very long time."

"If Amanda is still as high spirited as I remember her to be this isn't going to be easy," Claire said. "She'll fight off any attempt to forcibly remove her every step of the way."

"I'm sure she would, and we'll be prepared for that. That's why we need to gain her trust. To make her believe we're there to help her, not hurt her."

"How can you expect her to do that when she doesn't even know you?"

"Through you. We'll need you to provide us with the family picture you brought with you. And one more thing."

"What's that?"

"We'll need a tape recording of your voice. A personal plea from you to cooperate and come with us. If she doesn't recognize you from the picture she'll probably still remember the sound of your voice. You see, for most of us voices are like auditory fingerprints. We have a built-in capacity for the long-term retention of them, like when you get a phone call from someone you haven't heard from for a very long time. You know you know the voice. You strain to place its familiarity, and eventually you do. Hearing your voice may be the key to unlocking Amanda. That's what we want – to create an emotional or psychological connection with her that is so strong and compelling she will trust us and come along freely."

"I can do that," Claire agreed. "How soon will it be before Mark and his team can get started?"

"As soon as we've identified her exact location we'll arrange the extraction."

"How will you do that?"

"It's all a matter of planning - and patience. First, an operations or 'ops' team will engage in a reconnaissance of the area where we believe Amanda is being held. They'll make note of her surroundings, watch the comings and goings of the other members of the group, their daily routines, and most importantly, they'll identify if she has a handler."

"A handler?"

"Yes. In some cases a high-profile cult member is assigned a handler by the leader of the group, usually a senior lieutenant within the chain of command. It's their job to watch the person they have been assigned to twenty-four seven."

"I thought they maintained control over the group as a whole?"

"Yes, absolutely. But a person like Amanda is different. If the countries best law enforcement agencies tried to find her and came up empty it's obvious she's purposely being hidden by these people. They know that if she's found by the authorities living amongst them it will mean the end of life for them as they know it. Their freedom would be gone in a heartbeat. In Amanda's case, federal authorities would pursue an action against them, most likely implicating them on charges of obstruction of justice, conspiracy and kidnapping, just to name a few. Should that happen, the cult would crumble. Without leadership and guidance they're lost, and that would be a fate equal to death. If they know who Amanda is, and my best guess says their leaders do, believe me, they'll use her to further their own agenda, whatever that may be. They'll protect her at all costs. To them, Amanda is a valuable property - a commodity they won't have any problem using as a bargaining chip, if and when things get ugly. That's why we have to get in, find her, and get out as quickly as possible. If something goes wrong with our plan she will be in danger. It'll be her life for their safe passage. Make no mistake about it."

"We can't let that happen Martin. I don't want to have come this far only to lose her now. I don't know if I could live with that."

"Don't worry Claire. I have no intention of having anything go wrong. Before we make our move we'll have double and triple-checked the plan. Amanda's safety and security will be our top concern."

"Are you going to be part of the extraction team?"

"Yes. I really want this guy. I have a feeling Joseph Krebeck has more than one skeleton in his closet, and I want to be the one to expose him."

Claire stood up and walked to the edge of the gazebo, staring up at the pale moon. She turned, folding her arms across her chest.

"Then if you're going in after her, so am I."

Martin scoffed. "Are you insane? That is totally out of the question. You have absolutely no training in these matters. For all intents and purposes, this is a tactical operation - a hostage rescue. Your inexperience could get you hurt, or if things go wrong, killed. Just in case you haven't figured it out yet we are, by definition of statute, *kidnapping* Amanda. The fact that you're her sister and we're doing this at your request has no bearing on the matter whatsoever. We're going to go in and remove her - likely against her will. If we're caught in the act trying to extract her no one's going to ask if we'd like to chat about it first over a friendly cup of coffee. Cults govern themselves according to their rules, and a violation of this magnitude will have very serious repercussions."

"Meaning …?"

"Meaning you could be made to disappear … permanently. In all likelihood your next of kin may not even find your body to bury."

Claire drew her arms to her sides, her voice shaking. "My family is dead Martin. Amanda is all I have left. So if I have to die, or be left for dead in some godforsaken area never to be seen again, then I bloody well want to know it was for a good reason. And I can't think of a better one than trying to rescue my only sister from the hands of a bastard like Joseph Krebeck!"

"I'm sorry Claire," Martin said. "I shouldn't have put it that way. I know how much Amanda means to you, and that you want her back in your life. But that still doesn't change the situation. You can't go in. I won't allow it. It's just too damn dangerous."

"Then train me."

"What?"

"Train me. Teach me what I need to know. You name it, I can learn it."

"That's absurd! We don't have time to train you for something like this!"

"Then just give me the basics if you have to. But I'm telling you right now, trained or not, I *am* coming with you."

Martin sighed. "You're not going to give up on this, are you?"

"I'm going in with you to get her Martin," Claire replied coolly. "That's final."

"You don't know what you're getting yourself into Claire."

"I'm a big girl. I'll take my chances."

NIGHT CRIES

Martin let out a heavy sigh. "Something tells me I'm never going to figure out how I let you talk me into this. Not in a million years."

"You already know why."

"Why what?"

"Why you'll agree to let me come with you."

"This ought to be good."

"Because you find me completely irresistible." Claire winked and smiled, walking slowly towards him from across the gazebo. She sat in his lap.

"Yeah, but that's beside the point," Martin sighed. Her body was warm and inviting. He wrapped his arms around her, kissing her softly on her cheek. "I'm serious Claire. You could get hurt."

"No. I won't," Claire replied, comforted by the soothing tone of his voice and his gentle touch.

"What makes you so sure?"

She rested her head on his shoulder. Martin closed his eyes and stroked her hair. The smell of her was captivating.

"Because I know you'll be there to protect me."

From the wellspring of emotion rising within he knew she was right. He would protect her, no matter what the cost, and it scared him. No, it terrified him. Never before had he fallen in love so fast. Not even with Anne, and he had loved her to the very marrow of his being. But in this new life, this *life after Anne*, he had come to understand how quickly such a gift could be stolen. That this thief does not lay in wait in the shadows, but is daring, bold, brazen - as unbeatable as any foe he could ever face. He knew this because it *had* beaten him. In the aftermath of a battle he had been given no opportunity to defend against it had shorn his heart from his chest, emotionally leaving him for dead.

From the moment he met Claire he knew his life would never be the same. Everything about her warmed him - her smile, her touch, her very life force. And now, from a place deep within, where once remorse and despair had taken seed and flourished in greater abundance than he thought could ever be humanly possible now grew hope, passion, and desire. He wanted Claire in his life, for the rest of his life. He would not rush her. This moment had to be taken slowly, savored, *treasured*. He wanted to tell her he loved her. The words were on his lips, his next breath. He wanted to tell her that he would never, could never, let her go. That she was his world now, for all the right reasons, and for all the reasons he couldn't possibly begin to put into words.

They sat in silence, holding each other, immersed in unspoken words and desires. Claire lifted her head from his chest.

"Martin?"

"Yes?" *I could stay right here for the rest of my life, just holding you.*

"Thank you for everything you're doing to help me. I don't know how I'll ever be able to repay you."

"You'll never have to Claire. We do this because we can. Because we believe it's that important, and that it should never be allowed to happen to good people. Like you and Amanda."

"I know. But I believe it's more than that."

"What do you mean?"

"Do you believe in fate?"

"Fate? No, not really," Martin replied. "I believe we chart our own course. The decisions we make along the way, good and bad, determine who we are, and more importantly, who we become."

"Interesting. I believe just the opposite. I believe the life we live day to day cannot be changed. That there's nothing we can do to change the course of those events. Our future is a path we are predetermined to follow from the day we're born to the day we die."

"Is that your scientific opinion?"

"No. Just my personal philosophy. Take us for instance."

"Us?"

"Yes, *us*. You and me. Several days ago you knew nothing about me, had no idea who I was, had no connection to me in any way, shape or form. Now look at us. We couldn't be any more involved in each other's lives if we tried. Fate intended for us to meet. We had no choice in the matter."

"Of course we did," Martin said. "You could have declined Kelly's offer to attend the Janus party. If you had, we would never have met."

"That's not the way I see it. I believe I went to the party because I had no other choice but to go. Don't you see? I was destined to be there, to meet you, and for you to meet me. Fate brought us together."

"Tell me you're going somewhere with this, because there's a strong possibility this discussion could send *me* into therapy real soon."

"I'm serious!" Claire laughed. "Okay, let me try this on you. When you were young, didn't you ever wonder what your life would be like when you were eighteen? Or thirty? Or sixty? What you would do for a living? What your wife's name would be? What she would look like?"

"No. I grew up rich. Spoiled rotten. My father paid other people to think of those things for me."

"Very funny. Well, didn't you?"

"Well, sure. I suppose we all wonder about those things. But I still maintain they come to us as our life evolves. We choose whom to love, what to do with our lives, and how hard we're willing to work on improving ourselves determines whom we become. There's nothing predetermined about that."

"I disagree."

"Somehow I just knew you would."

"Our lives are governed by fate, and I can prove it."

"This should be interesting."

"Close your eyes."

"Excuse me?"

"You heard me. Close your eyes."

"Can I make a wish?"

"If you like, but it won't make any difference."

"Right. Fate. Absolutely nothing I can do to stop …"

Before Martin could finish speaking, Claire raised her head and kissed him.

"See?" she said, opening her eyes. "Told you so. There was absolutely nothing I could do about that. Couldn't have stopped myself if I tried."

"Fate."

"Absolutely."

They kissed again, more passionately than before.

"There's something I have to tell you. And I have to tell you now."

"I already know what you're going to say," Claire answered.

"You do?"

"Yes, I do. And I want you to know it's okay. You can trust me."

"Trust you? With what?"

"Your heart."

"You know how I feel about you, don't you?"

"I do."

"And that doesn't scare you? We barely know each other."

"Yes, it scares me. But not knowing where this could lead scares me even more. I haven't been in love in a very long time Martin. You need to know that up front so you don't expect more from me than I'm capable of giving right now."

"We'll take it one day at a time. One hour at a time, if that's what you want."

NIGHT CRIES

"Thank you. I needed to hear you say that. But I already know everything will be alright."

"Let me guess ... fate."

"Whatever gave you that idea?"

Martin smiled. "Come on. I'll show you to your room. We both need to get some rest. Tomorrow's going to be a long day."

10

STANDING IN THE doorway, Virgil concentrated on calming himself with each labored breath. Perspiration, and the cool, damp droplets of foggy mist which had penetrated every fibrous pore of his shirt and jeans now weighed him down, restricting his movement, as though he were an ancient knight struggling under the confines of an aqueous suit of armor.

The voice of Fallon and the cries of Blessing and Sky he expected to hear as he reached the building were strangely absent. The rooms above lay as silent and undisturbed as mausoleum vaults.

In his weakened state, the ascent to the second floor required considerable effort. Bracing his back against the wall for support, he tried not to think about the searing pain that threatened to steal him from consciousness and send him tumbling to the foot of the stairs. Tracing his hand along each splintered, beveled step he pushed up, up, up, until at last he reached the landing. He sat for a moment, gathering his courage with his thoughts, then struggled to his feet and crept around the corner.

NIGHT CRIES

At the far end of the long, narrow corridor tendrils of lamplight slithered beneath the door to his room, striking and recoiling from the wisps of air taunting the flame within. Virgil knew he was alone, but he did not *feel* alone. In his delirious state, the building had come alive. A wall of eyes he could not see but nevertheless knew were there, possessed no doubt in some demonic way by the spirit of Fallon himself, watched him from the end of the hallway. It would have been within Fallon's power to accomplish such a feat, Virgil thought. Any man evil enough to commit murder, or be party to it, would surely have made a deal with the devil that would empower him with such abilities. Another wave of pain rushed through his body, and Virgil could feel his ability to focus slipping away. The hallway ahead had transformed. No longer stable and solid, the floor had become a swirling, molten ooze, streaming around his feet, flowing under the door and into his room, carrying on it screaming souls of the damned. He knew what he was seeing was not real, could not be real - nothing more than a horrific manifestation of his imagination. Yet there it was. Pressing his back to the wall he fought to maintain both balance and sensory control. The foul acridity of bile rose up in the back of his throat and he smelled its noxious fermentation on his breath. He was sweating profusely, his eyes stinging from the acidity of the perspiration streaming down his face. *I'm losing control*, Virgil thought. *Got to keep it together… for Sky… for Blessing.* He closed his eyes and wiped the sweat from his face, drawing slow, deep rhythmic breaths. When at last he opened his eyes the corridor had resumed its familiar construct, and the dim light at the foot of his door ebbed and flowed with the familiarity of dancing lamplight. The constant pain emanating from his leg had caused a fevered rush, sending his imagination into overdrive. If he should fall he would not be swept into a river of darkness and damnation, roiling with the cries of Hell's newest cache of reluctant inductees. He would simply pull himself to his feet from the cold floor, again and again, as many times as necessary, because that was what he had to do. Even the Devil himself wasn't powerful enough to stop a father bent on protecting his family.

The room ahead lay still. Perhaps, Virgil thought, Fallon had heard him coming as he climbed the stairs, having opened the door just wide enough to catch a glimpse of him breaking the sightline of the landing and ordered Blessing and Sky to remain silent, or die. Or perhaps they were already dead, and Fallon was waiting for him now. Finish the family. Bury the truth.

Assessing his options, Virgil knew he would have to surprise Fallon. Catch him off guard. Do what he would not expect him to do.

Pushing off from the wall he ran for the door, gathering speed with each agonizing, erratic, lop-sided shuffle-step, smashing his way into the room, fueled by adrenaline, driven by instinct, screaming as he broke through the threshold, the war cry of pain and fury emanating from him a manifestation of his deepest fears.

Virgil's assault on the room ended as abruptly as it began. He fell, tripping on the scattered debris of the fallen doorframe. Against the wishes of writhing pain he clambered to his feet, striving to regain his bearings as quickly as possible. Fear pumped his heart like a bellows, and the constriction in his chest reminded him he had forgotten to breathe. Through heaping gasps he surveyed the dimly lit room, steadying himself against the bedpost.

No Blessing ... No Sky.

No Fallon.

He had not been preceded to his room. The danger to his family had been a figment of his imagination. Or had it? He needed to find them. To know they were safe.

He raised his pant leg and examined the gash below his knee. The mist-drenched compress had done its job. The wound had clotted.

NIGHT CRIES

Standing beside the bed, he again tested his leg under his full weight. He was able to move with greater freedom than before, and walked stiffly across the room to the bureau where Sky kept a safety kit of Band-Aids, gauze, and first aid supplies. Opening the top drawer he removed the white metal box and placed it atop the bureau. Unlocking the clasps, he flipped back the lid and rummaged through the container, removing a wide sleeve of medical gauze, several fat sterile cotton balls, a roll of cloth adhesive tape, a brown bottle of hydrogen peroxide and a thin tube of Polysporin. He stripped off his clothes, depositing them in a wet pile by his feet and placed his foot on the edge of the bureau, examining the wound carefully. It was deep and would require stitches, but not right now. At this moment he needed to clean and dress the wound the best he could, and get back to Communion Hall as quickly as possible.

Dousing the cotton balls in the peroxide, Virgil held his breath as he pressed the clammy mass into the wound. Pain jumped from his leg to his brain as though completing an electrical circuit, ricocheting from nerve ending to synapse like lightening through a storm cloud. He fumbled with the tube of greasy ointment, squeezing a generous amount of the clear gel into the crevice of the wound and placed a sterile pad over the gash. He wrapped the wound with fresh gauze and taped it in place. Slowly, the pain began to subside. He changed quickly, putting away the medical kit and discarding the damp, bloody, dirt-stained clothes into the hamper.

The broken door hung precariously in its frame, saved from total collapse by the tenacity of a single bottom hinge. With little effort the broken door pulled free of its frame, and Virgil stood it against the wall. An explanation for the damage would be necessary, of course, but presently a broken door was the least of his concern.

Going down the stairs required considerably less effort. His leg still burned with the intensity of white-hot embers, but the combination of peroxide and analgesic gel had succeeded in reducing the inflammation, allowing him to move much faster than he had anticipated.

The broken asphalt road with its dilapidated, jagged stones offered few if any level footholds, and Virgil winced in pain every time he would misstep, pulling on the ligaments and tendons surrounding the wound. He traveled close to the buildings, cloaked in the safety of their shadows.

Voices in the distance. Laughter. The clatter of pots and pans. Communion Hall.

Virgil peered around the corner. It was fifty yards to the front steps, maybe less. He rolled up his pant leg, examining the dressing in the pale light of the moon. No blood. No visible evidence that he had been hurt. No reason for Fallon to suspect he was the quarry he sought.

Stepping out from the shadows of the building, Virgil walked briskly to the front steps and climbed the stairs, defying the ravaging pain coursing through his leg.

Reaching the landing, he opened the door and stepped inside.

"'Bout time you got here. Prophet was just askin' where you'd gotten to."

The booming voice took him by surprise, made him jump. Reisa Stone, his closest friend, stood in the doorway to the dining hall. Shirtsleeves rolled to his elbows and holding a roasting pot, Stone all but absorbed the light attempting to peer out from behind him. He was a mountain of a man, nearly three hundred pounds, with a bodybuilder's physique and a Hell's Angels temper. Tattoos adorned both arms, running from his wrists to his neck. He wore his round, wire-rimmed glasses precariously balanced on the bridge of his nose, and a reddish-brown beard cascaded to the middle of his generously care-for stomach. Over the years, Virgil had come to know and respect the man under the colorful mosaic and found him to be a dependable friend, an honest man, and a deeply devoted follower of the ways of the Brethren. In the dim candlelight of the vestibule however, hands adorned by gaily-flowered oven mitts and sporting a pink and blue cotton apron with frilly lace trim, Reisa Stone looked as menacing as a biker at a country bake off.

"Dolled up for the prom I see," Virgil joked. "Did you remember to shave your legs?"

"Very funny," Reisa replied uncomfortably. "While you've been out for a stroll, the rest of us have been makin' dinner."

The aroma of the covered pot roast simmering in Stone's hands reminded Virgil how hungry he was. "Smells good," Virgil said, lifting the roaster lid and peeking inside.

"It should. It's been simmering for the last hour. What took ya anyway? Fallon's been runnin' around here botherin' everybody, doing a headcount. Gettin' on my nerves actually, damn little weasel."

"Fallon gets on everyone's nerves, Reisa. What do you mean, doing a headcount?"

"It's probably nothing. I overheard him talkin' to Prophet, saying somethin' about suspecting an intruder on the grounds. Said he thought he heard somethin' out back of the workshop earlier. Whatever it is has got him wound up tighter than the strings on my old Gibson. He's been walkin' around puffed up bigger than a rooster in a henhouse, checking everybody out." Stone shook his head. "Never did like that little guy. Too weasely for me. Even looks a little like a weasel, don't he? Long, skinny face, and that spindly little toothpick body of his. All he's missin' is a tail. Like I said, just plain ... *weasely*."

"Fallon's never topped my list of favorite people either," Virgil replied, "but I wouldn't worry about it. He's probably overreacting, as usual. I didn't see anyone out there."

"I suppose you're right," Reisa shrugged. "Well, don't just stand there like you're expectin' me to set the table for ya too. Sky and Blessing are inside."

Safe. Thank God.

"They've been waitin' for ya for the past half-hour, so get a move on. By the way … you hurt your leg or somethin'?"

"No," Virgil lied. "Why do you say that?"

"You got a spot on your jeans, just below your knee," Reisa said, gesturing with his elbow to Virgil's wounded leg. "Look's like ya cut yourself. Anyway, hurry up. While we're standin' around here yappin' my roast is gettin' cold!"

Virgil waited as Reisa turned and walked through the doors into the dining room. "Yeah. Right," he said. "Go ahead old buddy. I'm right behind you."

He leaned forward, checking his jeans. *I shouldn't have pushed it, damn it! Too much pressure coming up the steps.*

Virgil touched the spot of blood with his finger.

Warm.

Damp.

Spreading.

"Daddy!" Blessing's tiny voice trumpeted Virgil's arrival from across the room. She ran to greet her father, nearly colliding with Reisa.

"Whoa! Slow down, little darlin'!" Reisa laughed, hoisting the roasting pan above his head, spinning sharply to his left, deftly avoiding Blessing's charge.

"Hi angel," Virgil said. "How's my best girl?"

"Fine Daddy, but I was worried about you."

"You were? Why would such a pretty little girl like you be worried about me?"

NIGHT CRIES

"I asked Mommy where you were and she said she didn't know. How come you're late?"

"I had a little accident princess. Nothing important."

"An accident?" Blessing paused. "What did you do? Wet the bed?"

Virgil tried not to laugh. "No honey. I just fell down. Now I've got a great big boo-boo on my leg."

"Yuck!" Blessing exclaimed sourly. "I hate boo-boos. Does it hurt?"

"As a matter of fact, it does hurt a little."

"I'll go tell Mommy you're here."

Across the room Sky was setting cutlery beside the dinner plates on the long banquet table. She smiled and waved.

"You do that angel. Tell Mommy I want to talk to her right away. Okay?"

Too late. Blessing was already off and running.

"Quite a girl, isn't she?"

Virgil turned to find Fallon standing behind him.

"Do you always sneak up on people?"

"Forgive me. I apologize if I startled you." Fallon's tone was insultingly insincere. "I was just coming from the downstairs storeroom. Thought I'd take a last look around before dinner."

"Look around?" Virgil said. "For what?"

"Oh yes, that's right. You weren't here. I guess you wouldn't know."

"Wouldn't know *what*? Stop speaking in circles, Fallon."

"My, my! Aren't we touchy tonight! You seem nervous, Mr. Lutt. A little ill at ease. Is something bothering you? Anything you'd care to talk about? Confession is good for the soul you know."

"It's been a long day Fallon. You should know. You were with me."

"Yes, as a matter of fact I was. Until the last hour or so anyway."

"What's that supposed to mean?"

"It means that within that brief period of time I believe someone has compromised our property."

"Compromised?"

"Yes, compromised. As in broke in. Trespassed. Accessed without permission." Fallon paused as though assessing Virgil. "Am I speaking in a manner you are having difficulty comprehending? I can slow my speech if you like. Use smaller, less intimidating words perhaps."

"Don't insult my intelligence Fallon. I know exactly what you mean and you know it. What are you rambling on about? S*pecifically.*"

"I heard a commotion out back earlier. When I investigated the situation further, I found evidence of an intruder."

"What sort of evidence?"

"The kind that leaves a trail."

Virgil turned to walk away. "Are we going to do this all night? Banter back and forth? Because if we are I've got more important things to do."

Fallon grabbed him by his arm, burying his thumb deep into his forearm, halting Virgil mid step.

"What the …"

"I'm sorry Mr. Lutt," Fallon said, slowly relaxing his grip, "but I don't believe we've finished our discussion."

Virgil pulled back his arm, a tingling mass of swollen nerves.

"Oh yeah, we're done," Virgil said. He placed his aching arm around Fallon and whispered in his ear. "Understand something, you little fuck. If you ever try that shit with me again the only thing compromised around here will be your balls on a fence-puller. Am I making myself perfectly clear, or am I speaking in a manner *you* are finding difficult to comprehend? Maybe I should slow down my speech for you. Use smaller, less intimidating words."

Fallon looked him in the eyes and smiled. "Yes, Mr. Lutt. I believe we have arrived at a mutual understanding."

"Right answer," Virgil said. "Now run along like the good little whipping boy you are. I'm sure Prophet's waiting for you. You wouldn't want to be accused of shirking your responsibilities."

"One last thing," Fallon said.

Virgil turned around in silence.

"The evidence I mentioned earlier. The kind that leaves a trail? I was referring to blood, Mr. Lutt. Like the kind running down your leg as we speak."

Virgil looked down at the smearing mass below his knee. "What about it?"

"Anything you'd care to explain?"

"Not to you," Virgil replied, walking away.

#

"Where have you been? I was expecting you an hour ago," Sky said, hugging Virgil.

"Sorry. Something came up."

"Is anything wrong? You don't seem yourself."

Virgil looked down at his knee. "Guess I'm still a little shook up."

Sky gasped at the sight of the blood on his pant leg. "Good Lord, Virgil! Did you cut yourself putting up the fence?"

"No, nothing quite so macho. I tripped in the dark and fell down the stairs," he lied. "Why do you think you always lead when we dance? Two left feet, remember?"

"Are you sure you're okay?"

"I'll be fine."

"Maybe we should go back to the room. I'll clean it up for you."

"Don't be silly honey. It's just a scratch. Besides, I ran into Reisa walking in and got a first hand look at his pot roast. Nothing short of amputation could keep me from that right now."

"You're sure?"

"Sweetheart, I'm fine. Let's go round up Blessing and eat. I'm starved!" Virgil looked about the room. "Where is the little munchkin anyway?"

"Probably helping Uncle Reisa in the kitchen. When you're not around he dotes on her like she was his own daughter, and naturally she soaks up the attention by the bucketful."

"That sounds like Blessing. By the way, have you seen Prophet's daughter?"

"Amanda?" Sky replied. "Not recently. She was helping in the fields earlier though. Why?"

"No reason. I just haven't seen her around much. She tends to keep to herself quite a bit, don't you think?"

"Yes. Now that you mention it, I've noticed that too. Even today, she hardly said a word the entire afternoon we were in the field."

"This may sound a bit odd, but do you know if she was adopted by Prophet and Cassandra?"

Sky stopped and looked at Virgil. "Not that I'm aware of. Why would you think she was adopted?"

"Just curious." Virgil's troubled look belied the indifference in his voice. "She never said anything to you about her past that may have struck you as out of the ordinary?"

"No."

"You're *sure*?"

Sky pressed. "Virgil, there's something you're not telling me. What is it?"

NIGHT CRIES

Virgil hesitated. "It's nothing. I shouldn't have brought it up. Forget about it."

"Nothing? You don't ask a question like that out of the clear blue without reason. What's wrong?"

In his mind, Virgil replayed the conversation: *'We've had a hard enough time concealing her identity... You should have killed her after you killed her parents... The FBI will come looking for her – again.'* What in the world was going on? Should he tell Sky what he had heard? He knew Fallon well enough to know he knew it was Virgil he had been tracking. He simply hadn't put it together until now. *If only I hadn't fallen! If I hadn't cut my damn leg on the woodpile Fallon would never have known it was me he was after. He'd still be running around, chasing phantom intruders in the dark.* But the fact remained the conversation he had heard *was* real, and the consequences that could come from his knowledge of the facts would be grave. According to Fallon, Amanda's parents had been murdered by Prophet, and Amanda was either involved, or a victim herself in some way. They all knew about the killings - Cassandra, Prophet and Fallon. Were they co-conspirators as well? And now *he* knew. Why would Prophet want Amanda's parents dead? What could they have possibly done to bring about such a fate? Prophet wasn't a street punk, not a hired gun. He was a man of God: a seer, a visionary. His strength and leadership had kept them together, through good times and bad. He had led them away from the anarchy of the outside world, from the evil that men do, to this small parcel of land they would make into paradise. No, this was impossible! He was wrong. Mistaken. That was all there was to it. He had misunderstood their conversation. Simple as that … wasn't it? Virgil's mind whirled with indecision. No, he had heard them correctly. Something was very wrong. He knew, because the churning in his stomach confirmed it. And there was Blessing and Sky's safety to think about, not to mention his own. For a moment he wrestled with the thought that maybe he should keep his mouth shut. Leave it alone. Forget what he had heard. No, he couldn't do that. He couldn't walk away from this. Not now, knowing if what he suspected to be true *was* true. If he was unwittingly living in the company of killers, then his world had become paradise *lost*, and this he would not, could not accept. His stomach rolled again. Fight or flight.

"Alright," Virgil said at last. "Yes, something *is* wrong. Very wrong. But we can't discuss it. Not here. Not now."

"What are you talking about Virgil?" Sky persisted. "And what has this got to do with Amanda?"

"Later, after Blessing goes to bed, I'll explain everything to you then."

"Why not now?"

"It's not safe to talk now."

"Not *safe*?"

Virgil cupped his pretty wife's face in his hands. "Listen to me. Everything's going to be just fine. But you're going to have to believe what I tell you later, even if it seems, well, … crazy. Will you do that for me? Please?"

The frightened look on Sky's face spoke for her.

"But Virgil …"

Virgil gently pressed his finger to her lips. "I'll tell you everything later Sky. I promise."

#

"He knows."

"What are you talking about?"

"Lutt. He overheard our conversation. He knows you killed Amanda's parents."

"How can you be certain? Did you confront him? Did he admit to it?"

"He didn't have to. Remember the blood I showed you? Out back?"

"Yes."

"Take a look at his leg. It's a mess."

"That doesn't mean he knows anything. It means he cut his leg."

"Don't be a fool, Joseph. And don't speak to me like one. I'm not one of your catatonic followers. I'm the guy whose kept your ass out of the gas chamber."

"You're not exactly cut from holy cloth yourself," Krebeck replied. "The woman and the child? Remember?"

Prophet's words resuscitated fond memories. Musty smelling bales of hay stacked high in an old barn. The occasional whinny of horses in the adjoining stalls. The woman, her legs splayed, rocking to the hard thrust of him. The chanting of the witnesses during this ceremony of purification and indoctrination. He had forgotten the woman's name, hadn't he? No, wait ... *Anne*. Yes, that was it - Anne. Not that it really mattered. He'd been paid well for recruiting her. He hadn't wanted to take the girl. She was just a toddler. Collateral cargo. Of no particular use. But the mother insisted. And with all due respect she had been an excellent fuck. It was the least he could do.

Finally, he spoke.

"You and I both know this is bullshit, Joseph. Engage their trust. Sprinkle in a little God the Father this and Praise the Lord that, then watch them follow like lambs to the slaughter. That was the plan. It's quite pathetic when you realize the only purpose they serve is to insulate us from the outside world. *'Those who can't be found can't be prosecuted.'* Isn't that what you said?"

"You've benefited as much from this as I have Fallon."

"I'm not denying that. But I'm telling you, we have a problem. And its name is Virgil Lutt."

Prophet paused. "How do you propose we handle this … problem?"

Fallon shrugged. "No differently than any of the others."

"Fine. But do it quickly … and quietly. Make it look like an accident."

"Stone and I plan to explore the west ridge of the mountain in two days," Fallon replied. "I'll bring Lutt. The paths around the ridge are narrow - two feet wide, at best. They can be dangerous if you don't know where you're going. One wrong step and the fall could be … fatal."

"Spare me the drama," Prophet replied. "Just get it done. Soon."

#

"Goodnight Mommy."

"Goodnight precious," Sky said, kissing Blessing on her nose and tucking the bed sheets tightly around her. She blew out the lantern beside the bed. Darkness fell upon the room.

"I love you sweetie."

"I love you more Mommy."

"Want me to leave the door open?"

"No. You can close it. I'm a big girl now."

"I know you are. Goodnight."

As Sky closed the door Blessing called out nervously. "Mommy?"

"Yes honey?"

"Maybe you could leave it open … just a *little*."

Virgil sat on the edge of the bed, his leg turned in the direction of the pale glow of the lamp, examining the wound.

NIGHT CRIES

"How can you be certain? Did you confront him? Did he admit to it?"

"He didn't have to. Remember the blood I showed you? Out back?"

"Yes."

"Take a look at his leg. It's a mess."

"That doesn't mean he knows anything. It means he cut his leg."

"Don't be a fool, Joseph. And don't speak to me like one. I'm not one of your catatonic followers. I'm the guy whose kept your ass out of the gas chamber."

"You're not exactly cut from holy cloth yourself," Krebeck replied. "The woman and the child? Remember?"

Prophet's words resuscitated fond memories. Musty smelling bales of hay stacked high in an old barn. The occasional whinny of horses in the adjoining stalls. The woman, her legs splayed, rocking to the hard thrust of him. The chanting of the witnesses during this ceremony of purification and indoctrination. He had forgotten the woman's name, hadn't he? No, wait … *Anne*. Yes, that was it - Anne. Not that it really mattered. He'd been paid well for recruiting her. He hadn't wanted to take the girl. She was just a toddler. Collateral cargo. Of no particular use. But the mother insisted. And with all due respect she had been an excellent fuck. It was the least he could do.

Finally, he spoke.

"You and I both know this is bullshit, Joseph. Engage their trust. Sprinkle in a little God the Father this and Praise the Lord that, then watch them follow like lambs to the slaughter. That was the plan. It's quite pathetic when you realize the only purpose they serve is to insulate us from the outside world. *'Those who can't be found can't be prosecuted.'* Isn't that what you said?"

"You've benefited as much from this as I have Fallon."

"I'm not denying that. But I'm telling you, we have a problem. And its name is Virgil Lutt."

Prophet paused. "How do you propose we handle this … problem?"

Fallon shrugged. "No differently than any of the others."

"Fine. But do it quickly … and quietly. Make it look like an accident."

"Stone and I plan to explore the west ridge of the mountain in two days," Fallon replied. "I'll bring Lutt. The paths around the ridge are narrow - two feet wide, at best. They can be dangerous if you don't know where you're going. One wrong step and the fall could be … fatal."

"Spare me the drama," Prophet replied. "Just get it done. Soon."

#

"Goodnight Mommy."

"Goodnight precious," Sky said, kissing Blessing on her nose and tucking the bed sheets tightly around her. She blew out the lantern beside the bed. Darkness fell upon the room.

"I love you sweetie."

"I love you more Mommy."

"Want me to leave the door open?"

"No. You can close it. I'm a big girl now."

"I know you are. Goodnight."

As Sky closed the door Blessing called out nervously. "Mommy?"

"Yes honey?"

"Maybe you could leave it open … just a *little*."

Virgil sat on the edge of the bed, his leg turned in the direction of the pale glow of the lamp, examining the wound.

NIGHT CRIES

"Better let me take a look at that," Sky said.

As she pulled away the gauze, Virgil winced.

"Not so tough now, are you big guy?"

"Very funny, Florence Nightingale. Truth is, it hurts like hell."

"You didn't fall down the stairs, did you?"

"What gave you that idea?"

"Let's just say you're a worse liar than you are a dancer. How did you do this? What really happened?"

Virgil grit his teeth as Sky patted the gash with a hydrogen peroxide compress she had prepared from the safety kit.

"I fell over a pile of wood out back of Communion Hall. I was running."

"Running? Why?"

Virgil put his leg down to the floor.

"But I'm not finished ..." Sky said.

"It's okay," Virgil smiled, motioning with his hand to the bed. "Feels better already. You'd better sit down honey. Remember earlier when I said what I had to talk to you about might seem a little crazy?"

"Yes."

"Well, here goes. When I was making my rounds tonight, I overheard an argument coming from Prophet's room. I couldn't help but hear what they were saying."

"They?"

"Prophet, Cassandra and Fallon. Fallon was doing most of the talking. He accused Prophet of ... murder."

"*Murder?* You can't be serious."

"I know how it sounds," Virgil said, sitting back down on the bed. "But that's what I heard. He said Prophet should have killed Amanda when he killed her parents."

"How did Prophet respond to this?"

"That's the thing. He didn't. Cassandra knows about the murders as well. According to her, he had a right to kill them. It has something to do with Amanda - exactly what I don't know. But I do know this much; they didn't come here for our benefit. They came here to hide."

"What are we going to do?" Sky said. "If what you heard is true we have to go to the police. And that means we can't stay here anymore. It's not safe."

Virgil put his head in his hands. "I know."

"Then we'll leave. I'll pack what we need. Tonight. Right now. We'll be gone before the sun comes up. By the time they realize we're no longer here we'll be well on our way, and they won't know where to begin to look for us."

"There's one complication. Fallon suspects I know their secret. He tracked me earlier and almost found me, but I managed to get away. He questioned me about my leg before dinner. He asked me if I had heard or seen anything unusual in my rounds."

"What did you tell him?"

"I told him no. But I know he didn't believe me."

"I knew Fallon was dangerous," Sky said. "We have to get out of here. The sooner the better. Besides, we have Blessing to think about."

"And Amanda."

Sky paused. "You're right. We can't leave her behind. If her life is in danger she's safer with us."

"Mommy?" The tiny voice at the door made Sky jump, and she realized how deeply afraid she had suddenly become. Blessing stood in the doorway to their room.

"Yes baby?"

"Goodnight."

NIGHT CRIES

"I thought you were already asleep sweetie," Virgil said. "Why aren't you in bed?"

"I was," she said, wiping her eyes. "I wanted to go to the bathroom, but it was dark, and I was scared."

"It's okay honey," Sky said. "I'll take you down the hall to the bathroom."

"That's alright Mommy. I already went."

Sky looked at Virgil and smiled. "Well, I guess you *are* a grown up girl now. Able to go to the bathroom in the night all on your own."

"I didn't go on my own," Blessing answered. "Mr. Fallon took me."

"What did you say?" Virgil said.

"He was standing outside the door when I got up." Blessing ran to the window. "See?" she said, "There he goes now. I guess it's his bedtime too." Blessing waved.

Virgil watched Fallon disappear into a mist of dense mountain fog.

"No, Virgil" Sky cried. "*Don't!*"

Heart pounding like a timpani, Virgil ran out of the room, struggling down the stairs as fast as he could manage, shoulder-sliding along the wall for support. He shuffled out of the building and into the thick mist. Fallon was gone. Gasping, Virgil knew he was in no shape to give chase. He would need his strength for later. For their escape from Eden.

Walking back to his room, he shuffled up the stairs and froze at the sight of the broken door.

An unwelcome adornment graced its tarnished brass handle.

The bloodied plastic strip Virgil had earlier used as a tourniquet swung back and forth on the doorknob, like a hangman's noose awaiting the neck of a condemned prisoner.

"He must have followed us back," Virgil said, his voice shaking. "He was standing in the hallway all along. Listening to us."

Sky stood by the bedside, clutching Blessing. "I'm scared Virgil. What are we going to do?"

"We need to get out of here. But not tonight. It's too dangerous right now. I know Fallon. He's out there somewhere, hiding in the shadows, just waiting for me to make a mistake. Pack whatever you can tonight that will allow you and Blessing to travel light. We'll leave tomorrow night."

"What about Amanda? We can't leave her here."

"We won't. I'll come back for Amanda. She trusts me, and she knows I wouldn't lie to her. First, I need to get you two someplace where you'll be safe."

"But where will we go? We have no car, and we barely have any food."

"There's an old hunting cabin up on the mountain. Reisa and I came across it a few weeks ago. I think it's abandoned. It doesn't look like anyone's used it for years. We can stay there, at least for a couple of days."

"And then?"

"Then we go to the police."

11

MARK OYAMA EASED into his chair at the head of the boardroom table as the members of his team entered the room and took their seats. From the one hundred operatives on his payroll he had selected his top ten.

"Before we begin, I'd like to introduce you to our client, Dr. Claire Prescott," Mark began.

The attention of the room fixed on Claire. Below the level of the table, Martin held her hand. He squeezed it reassuringly.

Mark motioned to the switch on the wall, and Justin turned out the lights. The room fell dark as the projector on the ceiling whirred to life, filling the large screen at the front of the room with the image of a newspaper article taken from the Paulo Brava Examiner. The headline read, WITHOUT A TRACE.

"Each of you will find dossiers in front of you. Please open them now." He rose from his chair, pacing about the room as he spoke.

"Twelve years ago, Dr. Prescott's younger sister Amanda disappeared. The Prescott's contacted the authorities, and a full investigation was launched. No ransom demand was ever received, and no further contact was ever made with the family. In the end, state and federal came up dry. Now, we think we know why. Next slide please."

The image of the newspaper article dissolved, morphing into the file photo from Martin's book. The blurry visage of Joseph Krebeck and Amanda Prescott captured by the telephoto lens filled the screen.

"We believe from recent information provided to Dr. Prescott, her sister was taken against her will by the man you see here. His name is Joseph Krebeck. The girl is our extraction target. Until this morning we knew very little about Krebeck. Seems he's managed to dodge our radar very well over the years. I'll ask Justin to take us through his findings."

"Thanks Mark," Justin replied, opening his file folder and removing a photocopy of an official looking document. He held it up. The cover page read:

**CENTRAL INTELLIGENCE AGENCY
EYES ONLY
OPERATION DELIVERANCE**

"What you're looking at is a copy of a de-classified report outlining the involvement of the CIA in Uganda twelve years ago. The United States government agreed to assist in a military coup to oust a radical fundamentalist by the name of Mustafa Mensah. Mensah and his cronies had taken it upon themselves to redistribute Red Cross food and supplies to the people living in his territory. Those who could afford to pay with land, women or children received the blessings of his generosity. Those who couldn't died ... by the hundreds. Operation Deliverance was put in place to topple Mensah's regime and restore aid to the people who needed it. That's where Krebeck comes in."

Justin advanced the projector to the next picture, a copy of a CIA identification card.

"Joseph Ulysses Krebeck," Justin said, reading the name on the photo identification. "A bona-fide spook, ghost or any other cold war name you want to call him."

Dan Raines sat forward in his chair. "Let me get this straight. Our bad guy's a fed?"

"More than that. Joseph Krebeck was one of Uncle Sam's finest covert operatives."

"Was?" Cynthia asked.

"Yes. Krebeck was sentenced to life imprisonment for murder as a result of his actions during Operation Deliverance."

"How is that possible?" Martin asked. "CIA sanctioned ops carry impunity from prosecution."

"Ordinarily that would be true," Justin replied. "But Krebeck went rogue. That's when the government stepped in."

"What exactly did he do?" Karen asked.

"Krebeck believes himself to be a religious deity. That's the story according to his psyche evaluation anyway. The key difference though is most religious leaders don't lock hundreds of their followers in a tinderbox of a church, poison them, set fire to the place and stay around to watch it burn to the ground."

"Christ!" Karen replied.

"There's something I don't get," Raines said. "How is it possible for an American CIA operative to create a religious following in a foreign country?"

"With a little help from his friends," Justin replied. "Turns out Krebeck would meet with members of Mensah's inner circle and provide them with intel updates on Operation Deliverance in exchange for protection, and a quiet place to play God."

"So he's a fed *and* a traitor. Why didn't someone lock this sonofabitch up and throw away the key?"

"We did just that, only five years ago Krebeck and four other inmates went down in a plane crash just south of the Oregon-California border east of Mt. Hebron while on transfer to a maximum-security installation. Three were confirmed dead at the scene, but Krebeck and another inmate, Reginald Fallon, escaped the crash. The feds have been looking for them ever since, without success. I guess they fail to remember they were the ones who taught these guys how to disappear in the first place."

"So Fallon is CIA too?" Raines asked.

"Yes. The two of them were assigned to Operation Deliverance."

"Then shouldn't we be calling the feds? They're their boys. Under the circumstances, I'm sure the Agency wants them back real bad."

"Without a doubt," Mark interjected. "I don't give a rat's ass about Krebeck and Fallon. The CIA can have them. But bring them in too soon and this will become a military exercise, and I don't want to put Amanda Prescott at unnecessary risk. We've got to keep our objective top of mind: We go in, get her, and get out. Then we call in the cavalry."

Heads nodded in agreement.

"What do we know about the people she's involved with?" Raines asked.

"They call themselves The Brethren," Justin answered. "Quite honestly, we have no intel on their ideology - whether they're paramilitary, anti-government, or how heavily armed they may be." Justin turned to Mark. "For that reason, when we do locate them I suggest your teams go in hot. Sidearms and body armor. No exceptions."

NIGHT CRIES

Karen Lassiter raised her hand. "What about a location on the subjects."

Mark turned to Cynthia. "Care to bring us up to speed?"

"Certainly," Cynthia replied.

A picture showing several individuals handing out leaflets to student passers-by on the university campus flashed on to the screen.

"In your dossiers you'll find a copy of this photograph. It was taken approximately two weeks ago at Sonoma State University. Biometric comparisons confirm the girl on the right to be Amanda Prescott. I've had personal contact with the subject, though I didn't know we'd be looking for her two weeks later. So the good news is we can confirm she's alive and possibly still in the area. The bad news is we've never had her under active surveillance, so we don't know specifically where she is. The fact I took this photo was a complete fluke. Something about the group just didn't sit right with me, so I snapped their picture."

"Lucky for us you did," Raines said. "But if you ask me, I'd say we've got a major problem. We may know who the subject is and what she looks like, but she's on the move and we have no active intelligence to work with. I wouldn't exactly call that a winning combination."

"Dan's right," Karen added, turning to Mark. "Amanda Prescott could be long gone by now. If the group is transient we're beat already."

"I know," Mark replied. "That's why I'm pairing everyone into base and field reconnaissance teams. You and I will be field team one. Cynthia and Dan, team two. Starting today, we're going to establish surveillance on the university campus and the general vicinity. Start asking questions and poke around a bit. Show the photos in your file around campus. Perhaps one of the students will remember seeing Amanda or speaking to her. Talk to campus security. My guess is if the Brethren are using the university as a recruiting area they may not be transient after all. I know the timeline is tricky, only two weeks out, but we could catch a break. If you do locate her, no one is to even breathe in her direction without my authorization."

Turning on the lights, Mark addressed the remaining operatives in the room.

"The rest of you will work with Justin. Hit the computers, beat the drums, rattle your contacts, send up smoke signals if you have to, but dig up as much information on this organization as you can. The more we know now the better prepared we'll be when we go in. Like Dan pointed out, our timeline is fading. We've got to turn up something on this right away. Field teams, pack whatever gear you'll need. We leave for the university in two hours. Claire, you'll travel with Martin. If we should be lucky enough to run into Amanda and she recognizes you, this could be over today. I only say that as a possibility, so don't get your hopes up, okay? We've still got a lot of ground to cover, and as you know, not much to go on."

"I understand," Claire replied.

"And Martin?"

"Yes?"

"I'm putting you in charge of Claire's personal safety. She stays by your side at all times, like glue. Photographs and leads aside, her input is critical to the success of this operation. Don't let her out of your sight."

"Count on it," Martin replied.

Mark turned to the group. "By now everyone should know the severity of the situation. Anything less than one hundred percent commitment to this operation is unacceptable. Got that?"

Dedicated faces stared back. Silent. Attentive.

"Good," Mark concluded. "Then let's go find Amanda Prescott."

NIGHT CRIES

By early afternoon operations were in high gear. Every station in the computer lab was manned, every phone line in use. Operatives conducted extensive searches on lesser-known cults, building profiles on their leaders, speaking with their contacts in local, state and federal police agencies as well as the media, cross-referencing their findings and plotting prospective geographic locations on a plexiglas grid map of the state placed outside Justin's office. While Justin coordinated their efforts, the field teams prepared to leave for the university.

Martin tapped on the glass door to Justin's office. "Got a minute?"

"Sure Martin. What's up?"

"I've been thinking about what you said earlier ... about Krebeck, and the information you obtained from the CIA."

"Not from the CIA. From a web site that follows de-classified intelligence operations of the government. Everything from the Department of Naval Intelligence to Foreign Affairs. Eventually those reports become a matter of public record." Justin removed the CIA report on Operation Deliverance from his dossier. "Or at least as much as they'll allow us to read."

Heavy black lines had been struck through the majority of the report. Of the eighteen pages, the amount of readable text accounted for twelve pages of the document.

"It's their way of appeasing our curiosity," Justin continued, referring to the blacked out portions of the report. "We get to take a peek at the official records, and they get to share as little with us as possible."

Martin examined the report. "Just how reliable *is* this document?"

"Very reliable actually, compared to most. We're not talking downed spacecraft or little green men here. This is different. At the time, CNN was covering the difficulties with the relief effort in Uganda daily. Hell, they practically created a mini-series from it, so the events can't be denied. The juice in this report however is the information on Krebeck himself, not just Operation Deliverance. A lot of detail was left in, including mentioning Krebeck by name. I guess they figured with the world watching they wouldn't be able to bury the truth even if they tried. In my opinion someone screwed up. Good for us, bad for them."

"That doesn't strike you as strange? I mean, we're talking about the CIA here. You're sure this report wasn't created in order to misinform?"

"The thought did cross my mind. But I've reviewed a lot of these over the years, and quite honestly, I think we just got lucky."

Martin's face tightened. "You're aware of the history behind my wife and daughter's disappearance?"

"Yes Martin, I am."

"The Ugandan authorities never confirmed or denied who was responsible for Anne's death. They just knew it was cult related. When you mentioned the fire and the church burning to the ground, I couldn't help think that maybe …"

"Krebeck was responsible?" Justin said. "I don't know if that's true or not Martin. There's no mention in the report about the name of the group Krebeck was involved with. It could just be a coincidence. Unfortunately, a lot of this type of activity was going on in Uganda at the time."

"You'll let me know if you turn up anything more on this?"

"As soon as I know, you'll know."

Karen placed two overnight bags and a utility case in the back seat of the Suburban and closed the door. Unfolding a map on the hood of the truck, Mark drew a tight circle around the vicinity of Rohnert Park.

NIGHT CRIES

"Sonoma State University is about one hundred miles from here. Should take us about an hour and a half to get there."

"What's our plan of attack?" Dan asked.

"Like I said, start poking around. Turn over a few rocks and see what crawls out. You and Cynthia take the east campus. Karen and I will take the west." Mark turned to Martin. "There's a small town just north of the university named Kettawash. It's mostly a one-horse, two-saloon kind of place, but apparently it's a popular hangout with the university crowd. Might be worth a shot. You and Claire check it out. Let me know if you come up with anything worthwhile."

"You got it."

"And Martin? No heroics. If you pick up a lead, you let me know. We still don't know what we're up against here. Understood?"

"Yes, Dad."

"I'm serious. You call me on my cell and wait for backup. You do nothing until we arrive."

"It's your operation Mark," Martin said. "You're the one calling the shots. Don't worry, we'll wait."

"Alright." Mark folded the map and tossed it on the front seat. "Saddle up and roll out."

Maggy lay in the backseat of the Navigator, chewing fiercely on her rawhide. In less than an hour they would arrive in Kettawash, yet in the thirty minutes that had passed since leaving the estate Claire had hardly uttered a single word.

"What's wrong?" Martin asked, attempting to break the barrier of silence between them.

Claire simply stared out the window.

"I don't know about you," Martin continued, "but I tend to find conversations much more interesting when two people are talking. Then again, I could just sit here chattering away, but I'd probably end up in an argument with myself, and spend the next ten minutes trying to figure out just how the hell *that* happened. If maybe you were to contribute a sentence or two …"

"They're going to kill her, you know."

Stunned by the blunt finality in Claire's tone, Martin struggled with his reply.

"You can't allow yourself to believe that, Claire. If Amanda's there we'll find her and we'll bring her home. No one's going to kill her. I promise you that."

"You shouldn't make promises you can't keep Martin."

"That's a promise I intend to keep."

"Justin said Krebeck is ex-CIA, right?" Claire asked.

"Yes. So?"

"That means he's trained to kill, and to cover his tracks as if he wasn't even there. He won't hesitate to kill Amanda when he realizes we've come for her. And then he'll kill us, because he knows the first thing we'll do when we're safe is contact the police. Only this time they'll lock him up so long daylight will become a foreign concept to him, and I don't think he's going to let that happen too easily. Do you?"

"Maybe you're right Claire. Maybe the odds are against us. But frankly I'd rather face those odds than walk away. I've got questions too. Krebeck may be my only link to finding Melanie, and I'll follow that bastard straight into Hell to find out if he's the missing piece of the puzzle I've been looking for. So I guess as much as I'm helping you, I'm helping myself too."

Martin's cell phone rang.

"Yes?" His voice was stern.

Mark hesitated. "You okay?"

"Yeah." The reply was curt, to the point.

NIGHT CRIES

"Doesn't sound like it," Mark insisted. "You sure everything's alright with you and Claire?"

"Sorry Mark," Martin said. "I guess you caught me at a bad time. Everything's fine."

Mark persisted. "If you've got differences Martin settle them now. You both need your head in the game if we're going to pull this off."

"I told you," Martin replied, "everything's fine. What's on your mind?"

Martin's tone told him he was lying, but the point had been made. "Call me when you get to Kettawash," Mark said. "By the time we reach Sonoma State we'll have had about a twenty-minute head start on you. I want to meet up and compare notes after we've worked the campus."

"No problem. I'll call you soon."

"Good. And Martin?"

"What?"

"I understand the pressure you're under right now. Believe me, I do. But you and Claire have got to keep it under control and not let it get the better of you. If we turn up nothing and end up chasing ghosts then we'll follow up on the next lead, and the lead after that. Alright?"

"Thanks Mark. I needed to hear that."

"Tell Claire to keep her chin up. Everything's going to be okay."

The sign for Kettawash drifted past as Martin exited the interstate, slowing to negotiate a gauntlet of flashing construction lights as repair crews tended to steaming ribbons of freshly pressed asphalt. Maggy sat up, sniffing the air. She snorted her disapproval of the foul smell.

"Keep your eyes open for a gas station," Martin said. "I could use a cold drink and Maggy should probably stretch her legs, if you know what I mean."

Claire looked over her shoulder. "Need to tinkle, girl?"

Maggy wagged her tail, panting eagerly.

Martin smiled at Maggy in the rear view mirror. "Wash your hands when you're done, fur face," he said.

"One mile ahead."

"Say again?"

"The sign we just passed says there's a gas station one mile up the road."

"We passed a sign?"

"You were looking at Maggy. I guess you didn't see it."

"You're *sure*?"

"No," Claire teased. "I see gas station signs where there are none. You know," she whispered in her best Haley Joel Osment impersonation, *"I see dead people!"*

"Very funny," Martin said.

Claire pointed to the Exxon sign as they rounded the turn. "See? Just where I said it would be."

"You are truly gifted."

Martin pulled into the gas station, parking between two tractor-trailers. Maggy jumped into the front seat as Claire opened her door, following her into the parking lot.

"I better put her on her leash," Martin said, snapping the metal clasp to Maggy's collar. "Grab a bottle of water for me. I'll take her for a quick bathroom break."

"Okay." Claire reached inside the SUV and picked up her dossier. Martin looked at her quizzically.

"What? Just a little light bathroom reading!"

Martin rolled his eyes. "I'll meet you back here when you're ready."

After Maggy had found her favorite spots, Martin returned to the truck. A tall, bearded man dressed in baggy overalls and a worn t-shirt

NIGHT CRIES

stood by the driver's door, hands cupped to the window, staring inside. Maggy snarled and the man stepped back, suddenly aware of the dog.

"Something I can do for you mister?" Martin asked the stranger. Maggy strained on her lead, uncomfortable with the man's presence, baring her teeth. Martin considered commanding her to settle down, but dismissed the idea for the moment.

"Your dog ... is it dangerous?" the man asked.

"That depends. If you're asking me if she's trained to attack, the answer is yes."

"I don't like dogs, 'cept them that like me," the stranger said. "Got bitten bad by one once. Guess I ain't never much cared for 'em since."

Placing his hands in his pockets, the old man shuffle-stepped back to the front of an eighteen-wheeler. "Sorry mister," he said. "I was just looking at your car. I always wanted one of these but I suppose 'ol Nellie Blue here's the closest I'm ever gonna get to it." He patted the hood of his truck.

"This is your rig?" Martin asked.

"Yep," the man said proudly. "Bought and paid for twelve years now. Best maintained truck on the road, too. Do all the work myself. By my way of figuring, if I take care of her, she'll take care of me."

"Sounds like smart thinking." Maggy continued to growl, and Martin pulled gently on her collar. "Maggy: Control." Immediately the retriever lay down on all fours, facing the man.

"Say, she's smart. She a police dog?"

"Used to be. Now she's just a big baby. But she still remembers her training."

"Sorry. I really didn't mean to make her mad."

"I know you didn't," Martin said. "You're welcome to take a closer look inside, if you like." Martin released the locks with the remote control.

The old man walked to the Navigator. "You sure? I don't want to be a bother or nothing."

"No problem at all."

The man wiped his hand on his shirt and held it out. "My names Bentley ... Earl Bentley."

Martin shook his hand. "Pleased to meet you Mr. Bentley."

Claire walked across the parking lot to the two men. Maggy sat up, wagging her tail, assured the situation was under control and the danger she sensed had now passed.

"Claire, this is Mr. Bentley," Martin said. He pointed to the tractor-trailer. "He owns Nellie Blue here."

"Pleasure to meet you ma'am," Earl said. Extending his hand to Claire, he accidentally knocked the file folder out of her arms. The contents of the dossier fell to the ground. A gentle breeze lifted the sheets into the air, scattering them around the front of the rig, sending them scurrying across the parking lot.

"Oh my gracious! Look what I've done," Earl Bentley exclaimed. Together they corralled the loose papers and photographs. "I'm terribly sorry, ma'am. My wife always said I was clumsy enough to crack the eggs inside a chicken, given half a chance."

Claire laughed. "It's alright Mr. Bentley. No harm done."

Atop the pile of papers, the old man noticed the surveillance photo taken at the University. He stared at the picture.

"Something wrong, Mr. Bentley?"

"No ma'am."

"You're sure?"

"Well ... it's just ... I think I might know him."

"Know him? What do you mean?"

NIGHT CRIES

Earl Bentley pointed to the thin man standing in the background of the photograph to the left of Amanda.

"That guy."

Martin handed him the photo. "Take a closer look Mr. Bentley. You say you know one of the men in this picture?"

"Well, *know* him may not be the right way to put it, but he looks the splitting image of a fellow I gave a ride to a few days ago. His car had broken down about ten miles north of here. I saw him walkin' along the side of the road, so I offered him a ride. Strange sort. Truth be known, he kind of made me a little uncomfortable."

"Why's that?" Martin asked.

"Hardly said two words to me the whole way. I offered to drop him here where he could call for a tow, but he said it wasn't necessary. Just had me drop him off on the side of the road. Then he walked in through the woods and disappeared. Strangest thing I've ever seen. I've been driving these highways over forty years and gave a lot of rides in my time, but no one ever made me wish I'd just as soon kept on goin' the way he did."

"And you're sure this is the man you gave the ride to?"

"Sure as I can be. Why? You and your police dog lookin' for him?"

"Yes, something like that. Would you mind showing us where you dropped him off?"

"Sure, if you need me too. I'm always willin' to help the police."

"We're not the police Mr. Bentley. But we are looking for this man, and your instincts were right. He is dangerous. We need to know where you saw him last. Will you help us?"

"Hell, yes."

"Then lead the way. We'll follow you."

\#

On the second ring Oyama answered his cell phone, though he never got the chance to speak.

"Mark, its Martin. Forget the university. We may have found Reginald Fallon. Meet us in Kettawash. I don't have time to explain everything right now. Just get here. As quickly as you can."

#

Nellie Blue, unhitched from the restricting weight of the tractor-trailer she had faithfully carried for the past twelve years, rallied up the country road, plumes of dust billowing behind her. Martin followed the sandy wake at a distance. Corn stalks raced past the windows, as though they were driving headlong into the fields rather than between them.

"So what happens now?" Claire asked, gazing through the breaks in the stalk rows rushing by. In the distance, a rugged mountain climbed into the sky. Near its peak, a family of hawks soared graciously on isotherms of crisp, cool air.

"What do you mean?"

"If Mr. Bentley's right and it was Reginald Fallon he recognized, what do we do?"

"We do as Mark said. We wait until the rest of the team arrives."

Claire sat silently for a moment, then spoke.

"I disagree."

"Too bad."

Turning in her seat, she faced Martin. "Martin, listen to me. We need to find out if this is even worth following up on first, don't we? If Bentley is wrong and we drag the others away from the university for nothing then we've wasted valuable time – time they could have put to better use where they are now, showing Amanda's picture

NIGHT CRIES

around campus. I say we take a look around. Not long – ten, maybe fifteen minutes at the most."

Martin said nothing.

Brake lights beaming through a cloud of brown dust, Nellie Blue rumbled to a gentle stop. A whooshing *hisssss* escaped the air brakes.

"Fifteen minutes," Claire repeated. "That's all Martin. Please?"

"I don't think that's a good idea," Martin said, turning off the ignition.

Opening his door, Earl Bentley grabbed the steel handlebar on the side of his truck and climbed down the driver's steps to the ground, walking back to the Navigator.

"There," he said, pointing to a narrow clearing in the woods on the opposite side of the road. "That's where I dropped him off."

"Are you sure that's the spot?" Claire asked.

"Oh, yes ma'am. Sure as my wife makes the best peach cobbler from here to Seattle. Let me show ya."

The elderly trucker walked across the road to the clearing. A cluster of branches, brittle and gray, slumped down over the trunk of a once noble willow. Earl Bentley folded back the branches to reveal a numbered sign affixed to a fence post.

"See? Mile marker 14.5. Up the road is 15, down the road's 14. When you drive trucks for a living like I do, remembering things like your last mile marker can save your bacon. Broke down myself once, years ago, on a back road upstate just outside Ettersburg. I got on my CB and gave the towing company the number of my last mile marker. They had me and 'ol Nellie Blue hooked up and on our way to a steamin' bowl of truck stop chili in next to no time. Yep, one thing I never forget are mile markers. And your man walked into the woods right here. At 14.5."

"You're a very astute man, Mr. Bentley," Martin said.

Earl Bentley beamed. "Well sir, coming from you, I'd say that's a mighty fine compliment."

Martin turned to hear Claire closing the rear cargo door of the Navigator. In her hands she held his camera. Around her neck hung a pair of binoculars.

"Seems like a beautiful afternoon for a walk in the woods, doesn't it?" Claire said with a smile.

"Nice try," Martin said. "I can practically see the wheels spinning in that pretty little head of yours. You heard what Mark said. We stay put until we have backup."

"Who said anything about needing backup? I simply thought we'd take Maggy for a stroll through the woods, snoop around, do a little birdwatching, take a few pictures, snoop around some more ... "

"Funny, you seem to be understating the whole snooping around part, or did you think I missed that?"

"*I am?*"

Martin sighed. "I suppose you're right. I can't see what harm we can get into by taking a few pictures. But not for long!"

"Half an hour ... tops."

"You said fifteen minutes."

"Twenty minutes," Claire pressed, "and not a second longer."

"I am in such deep shit."

"Yes, but at least you're in it with me."

"Wonderful," Martin replied. "I feel better already."

"Maybe it's none of my business," Earl Bentley interjected, "but are you sure you two are going to be okay?"

"Yes, thanks Mr. Bentley," Martin said. "We'll be fine."

Bentley continued. "It's just I grew up in these parts. I know the woods and the mountains 'round here so well you'd think spring water ran through my veins. I could see to it you don't get lost.

NIGHT CRIES

Believe me, these woods take on a whole different look when you're not sure where you're going."

"I don't know, Mr. Bentley."

"It's Earl. Truth be told, I'd feel mighty terrible if I watched you two set off on your own, then hear on the radio tomorrow the Forest Service is looking for ya 'cause you got lost when I could have done something to make sure that didn't happen."

"I appreciate your wanting to help Earl," Martin said. "I really do. And no offense, but it could be a bit of a trek. You sure you're up to it?"

Earl Bentley took off his worn New York Yankees baseball cap and pointed to his thin crown of white hair. "Here's a lesson for ya, young fella. Just 'cause there's a little snow on the volcano don't mean there ain't plenty of fire burning down below."

Martin laughed. "Point taken."

"Earl's right," Claire said. "We'd be a lot faster if we had a guide."

Bentley smiled and took Claire by the hand. "Your wife's right. Let me show you missie," he said, walking her along the beaten path past the mile marker, down the embankment to the edge of the forest.

"She's not my wi--," Martin called out from a distance. He shook his head. "Oh, what the hell!"

Looking back toward the SUV, Martin whistled through his teeth. Maggy popped her head up from the back seat.

"Come on girl!"

Maggy bounded gracefully through the open window and ran past Martin, barking down the path after Claire and the sprightly old trucker. "Stay clear of skunks, for Pete's sake!" he called, watching her disappear over the top of the embankment.

"There ain't much about these mountains I don't know missie," Earl said to Claire as he led the way through the dense underbrush.

"Spent my youth as a park ranger in Sequoia. Had to go in deep one too many times I'm afraid, lookin' for city slickers like you. Sometimes it turned out good, sometimes not so good." With fox-like dexterity, the old trucker clambered down a steep slope at the end of the path, holding Claire by the hand, using his body to protect her from falling.

"I don't know what it is with some folks when it comes to the woods," Earl continued. "People who can barely recognize one end of a tent peg from the other would come visitin' for a weeks vacation. I'm talkin' about otherwise intelligent folks … doctors, lawyers, businessmen. Seems they all think the minute they drive through the gates and set up camp they're Daniel Boone or somethin'. Lose all touch with their faculties. They don't know what they're up against in the wild, and believe me, it don't get any wilder than Sequoia."

"How do you mean?" Claire asked, stepping over a fallen branch.

"Well," the old man began, pushing aside a low hanging bough, "there was one couple in particular I remember. He was a Wall Street financier. She was a stockbroker." Bentley shook his head disapprovingly. "Arrived at the park in a Mercedes Benz, of all things. Now, I'm not sayin' just because they were young and from the city, and drivin' a snappy sports car, that that made them any less capable than the next couple. But all they could lay claim to for camping gear was a pup tent, a couple of backpacks, a portable stove and barely enough rations to last out the week. They became friendly with another couple a few sites over and announce they're goin' into the woods to do a little exploring. Said that they'd be back later that evening. Well, sure as you can figure, the next day came and went. When no one had seen 'em after three days we got the call. Rangers organized a search party. Found 'em two days later."

"Were they okay?"

"Nope. Dead. Both of 'em."

NIGHT CRIES

Claire pulled Earl Bentley by the arm. The old man turned around, facing her. "What happened to them?" she asked.

"We figure most likely they was attacked by a mountain lion, but with the state the bodies were in we couldn't say for sure. Could've been a black bear or a bobcat. They were in far deeper than they should have been. We checked their clothes and their packs. No compass, no GPS, no cell phone ... nothin'. They were lost, for sure. The one thing you gotta remember about the mountains and the forest in these parts: they don't care who you are, and they never forgive you for being stupid." Bentley waved his arm in a wide arc. "Take a good look around missie. Out here, you're on your own ... for better or worse."

Martin shuffled down the slope, finally catching up.

"Geez! Slow down a little. I could have tripped and broke my neck back there. Meanwhile, you two are off skipping through the woods like Bambi and Thumper."

Earl Bentley winked at Claire. "C'mon, Daniel Boone. You sure *you* can make it?"

Claire laughed, following the old man as he turned away, quietly chuckling to himself, marching up the slope with the determination of a seasoned footsoldier.

"Don't worry about me," Martin replied, dusting off the seat of his pants. "I can manage just fine."

Negotiating the forest proved to be an arduous task. Martin and Claire followed closely on the footsteps of the old trucker as he traversed blankets of fallen branches and slippery moss-covered rocks, stopping periodically to break a low-hanging twig or pick a flower from the ground and place it in the middle of the path.

"These are trail markers," Earl explained. "Remember to look over your shoulder when you set them so you know what the path looks like on the way out. And count your way from marker to marker. I'm puttin' one every ten paces. They'll help you find your way back if you get lost or confused. Just turn around and walk straight back. No dilly-dallyin' or veering off the path. And pick yourself up a good, sturdy branch when ya see one. Makes a great cane if you should trip and hurt yourself, or worse yet, break somethin'."

"One thing's for certain," Martin observed. "No one takes this route if they don't know where they're going."

"Damn right," Earl Bentley agreed. "I didn't see any other markers on our way in. The fella you're lookin' for knows these woods as well as I do. Maybe better. Let's just hope he's not one of those marijuana pot-growin', drug dealer types. They'll shoot you sure as look at you if they find you in their patch."

The old man stopped suddenly, looked down at Maggy, then back at Martin and Claire.

"Wait a minute. Your dog … she's one of them *drug* dogs, ain't she? That's why she responds to you the way she does. She's lookin' for pot plants." The old man leaned against the trunk of a tree. "That's why you're after this guy. He's a drug dealer. And that would make you federal agents, right? And you're not his wife. You're his partner!" The old man slapped his cap against his leg as though suddenly discovering a closely guarded secret. "Well, I'll be snookered!" he said with a wide smile. "I ain't never met any FBI agents before. Say, if I'm gonna be out here trackin' this guy, don't ya need to deputize me or somethin'?"

"Sorry to disappoint you Earl," Martin said, "but like I said, we're not with the police. Besides, if it were a grow operation we were after, we'd be ATF, not FBI."

"Well, if you're not the feds, then just who are you? And why is this guy so important you're carrying around a file on him?"

NIGHT CRIES

Claire walked to the tree against which Earl Bentley stood, snapping a small branch and bending it down, marking the path.

"You're right Earl," Claire said. "I suppose you should know who we are and why we're looking for this man. But what I'm about to tell you can't be repeated – not to anyone. Do I have your word on that?"

"Yes ma'am. As a gentleman and a former officer of the law. You can trust me."

"I believe I can."

"That might not be such a good idea Claire," Martin warned.

Earl Bentley slipped his cap back on his head. "It's up to you whether you want to tell me or not, little lady. I gave you my word. Can't do much more than that. Besides, I did what I came out here to do. You just keep markin' the path the same way as I showed ya and you'll be fine. You'll find your way back out. No problem." The old man sighed. "Well, I've got a sixty thousand dollar rig sittin' back there, and up until an hour ago that was all that mattered to me, next to my wife and her peach cobbler. So, if you've got no further use for me, I think I'd best be on my way."

The old man walked past them down the path.

"We think he and another man may be responsible for the disappearance of my sister," Claire blurted out.

Earl Bentley stopped in his tracks, turning slowly. "Disappearance … as in kidnapped?"

"Possibly, yes," Martin interjected. "If the man you gave the ride to is the same one we're looking for, and he's bunkered down somewhere in these woods, then I guess your knowledge of the area and ability to track him makes you our best chance of finding out exactly where he's holding up."

"Remember the picture we showed you?" Claire added.

"Yes ma'am," Bentley replied.

"He and another man are responsible for the deaths of hundreds of innocent people. We need to find out whether or not my sister is with them, and if she isn't, what they may have done with her."

Earl Bentley stood silently, then addressed Martin.

"You said ya weren't with the police, yet you're organized. Binoculars. Backpacks. I even saw what looked like a couple of bulletproof vests in the back of your truck. If you're carrying those around you're probably also carrying the firepower to go with them too. Am I right?"

"Yes," Martin answered. "You're right."

"Then I'll ask you again, and this time I want a straight answer. If you're not the police, who are you?"

"Martin runs a private organization that is helping me find my sister Mr. Bentley," Claire replied. "The police can't help me. Not even the FBI. They say there isn't enough evidence to open an investigation. But we have proof. The girl in that photograph is my sister, Amanda. She's the one we're looking for. It was taken two weeks ago by one of Martin's operatives at Sonoma State University. Two weeks ago! That means Amanda's alive, and we think she's somewhere in this area. This is the closest I've been to finding her in five years, and I wouldn't be here if it weren't for Martin's help and that of the people who work with him. And we're not alone. We're to meet up with the rest of the extraction team in an hour. I'd like to be able to tell them we've got a solid lead to follow up on. But we need your help."

"Extraction team?" Bentley said. "Last time I heard that I was in the military."

"It's what we do," Martin said. "We rescue loved ones who have been taken from their families or gotten involved with psychopaths like Fallon. Give them a chance to get their life back. To start fresh."

"That's this character's name then? Fallon? The guy I gave the ride to?"

"Reginald Fallon, to be exact."

"And he's got your sister?"

"We believe so, yes. He and another man, Joseph Krebeck. And maybe others besides Amanda."

Earl Bentley scratched his long, scraggly beard, contemplating the situation. "Well, I guess I have no choice here, do I?"

"There's always a choice Earl," Martin replied. "You can do as you said you were going to do and leave. We're thankful for your help either way."

"Nope," the old man sighed. "Not in this case. There ain't a choice anymore. I got a code to follow."

"Code?" Claire asked. "What do you mean, a code?"

"Truckers code," Bentley replied. "Never leave a lady in distress. So, I guess you could say I'm duty bound to see this through."

Claire kissed him on his cheek. "You're a very sweet man, Earl Bentley. Thank you."

Blushing, the old man leaned over, picking up a crooked branch from the ground. He tested its heft, trying unsuccessfully to bend it. Satisfied, he turned to Martin.

"Well, don't just stand there sonny boy!" he said, taking Claire's hand and marching up the path. "Ain't you learned nothin' I taught ya today? Get a move on! I ain't got all day! We'll mark our way in a little further, then head back to meet your friends."

"You're sure about this Earl?" Martin said. "You don't have to get involved you know."

"Hell, son, I'm already involved."

"Thanks. Under the circumstances, we really could use your help."

"Well, come on then," Earl Bentley said, pulling aside a swath of branches and helping Claire over a fallen log. "We're losin' light the longer we stand around here doing nothin'. The sun drops like a stone this time of year." He looked up. "With those clouds rolling in over the mountain the forest will be black in no time."

"On second thought, maybe we should head back," Martin said, observing the gray clouds inching over the mountain peak. "You've had your fifteen minutes, Claire. Besides, Mark's on his way. We need to hook up with the rest of the team and plan how we're going to deal with this. It looks like there's a lot more ground to cover than we anticipated, and like Earl says, it's already getting late. We're probably better off to conduct a grid search in the morning after we've mapped the area by sector. There's no point in fumbling around in the dark."

"The man's got a point," Earl said. "We ain't got any flashlights."

"Let's just see what's beyond the tree line," Claire replied, pointing to the edge of the forest. "Look, you can see the clearing from here. We can be there in five minutes."

"Sorry Claire," Martin replied sternly. "I don't care if it's five more seconds. I told you before, this is Mark's operation. You're along for the ride, remember? Frankly, so am I. He made it very clear to both of us your safety is my responsibility."

Claire turned, walking deeper into the woods. She picked a wildflower from the edge of the trail and dropped it at her feet.

"You heard what Earl said Martin. The sun's going down soon. We're wasting time."

"I don't care. We'll be back first thing in the morning. We know the way in, and the path is marked. Now let's go."

"Not yet."

"Perhaps you didn't hear me amidst the deafening silence, Claire. I said we're leaving … now."

"I hate to get in the middle of what clearly ain't my business," Earl Bentley said. "But maybe I can offer a compromise."

NIGHT CRIES

"I'm all ears," Martin replied.

Claire stood stone-faced on the path, looking back at the two men.

The old man produced a penlight from a small pouch attached to his belt and clicked it on. Its narrow beam was barely visible in the fading twilight.

"It ain't much, but it'll do for the next five minutes or so. The batteries are low, but it should give us enough light to find our markers if we lose the light completely."

"Alright," Martin reluctantly agreed. "But in five minutes we're out of here. Clear?"

Claire turned away, heading into the woods, offering no reply.

"Feisty young thing, ain't she?" Earl said to Martin as they walked together through the woods.

"No, she's just scared."

"Scared of what? Finding her sister?"

"Of *not* finding her."

"You really think this Fallon fella's the key?"

"Yeah, I do."

"Then we'll find him. Ain't nobody this old dog can't sniff out. Speaking of dog's ... where's yours gotten to?"

Martin whistled, and from a distance arose the sound of crackling leaves and snapping twigs. "Maggy ... *track*," Martin called out as the retriever ran alongside the two men, then bounded back into the woods.

"That some kind of command?" Earl Bentley asked.

"It used to be, when she was in active duty. Now it's more like *hide-and-seek* to her. If I tell her to track she'll stay out of sight but keep an eye on me from a distance. The same way a police officer covers his partners back."

"How come she's not still active?"

"Maggy was involved in a raid on a methamphetamine lab five years ago that went bad. The cops didn't know the bad guys had a pit bull inside when they broke the door down. It took one officer by the leg and brought him to the ground. As soon as it saw Maggy coming through the door it released the officer and went for her. The cop put six rounds into the pit bull. Maggy needed seventy stitches to close her wounds. She almost died on the table from the blood loss. Her career ended that day. They couldn't take the chance on her freezing if a similar situation occurred in future. That's when a friend of mine told me about her. I arranged to adopt her from the department, and we've been together ever since."

"I didn't think the police department used golden retrievers."

"Usually, they don't. Typically they use German Shepherds because of their intelligence, size and strength. Maggy's first master was a DEA agent, and she was just supposed to be a family pet. Out of curiosity he put her through some basic tests when she was still a puppy, and realized she possessed the ability to sniff out narcotics - meth and cocaine in particular. That's how she ended up in law enforcement."

Standing atop the crest of a steep hill and looking back from the edge of the treeline, Claire called out in an excited whisper. "Martin, come quickly. Take a look at this!"

The two men ran up the hill, standing beside her. Night had fallen. The magnificent glow of the moon silver-plated the valley below.

An enclave of buildings arose from the mist at the foot of the mountain, smoke churning lazily from a chimney in the largest structure. Candlelight danced in the windows.

A lone figure appeared, then disappeared between the buildings.

"There he is again!" Claire pointed. "Did you see him?"

"Yes, I saw him," Martin replied.

"That's Reginald Fallon!"

NIGHT CRIES

"Hard to tell from this distance," Earl Bentley added, "but if I had to guess I suppose I'd have to agree with you missie. Sure looks like him to me."

Claire took Martin by the arm. "We can't run the risk of losing him Martin. We need to know for certain if it is Fallon." Claire looked up at the bright moon. "What do you think Earl? Is there enough light to make our way back if we go down for a closer look?"

"Yeah," the old man agreed. "We'd be fine. As long as we stick together."

"Then let's check it out," Claire said, starting down the hill.

"Forget it," Martin called out. "I told you Claire, it's Mark's op. We go on his say-so, not yours!"

"I don't think anyone is going anywhere."

The voice came from behind. A man stepped out of the shadows into the light of the moon. In his hand he held a gun. Martin slipped his hand into his pocket, pressing a button on the remote control for the Navigator.

"Keep your hands where I can see them," the man ordered. "Down the hill to the compound. Move ... *now!*"

Martin recognized him from his picture. It was Joseph Krebeck.

12

MARK'S CELL PHONE rang as Kettawash came into view. Justin was calling from the command center. His tone was serious, anxious.

"Is Martin with you?"

"No. Karen and I are on our way to meet him now," Mark replied. "He called me forty-five minutes ago. Said he had a lead on Reginald Fallon. He wants us to meet him in Kettawash."

"Something's wrong, Mark. We picked up an emergency signal from the GPS transmitter in his SUV three minutes ago. He wouldn't have activated it unless he was in trouble. I tried his cell. Claire's too. No luck."

Mark pulled the truck to the side of the road. He struck the steering wheel with the palm of his hand. "Son of a bitch!" he said. "I knew something like this was going to happen." He stepped out of the truck and slammed the door closed. Dan and Cynthia pulled in behind the Suburban. "I told them specifically to wait for backup. Damn it!"

"I've got his position," Justin continued, ignoring Mark's anger. "Looks like he's about four miles outside Kettawash. I'm tracking your signal as well. By my estimate you're about fifteen minutes away from him."

"I'll call you back in five," Mark said. "I need to talk to the team. Don't take your eyes off that screen Justin!"

"Not a chance."

"*Five minutes*," Mark repeated. He hung up.

"What's going on?" Cynthia asked.

"Everybody gear up," Mark replied. "Vests and sidearms. And bring your night vision equipment. We've got more than the extraction target to deal with now. That was Justin. Martin and Claire might be in danger."

"What king of danger?" Dan said.

"Martin's emergency GPS has been activated. He called me earlier. Said they thought they'd found Reginald Fallon. Now I'm beginning to think Fallon found *them*." Mark checked his watch. "Let's hope we're not too late. Justin's going to lead us to their location via GPS. Follow me, and when we get there, remember: Keep your eyes open …"

" … and your head down," Dan finished, slipping his bullet-proof vest over his head, securing its velcro straps in place.

#

"Mommy, where are we going?" Blessing asked as her mother quickly buttoned her coat.

"We're going on a little adventure honey," Sky replied nervously, tying her daughter's shoelaces. "Daddy's going to take us on a little camping trip to the mountain. Like we did before, remember?"

"Y-yes," Blessing said. "But it was daytime, and we went swimming. It's too cold to go swimming at night, and it's dark. I don't like the dark – it's scary."

"There's nothing to be afraid of sweetheart," Sky lied. "Besides, part of the fun of camping is looking up at night and seeing all the stars. And you can't see stars during the day, can you?"

"I suppose not."

"Of course you can't, silly. Stars sleep during the day so they can stay awake all night."

"Why would they do that?"

"So they can watch over you when you sleep, and keep you safe in your dreams. Chin up."

"*Really?*"

"Really," Sky said, tying the strings of Blessings cap under her neck. "That's a star's job. And tonight, if you're especially lucky, you might even see shooting stars."

"What's a shooting star?"

"Those are very, very special stars. They're *magic* stars. If you see a shooting star and make a wish, maybe it will come true."

"I already have a wish."

"You do? Well, keep it a secret! Wishes won't come true if you tell …"

"I wish that you and me and Daddy will be together, forever and ever!" Blessing blurted out, arms stretched as wide as the tips of her tiny fingers could manage.

Sky pulled her daughter close, hugging her fiercely.

"Thank you baby," she said through glistening eyes. "That's a wonderful wish. Mind if we share it?"

"I suppose. But is it good luck to share wishes Mommy?"

"When they're wishes like that … absolutely!"

Shuffling up the stairs, Virgil entered the room. "You two almost ready?"

"Ready as we're going to be," Sky sighed. Virgil helped her on with her jacket.

NIGHT CRIES

"Good. Now listen to me, both of you. Everything's going to be fine. *We're* going to be fine. We'll get through this, just like we've gotten though everything else."

"I know," Sky said. "But right now I don't mind telling you - I'm scared to death."

"So am I. But we have no choice. Staying here isn't an option anymore. The cabin is the safest place we could be right now." Virgil picked up the bundle of food and clothes his wife had wrapped in a blanket, slinging it over his shoulder. "When we get outside, stay close to the wall of the building. There's a trail about thirty yards away. It leads into the woods. From there it's about a twenty-minute hike. Blessing, hold Mommy's hand and don't make a sound, okay? We've got to be *very* quiet."

"Like playing hide and seek!"

"Yes baby," Virgil replied, kissing his daughter on the forehead. "Just like hide-and-seek."

A familiar blanket of cool, mountain mist swirled at Virgil's feet as he opened the door and stepped outside with Sky and Blessing beside him. Dewdrops clung to the tall grass along the trail, glistening like strung pearls in the moonlight.

"Like I said, stay close."

"Virgil, wait!" Sky said, grabbing him by the arm.

"What's wrong?"

"Shhh! Listen … someone's coming." Sky pointed. "There! By the edge of the forest."

Four silhouettes stepped out from the perimeter of the treeline.

"Back inside … now!" Virgil said.

From behind the crack in the door Virgil watched the four figures walk single file along the trail, past his building and out of sight.

"Who are they?" Sky asked.

"Outsiders," Virgil replied. "Two men and a woman. And Prophet." He turned to Sky. Even in the shadows she could see the taught expression on his face. "He's holding them at gunpoint."

"Gunpoint?" Sky gasped. "What is going on Virgil?" She looked as though she were on the verge of crying.

Pulling her close, Virgil held his wife tightly in his arms. "I'm not going to let anything happen to us honey. Understand? *Nothing*. I promise you that. We're still leaving here ... tonight."

"But how? If we leave now we'll be seen for certain."

"We don't have a choice Sky. We have to get out of here, for Blessing's sake if for no other reason." Virgil paused. "Take Blessing back upstairs and wait a few minutes. I have an idea."

"What are you going to do?"

"Get help. I'm going to tell Reisa what's happening. Then I'm going to find out where Prophet's taken the Outsiders."

"But if he catches you ..."

"He won't. Besides, it's dark, and I'm on lamp lighting duty - remember? If I don't go they'll begin to wonder where I've gotten to, and they'll be suspicious for sure. This way no one's the wiser."

"I'm not sure about this ..."

"Look," Virgil replied. "I know it might not be the best plan, but it's my *only* plan." He kissed his wife goodbye. "Sit tight. I'll be back soon."

#

"Speak to me Justin!" Mark barked into his cell phone as he sped along the county road. "Tell me where the hell I'm supposed to be going here."

Adjusting the microphone on his headset, Justin studied the locator blips pulsing on the GPS base station monitor. "You should

NIGHT CRIES

practically be on top of him Mark. Your position locator is directly over top of Martin's signal. He's got to be there. Keep looking."

"You're not helping me much kid. It's pitch-fucking black out here. All I can make out is row upon row of godforsaken corn and ... wait just a minute ... I think I see his truck. Yes, okay, I've got him. I take it back. Nice work kid."

Jumping from the Suburban, Mark and Karen drew their weapons, taking cover behind the doors of the truck. Dan and Cynthia pulled in behind, and Mark heard a *thunk-thunk* sound behind him as they closed their doors. The Navigator was parked behind the cab of a transport trailer, the name *Nellie Blue* emblazoned across its wind dam. Mark looked back and pointed to Cynthia and Dan, motioning them to cover the cab while he and Karen proceeded to the Navigator.

Both vehicles were empty.

"This doesn't make sense," Dan said, returning his gun to its holster. "Martin left the Nav wide open. The back window's down and all his stuff's inside."

"Check this out," Cynthia added, holding up Martin's vest. "Claire's vest is in there too. Looks like his weapon is still in the lockbox."

"No skid marks," Mark said, inspecting the shoulder of the dirt road with his flashlight. "It doesn't look like they were forced off the road."

"Why would he be parked behind a transport in the middle of nowhere?" Karen asked.

"Good question," Mark answered. "My guess is he was following this cab."

"Do you think they were set up?" Dan asked.

"What do you mean?"

"You said Martin was outside Kettawash when he called and told you he was following up on a lead, right?"

"Yeah."

"So maybe the owner of this rig radioed the details of their conversation to someone else, like Fallon. We don't know how far the Brethren hand reaches in these parts. Maybe the lead Martin picked up was from one of their people. They convinced him to follow and wound up here."

"You could be right," Mark said. He paused. "Wait a minute. Wasn't Maggy with Martin and Claire?"

"Yes, she was," Cynthia said. "I saw her in the back seat when we were examining the map at the estate."

"Then where the hell is she?" Mark opened the back door of the Navigator. Maggy's leash lay in a rumpled coil on the floor. Kneeling down, he examined the ground outside her door. "No blood, so there couldn't have been a fight. Maggy's trained to attack on command. If someone had tried to take them by force Martin would have given her the word. That tells me they had no reason not to trust the lead." Mark looked toward the forest, panning the beam of his flashlight across the distant treeline. Shards of halogen light fell in fractures through broken limbs and fallen branches. "My guess is they're out there. Somewhere."

From the distance, a low growl. Red eyes glared back from the crest of the hill.

"Wolf!" Dan cried, drawing his gun, training it on the silhouette starting down the hill towards Mark.

"Hold your fire!" Mark yelled, raising his hand. Walking across the roadway, he stopped at the edge of the embankment. "Maggs? ... is that you girl?"

The growl abated. An uncertain whimper escaped the forest floor.

"It's alright Maggy. It's me girl."

"She's scared," Karen said, crossing the road and standing at his side. "Be firm with her Mark. She's confused. She needs to know you have control, and most of all that she's safe."

"You're right." Mark called out sternly: "Maggy! *Service!*"

Woof! came the reply, accompanied by a scuttling of leaves and twigs. The retriever bounded up the hill through the darkness and into the beam of the flashlight, rounding behind Mark, sitting by his side.

Karen knelt down and hugged her, scratching her head. "Good girl Maggs! Good girl baby!"

"You think she knows where Martin and Claire are?" Dan asked.

"We're about to find out," Mark answered. "Okay Maggy. We're counting on you girl."

Maggy looked up at Mark, cocking her head quizzically.

Mark commanded: *"Track."*

The retriever ran ahead several paces, then stopped and looked back.

"Find Martin girl," Mark said, following close behind. Maggy ran to the top of the embankment, waiting momentarily, then disappeared over the peak of the hill.

The team slipped into the black depths of the forest, following their canine guide.

#

Virgil tapped lightly on the door to Reisa's room and waited. As the door creaked open he forced his way inside, struggling past the big man.

"Come on in. Make yourself at home," Reisa scoffed, stepping out of Virgil's way as he brushed past. "Geez! What's eatin' you, anyway?"

"I need your help, and I need it now!" The words poured from his mouth. Virgil's usually calm demeanor had vanished. An uncommon measure of fear played in his voice.

"Alright," Reisa replied, placing his hand on his friend's shoulder and helping him to a chair. "That's good enough for me. But ya won't mind if I ask what the hell's going on?"

"Amanda is not Prophet's daughter. He killed her parents. Fallon's in on it too. Prophet's holding Outsiders hostage, and --"

"*Whoa!* Hold on partner," Reisa interrupted. "Slow down. Take a deep breath and start from the beginning. What's this about Prophet and Fallon, and ... *hostages?*"

"We need to get out of here, right now!"

"You haven't answered my question Virgil. What's wrong? Why are you so upset?"

"You're never going to believe me."

Reisa sighed. "Try me."

"I overheard an argument between Prophet and Fallon. Prophet admitted he killed Amanda's parents."

"He *what?*"

"It's true. She's not his daughter like we thought. He and Cassandra have been keeping her hidden from the police. Remember the reporter who took a picture of us at Sonoma State?"

"Yeah. What about it?"

"The newspaper printed that picture. Now Fallon is worried when the police see it they'll recognize Amanda and come looking for her. They'll speak to the reporter first, then to students at the university. That will lead them here, to us. We're in danger, Reisa. And I'm sure Fallon knows I know about Amanda."

"How could he? Did he see you?"

"No. I heard someone coming down the stairs from Prophet's building after I overheard the argument. Turns out it was Fallon. I

NIGHT CRIES

didn't want anyone to know I was there so I ran. I tripped in the dark and fell over a pile of wood behind the workshop. That's how I messed up my leg. He heard me fall and came looking for me, but I was able to stay out of sight. Fallon's mad, maybe Prophet too. He'll kill me if he finds out I know the truth."

"You've got to talk to the police about this Virgil," Reisa said.

"I will, but only after my family is safe. That's why I need your help."

"Name it. What do you want me to do?"

"Get them out of here. Tonight. Remember the old hunting cabin we found up on the mountain?"

"Yeah."

"Take them there. Stay with them until I arrive." Virgil removed the bloodied plastic strip from his pocket, handing it to Reisa.

"What's this?"

"I used it to tie off my leg and stop the bleeding when I cut myself. I threw it away, but Fallon found it. He left it hanging on the doorknob to my room. It's his way of telling me he knows it's me he's looking for."

"It's not safe for you to stay here Virgil. You should be coming with us."

"I know, but I can't leave Amanda behind. Her life may be in danger, and I can't walk away knowing that. I'll find her and convince her to come with us."

"How?"

"I don't know yet. Guess I'll deal with that when I have to. Besides you and Sky, I'm the only one who knows there's trouble. That should work in my favor. If I just go about my business quietly maybe I can buy some time."

"What about the Outsiders?"

"Leave that to me. Prophet and Fallon were leading them in the direction of the supply shed, which would be a likely place to keep them under guard. For all we know they're the authorities. I'll let them out. We could use their help."

"You're in no shape to do this on your own, Virgil. Let me help you. Then we can leave for the cabin with your family. Together."

Virgil smiled. "You're a good friend Reisa, but the best way you can help me right now is to get my family out of here. Don't worry about me. I can take care of myself. I'll meet you at the cabin in an hour."

Reisa stood up and slipped on his coat. "Don't worry about a thing Virgil. We'll be there. You have my word on that."

Virgil shook the big mans hand. "I know. Thanks." At the door, Virgil turned back. "Listen, Reisa. If anything should happen to me …"

Reisa cut him off. "Nothing's going to happen to you so long as you don't do anything stupid. You get my meanin'?"

"Just the same … watch over Blessing and Sky for me. Okay?"

"Like they was my own. Now get out of here. I got a job to do."

#

Hidden in the very shadows that earlier had proven to be his ally, Virgil pressed his back to the wall of Prophet's building, listening.

Distant footfalls. Moving away.

Peering around the corner, he watched his family and friend reach the end of the path and disappear into the woods. They would soon be out of harms way, safely tucked away in the mountainside cabin under Reisa's watchful eye.

The pain in his leg flared to life again. Virgil pressed his fingers around the pulsing area, massaging the wound. *Not now, dammit!* he

NIGHT CRIES

thought. He unwound the compress carefully, releasing the pressure on the gash. The bleeding had resumed. The lightheadedness he had suffered earlier was returning and he sat down, allowing himself a few seconds rest, once more battling the desire to slip into unconsciousness. Taking a deep breath, he braced himself against the searing pain to come, and reapplied the compress as tight as he could bear.

"Virgil? ... Virgil? ... Are you alright?"

The voice belonged to a young woman. She was kneeling beside him.

Arousing from his confused state, Virgil realized he had passed out from the pain. He lay on his side, slumped against the wall of the building.

"It's me ... Amanda." Amanda looked at the unraveled, blood-soaked compress on his leg. "Virgil, you're hurt," she said, putting her arm under his shoulder, helping him to his feet. "Come inside. Let me take a look at that leg."

"No ... time." Darkness threatened to envelop him again. Virgil struggled to hold it at bay.

"No time for what Virgil?"

"You're in danger. So am I. We need to get out of here. I was coming to ... help you." Virgil looked down at his leg. "Now it looks like it's your help I need."

"What are you talking about? We're perfectly safe here. You know that."

"I wish that were true, but it's not, and I can prove it. But you have to help me. You need to come with me. To the supply shed."

"Virgil, you're obviously not well," Amanda replied. "You're in no condition to be going anywhere. Come inside. Rest. I'll get Sky and explain you've been hurt. Then we'll get you back to your room."

"Blessing and Sky have left the compound. Reisa too. And they're not coming back."

"What do you mean?"

"I've been trying to tell you all along. We're in danger. I need you to come with me. Now!"

"I'm not going anywhere with you Virgil until you tell me what's going on," Amanda said defiantly.

"I will Amanda. Soon. I promise. But right now we have to get to the supply shed."

"What's so important about the supply shed that we have to go there this very second?"

"That's a question I'd like to know the answer to myself, Mr. Lutt."

Fallon and Prophet stood at the corner of the building.

"Virgil, Virgil, Virgil," Fallon mocked caustically. "I'm surprised at you. You struck me as an intelligent man, but it seems I was wrong. You just couldn't leave well enough alone, could you? Had to stick your nose in where it didn't belong."

"Let the girl go," Virgil said, hobbling in front of Amanda. "She doesn't know anything. It's me you want."

"How heroic," Fallon scoffed.

"It's too late for that Virgil," Prophet said.

"Will somebody please tell me what's going on?" Amanda said.

"There's no easy way to tell you Amanda," Virgil said. "Prophet killed your parents. I don't know why, but he did. Now they're afraid the authorities will come looking for you."

"Don't be silly," Amanda laughed. "Joseph would never do that."

"*Joseph?*" Virgil replied.

"You didn't know?" Amanda said. "Virgil, Joseph is my husband."

NIGHT CRIES

Fallon walked over to Virgil and leaned forward, whispering in his ear. "That's right. Her *husband.* And you know what? A wife can't testify against her husband."

"Maybe not," Virgil replied. "But I sure as hell can."

"Only one small problem with that," Fallon said, leaning forward, pressing his thumb deep into Virgil's wound. "Dead men can't testify."

Screaming in agony, Virgil crumbled to the ground.

"Take your hands off him!" Amanda cried, trying to push Fallon away. Grabbing her by the back of her neck, Fallon twisted her hair until she screamed. He threw her into Prophet's arms.

"Put your dog on a leash Joseph!"

"How dare you touch me!" Amanda screamed as she tried to strike out at Fallon.

"Shut up!" Fallon yelled as Prophet held her back. "You made this mess Joseph!" he said, pointing his finger at Amanda. "Clean it up. Once and for all!"

Pulling the semi-automatic from his waistband, he chambered a round and forced the gun into Prophet's hand.

"I tried to tell you but you wouldn't listen! She's a fucking liability! Cap the bitch, right now. Be done with it!"

Amanda turned to Prophet. "What are they talking about? What did you do to my parents? Tell me this isn't true. Tell me they're lying." She began to sob. "Look at me Joseph. Tell me ... *please!*"

Prophet stood before her in silence.

"What's the matter Prophet?" Virgil said, his breathing heavy. "Too much blood on your hands? It's a little late to be developing a conscience, isn't it? The girl wants an answer to her question. What are you waiting for? Tell her the truth, if you've got the guts."

"Shut up, Lutt!" Prophet replied.

"You know why he won't tell you the truth Amanda?" Virgil said, pushing himself to his feet. "Because he's afraid you'll see him for what he really is - a murderer." He turned to Prophet. "You took advantage of us ... all of us. You and your lackey here! Everyone believed you. But it was all a lie, wasn't it? Well, it's over. I'm leaving, and Amanda's leaving with me."

Prophet threw the weapon to the ground. "I'm sorry Amanda. Falling in love with you was not part of the plan."

"The *plan?*" Amanda cried. "Then what Virgil is saying is true? You killed my parents? You son of a bitch!"

Fallon picked up the gun. "Enough of this bullshit!" he yelled. "If you don't have the balls to do it, then I will."

"No!" Prophet cried, pushing Amanda to the ground, forcing Fallon's arm into the air. The two men struggled for control of the weapon.

"Amanda ... run!" Virgil yelled. "The woods ... run for the woods!"

"I can't," she cried, trying to stand. Fear held her down.

"You've got to! Run, and don't look back. I'll find you."

Fallon locked his thumb into the trigger guard of the gun, preventing it from firing. With a quick thrust, he rammed his knee into Prophets ribs. Prophet fell to the ground, clutching his side.

"On your feet! Both of you," Fallon yelled, grabbing Amanda by the arm, forcing the gun to her temple. "Or do I do her ... right here, right now?"

"Hurt her," Prophet gasped, rising to his feet, "and I'll squeeze the last breath out of you with my bare hands."

"You're forgetting which side of the barrel you're on," Fallon replied, waving the gun. "The supply shed. Move!*"*

#

NIGHT CRIES

"On three. Ready? One … two … *three!*" With a running start, Martin and Earl tried breaking down the door to the supply shed.

"It's no use," Martin said. "Must be a cross beam in place. We can't even budge it."

"Try this," Claire said, holding two wooden dowels in her hand. "It's all I could find. Maybe if you shimmied these through the cracks in the frame you can lift the beam enough to knock it out of its brackets."

"It's worth a shot," Martin replied. He handed the trucker one of the wooden sticks. "See if you can find an opening on your end."

The spacing between the planks of the old wooden door formed irregular channels between the timbers. Earl tried fitting the length of dowel between several boards, finally finding a space wide enough to accommodate the narrow shaft.

"Ready on my end," Martin said.

"Me too."

"We're probably only going to get one shot at this, so lets take it slow and easy. The beam's about ten inches wide. Claire, when Earl and I raise it clear of the brackets I'll give you the word, then push hard against the door. That should knock the beam away from the brace."

Claire stepped between the two men and placed her hands against the door.

"Alright Earl. Like I said, slow and easy."

Immediately, the dowels began to bend under the weight of the thick beam.

"Mine's too weak," Earl said. He could hear the sound of stressed fibers beginning to snap within the wooden shaft. "It can't take the load."

"Keep going. Just a little higher and we've got it. Get ready Claire. When I say push, *push hard*."

"It's breaking," Earl said. "I can't raise it any higher. It's stuck in the channel."

"I'm almost there," Martin replied. "Now Claire! *Push!*"

Claire pushed against the door as Earl's dowel broke in his hands. The beam teetered momentarily on the edge of its brackets, then fell back into its brace with a loud clatter.

"Damn it!" Martin yelled. "We almost had it. Try to find some more of those dowels Claire. We'll try again."

"Wait!" Earl said, raising his hand. He stepped back from the door. "Move back. Someone's comin'."

As shuffling footsteps stopped outside the shed door, the heavy beam rattled free of its brace. A voice called out to the prisoners inside.

"Step out, slowly," Fallon announced. "And if you have any ideas about rushing the door, forget it. You'll be dead before you see moonlight."

Martin, Earl and Claire stepped out of the confines of the supply shed and into the cool night air.

Claire recognized her sister immediately. "Amanda!" she cried. "It's me ... *Claire*. Thank God you're alright!" She tried to step forward to embrace her sister but Fallon blocked her path, training his gun on her. Martin pulled her back by his side.

"I *was* right," Earl Bentley said, pointing his finger at Fallon. "That's the fella I gave the ride to."

"And just who the hell are --?" Fallon said, turning his attention away from Claire. "Wait a minute ... I recognize you. You're that trucker."

NIGHT CRIES

"Guess I should have left ya right where I found ya," Earl Bentley replied. "Broken down by the side of the road. If I had, I probably wouldn't be in this mess right now."

"How very astute," Fallon replied. "I take it these are your friends. Let me guess ... CIA? FBI? INTERPOL?"

"Neither," Martin replied. He pointed to Amanda. "We're here for the girl. Let her come with us and we'll disappear. No one will know where you are. You have my word on that."

"Do you really think I'm that stupid?" Fallon replied. "The simple fact you were able to locate her means you've done your homework. You know who we are. That makes you a major liability. Besides Martin, I'm surprised you don't recognize me."

"How do you know my name?"

"Actually, I knew your wife and daughter quite well. Mind you, the last time I saw you you were laying on the ground. Remember the barn? Memories like that never fade, do they? Remember watching Anne leave? How she walked past you like you were a total stranger? I do. I was there. I'm the one who took her. Melanie too."

A vortex of memories whirled in Martin's mind with Fallon's words. *Little Melanie, alone and crying on the kitchen floor ... the surreal, chanting emanating from the barn ... the circle of hooded strangers ... Anne's vacant stare as she walked past him despite his pleas ... the final horrible blow to his head that left him unconscious and utterly alone ...*

"It was you?" Martin said breathlessly. "You took my family ... *my life.*"

"Yes, but for a good cause," Fallon replied nonchalantly.

"You mother --!"

"No, Martin!" Claire screamed.

Grabbing Martin by his outstretched arm as he lunged forward, Fallon stepped aside, twisting his wrist in a tight circular motion, sending Martin reeling head over heels to the ground several feet away. Walking to where he lay, Fallon buried the sole of his boot in his throat, pressing down with increasing force. Gasping, Martin clutched wildly at his leg until he thought he would pass out from lack of oxygen.

"No one *took* your life," Fallon said. Dirt fell in Martins face and eyes. "You fucking well gave it away." Releasing his foot, he stepped back. Rolling to his knees Martin grabbed his throat, sucking air in huge, gasping breaths, spitting the dirt from his mouth.

"You're a dead man, Fallon." Martin said feebly, forcing out the dry, raspy words, a trickle of bloody saliva hanging from his mouth to the ground. He looked up at his adversary. "I swear on Anne and Melanie's life, I'll kill you."

"Such a heartwarming sentiment," Fallon replied, unfazed by the cold threat. "I'll look forward to it. It'll be like a ... family reunion." Fallon turned his attention to Earl Bentley. "You ... trucker. Get over there and get him on his feet. Now!"

Earl walked over to Martin, helping him up from the ground. "Better do as he says, junior."

"I hope everyone's feeling energetic," Fallon said, clapping his hands together. "We're going for a little walk. Joseph, can you manage Lutt?"

"He's no problem," Krebeck replied reluctantly.

"Good. Then you lead the way. I'll keep an eye on our newfound friends. Take them to the cabin."

With Fallon's words, Virgil's legs grew weak.

God no! Not the cabin!

13

MAGGY STAYED AHEAD of the team, tracking through the dark forest until she arrived at the edge of the clearing where she lay down, an alert to her human companions she had reached her destination.

Dan and Cynthia remained with Maggy, taking cover behind the treeline at the edge of the woods. Moving along the inner perimeter of the forest, Mark and Karen observed the moon-shadowed buildings of the Brethren compound, jutting out of the ground like tombstones in a cemetery: cold, dark and silent.

Mark's voice crackled in the headsets of the team members. "Team two: Position report."

"Hard to say," Dan replied, surveying the meadow below for signs of activity. "Looks quiet enough, but I can't tell. Going to night vision."

"Copy that," Mark said. "Everyone, eyes on."

Dan slid his goggles in place, watching the mountain come to life. A family of deer, their presence previously undetectable in the dark, grazed in quiet solitude at the foot of Mount Horning. Suddenly aware of intruders in their midst, the buck raised it head and stopped chewing, looking in the direction of the forest. Instantly it bolted, followed in leaps and bounds by the rest of the herd.

"Did you see that, Mark?" Dan asked.

"Yeah. Karen and I are going to try to get closer. Maybe we can see what spooked them."

"Copy that. Let us know when you're in place and we'll assume your position."

Mark motioned to his partner. "Follow the path as far as you can. Let me know what you see."

Karen nodded, heading deeper into the forest.

Maggy growled. "Maggy ... *Control*," Dan said, trying to hush her.

"What's with Maggy?" Mark asked.

"Don't know. She jumpy as hell."

"Jumpy my ass. Something's got her bugged."

Karen's voice interrupted the channel. "We have movement. Southeast sector. Heading this way. Seven by my count."

"Confirming your visual," Dan replied, adjusting his goggles. "Copy that. I make five males, two females." He pulled the case photo from his pocket, examining it.

"Sonofabitch," he muttered. "Mark, you're not going to like this."

"I'm listening."

"It's Martin and Claire. Looks like they found our extraction target before we did."

"Amanda's with them?"

"Affirmative. Our unfriendlies too. Krebeck's up front with two unknowns. Fallon's got his six o'clock. He's armed."

"What about Krebeck?"

"Can't confirm if Krebeck's carrying or not."

"Alright," Mark replied. "Hold your positions for now. We can't risk any sudden moves with Martin and Claire in the line of fire. No one engages unless absolutely necessary. Clear?"

NIGHT CRIES

"Copy that," Dan and Cynthia replied.

#

"Where are you taking us?" Claire asked, trudging along the narrow path into the woods.

"Shut up and walk," Fallon replied.

"You can't be stupid enough to believe people won't come looking for us," Claire pressed, "or to think they won't find us."

"Bad for them. Guess that'll just add to the body count."

Turning, Martin looked back at Fallon. "Where's my daughter?" he demanded. "Where's Melanie?"

"Damned if I know," Fallon replied.

"Why won't you tell me?"

"What's the point?" he said casually. "You're never going to see her again anyway."

"Then it shouldn't matter to you to tell me, should it?"

Fallon paused. "Uganda, last I knew."

"Uganda?"

Fallon scoffed. "Please, Belgrade. Do I look like the fucking daddy type to you? Taking your kid was never in the plan. I could give a rat's ass about your brat. It was Anne that was important. The kid was baggage. But Anne refused to leave the country without her, so we took her with us."

"Where did you take her?"

"Does it matter?"

"It does to me."

"It shouldn't."

"Humor me."

"I don't know," Fallon replied. "Some orphanage. Sacred Light Mission - something like that. I dumped her with the nun's. Gave 'em some bullshit story about her mother being killed by guerrillas in the north."

"And they believed you?"

"Of course they did. They had no reason not to. Christian missionaries, especially whites working in-country, were disappearing every day. The LRA were wiping out entire towns. The Sisters had become so accustomed to taking in survivors and the homeless they didn't bother to ask questions anymore, and I'm sure you can appreciate the fact I wasn't particularly interested in whether or not the kid was getting tucked in at night. It was getting a little hot down there for us, and I'm not referring to the temperature."

"So I heard," Martin replied. "Selling out your country ... that's got to make your mother proud."

"Wake the fuck up, Belgrade!" Fallon replied. "Our politicians sell us out every damn day and get filthy fucking rich in the process. You think any of us down there really gave a shit? Krebeck and I weren't alone. Everyone was on the take. We just got busted anteing up a little info in return for a piece of the action. That's all."

"And aiding a murdering dictator in the process."

"A minor detail."

"I don't get it," Martin said. "You had top-secret security clearance, working under a presidential directive, and you all but pissed on the flag. You could have had your choice of any cushy job in the agency when the assignment was finished."

"Fuck the agency. We had the chance to live out the rest of our lives in style, so we took it."

"Yeah. Except your master plan was so well conceived you ended up enemies of the state. What a stroke of brilliance that turned out to be."

Ahead, Virgil stumbled and fell.

"On your feet, Lutt!" Fallon called out.

NIGHT CRIES

"I ... c-can't ... feel my leg."

Running past Martin to the fallen man, Fallon delivered a heavy kick to the side of his body. Virgil attempted to roll, to deflect the blow, but his damaged leg would not allow him to move. As though receiving an electric jolt he screamed, arching his back and collapsing to the ground.

"I said get your ass off the ground!"

Earl Bentley stepped between Fallon and Virgil. "Pretty tough for a pissant with a gun," he quipped, clenching his fists at his sides. "Maybe you'd like to try this old trucker on for size. I'll even give ya the first one free."

Fallon chambered a round, smiling. "You want a shot at the title?" he said, pressing the gun under Bentley's chin, forcing his head up.

Bentley struggled to reply. "Like I said, nothin' but a pissant. A gutless pissant."

Fallon removed the weapon from Bentley's chin. "I haven't got time for you now old man," he said, "but trust me, before the night is through, you and I are gonna dance."

"It'd be my pleasure."

"Now get him up," Fallon demanded, walking away.

"He ain't goin' anywhere, junior. Neither am I."

"Now you're really beginning to piss me off, grandpa!" Fallon yelled, grabbing Claire by the arm, pulling her out of the line, jamming the barrel of the gun against her temple.

"You have exactly five seconds to get your new found friend mobile or I reduce our happy hiking party by one. Four ... three ... two ..."

"*Fallon ... no!*" Amanda cried.

"Alright!" Bentley screamed. "Ya made your point." He knelt beside Virgil. "Leave the lady alone!"

Fallon pushed Claire aside and walked back to Earl Bentley. "I told you. Don't fuck with me, old man. Next time you don't get a count, understand?"

"Yeah, I understand."

"Good. Now let's go."

Martin helped Earl get Virgil back on his feet. "Don't worry mister. We got ya," Earl said.

"Thanks," Virgil replied, wincing. "I think he busted a rib."

"Better a rib than dead," Martin replied.

"Yeah, I suppose," Virgil said, hobbling along the path between the two men. He looked over his shoulder for Fallon as they approached the edge of the woods. "He's on the run, isn't he?" he whispered.

"By more organizations than you'd care to know," Martin replied. "Do you have any idea who you're involved with?"

"Until last night, no. But now I do."

"Fallon and Krebeck are walking laundry lists of criminal charges," Martin replied. "Escaping lawful custody, kidnapping, murder, espionage, treason ... take your pick."

"I shoulda kicked his ass when I had the chance," Earl Bentley said.

"That makes two of us," Martin replied.

"You came to arrest him, didn't you?" Virgil said.

"No. We came for Amanda."

"I heard them talking," Virgil confessed. "Krebeck killed her parents."

"Yes, we know. When this is over, would you be prepared to testify to that in court?"

"Absolutely," Virgil replied.

"Good," Martin said. "Then try to keep your cool. Help is on the way."

NIGHT CRIES

"You got somethin' up your sleeve I don't know about, junior?" Bentley quipped, "'cause as far as I can see, we're pretty much on our own out here."

"Yeah, I do," Martin said. "When Krebeck surprised us back in the forest I activated an emergency locator in my car. It's like a panic alarm. People from my office are already in the area looking for us. They'll find us – soon."

Bentley smiled. "You might just earn that merit badge after all."

"Just keep your eyes open, and be ready for anything. When it goes down, it'll go down hard and fast. You take care of our friend Virgil here. I'll watch out for the girls."

"You got it."

"If your friends can help us," Virgil said, "They better get here soon. We can't go to the cabin."

"Why not?" Martin asked.

"Fallon doesn't think I know about it, but I do. My friend is there … and so is my family. I told them about Krebeck and Fallon and what I had overheard. I sent them there for their own safety. Now I think I may have ended up getting them killed."

"No one's going to die tonight, Virgil," Martin replied. "Not your family, not us. I guarantee that."

"I wish I could believe that. I want to do something to help … to protect my family ... but I can't. Look at me … I'm useless. I can't walk, much less fight back."

"You just hang tough my friend," Earl said. "I'll do your fightin' for you. That includes lookin' out for your family. Everything's gonna be okay. You'll see."

"Everbody hold up!" Krebeck yelled as they entered the perimeter of the forest. "Stay where you are!" He walked to the end of the line, gesturing to Fallon. "Come with me."

The two men stepped a safe distance away from the group where their conversation could not be heard.

"What's going on?"

"Look straight at me," Krebeck whispered. "Don't look around."

"Okay," Fallon complied. "Why are we stopping?"

"We've got trouble. About one hundred yards to your left. In the woods."

#

Crouched behind the base of a tree, Mark placed a call on his cell phone.

"This is Pike," the voice answered.

"Jonathan, it's Mark. Joseph Krebeck and Reginald Fallon ... you want 'em back?"

"Hell, yes." Pike replied. "Hot or cold. Makes no damn difference to me."

"That's what I figured you'd say. I need your help pal, and I need it *yesterday*."

"Name it."

"We've found your boys. But if we move in now our target's gonna die. How soon can you deploy a tactical unit to my coordinates?"

"I've got a hot chopper and live-round team on the tarmac, as we speak. They're scheduled for a training exercise, but I can prep them en route. Where are you?"

Mark read aloud his GPS location to the CIA Special Operations Commander.

"Christ! You mean these bastards have been in our backyard all along?"

"I'm afraid it looks that way Jonathan," Mark replied.

NIGHT CRIES

"Well that just plain pisses me off," Pike said. "Inform your people we're on our way."

"Tell your pilot to look for several small buildings near a clearing at the base of the mountain," Mark said. "I can't risk a landing flare. You'll have to use infrared to locate our heat signatures."

"How long can you hang in?"

"Not long. They're on the move."

"Consider us in the air," Pike replied, hanging up.

#

Creaking open the cabin door, Reisa peered out into the rain-soaked forest. Droplets of water fell from the leaves on the trees, smacking loudly on the rickety wooden verandah and pooling on the path, streaming down the mountainside, drowning out the peaceful silence of the night.

He looked back at Sky.

"Cold?"

"Freezing!" she replied, her arms wrapped around Blessing, keeping her warm. The little girl sat in her lap, playing happily with her doll.

"Sorry I can't make the place more comfortable. I can't risk a fire. No one's supposed to be here. The smell of the smoke would be a sure-fire giveaway where we are. Anyway, Virgil should be here any minute. Then we'll decide whether to stay or go."

"I know," Sky replied. "Thank you for helping us, Reisa. Virgil should think himself lucky to have a friend like you."

Reisa shrugged. "I gave him my word I'd keep you both safe, and that's exactly what I intend to do. Besides, there ain't nothin' he wouldn't do for me. Just try to stay warm, best you can anyway.

We'll be out of here soon." He looked at Blessing as she played, talking quietly to her doll.

"How're you doin' sweetheart?"

"Fine," Blessing replied, stroking her doll's hair. "But Miss Emily's getting a cold."

"Really?"

"Yup. She's got the sniffles. And she's been coughing a lot, too."

"Well, you tell Miss Emily to keep herself wrapped up nice and tight in her blanket," Reisa said, playing along. "Soon as Daddy gets here we'll take you both someplace warm, and she'll be feeling better before you know it. Okay?"

"I guess," Blessing hesitated. "Where is Daddy, Uncle Reisa?"

Branches cracking, on the path beyond the sound of the falling raindrops.

"Sounds like him comin' right now honey," Reisa said, turning to Sky. "I'm gonna see if he needs help. You two stay put. Don't open this door until I get back. Understand?"

Sky nodded. "Be careful, Reisa."

"Nothin' to worry about. I'll be fine." Reisa pulled his jacket collar tightly around his neck and stepped outside, closing the door behind him.

A cold wind blew down the mountain and through the trees as Reisa walked down the path. The chilly night air passing through his jeans made him shiver.

The cabin's too damp and cold for Sky and Blessing, he thought. Got to get a move on … tonight.

The muddy path was slick from the rain. A fallen tree limb lay by the side of the path. He picked it up, using it for support as he negotiated the treacherous terrain. Several times along the way his makeshift cane saved him from falling as he stepped into unseen potholes, or slid over lichen-smoothed rocks hidden beneath the thick

NIGHT CRIES

black mire. Reaching a bend in the path, he stopped and listened. The forest felt preternaturally still, as though on guard.

"Virgil?" Reisa whispered. "Where are you?"

A figure, steeped in purple shadows, approached from the foot of the clearing, gradually walking into view.

"Geez!" Reisa exclaimed. "What took you so long? I was beginning to get worried that somethin' might have happened to …"

Stepping out of the shadows, the harsh glare of the moon glinted off the barrel of Fallon's gun as he trained it on the big man.

"Somehow I just knew you'd be as stupid as Lutt," Fallon said, advancing up the path until less than a few feet lay between the two men. "To assume otherwise would be an insult to my intelligence."

Reisa looked past Fallon to the small group assembled behind him.

"It's true Reisa," Virgil called out to his friend. "Everything I told you … about Prophet and Amanda … it's all true!"

"*Shut him up!*" Fallon yelled over his shoulder, his eyes never wavering from Reisa. "Now," he continued, "you're going to head back the way you came. My guess is you know about the cabin, so you've just been elected tour guide for this romantic evening stroll."

"That ain't gonna happen," Reisa replied firmly. "So why don't ya just put the gun away before ya shoot yourself with it."

Fallon ran his fingers through his wiry hair with feigned exasperation, "Now that is simply *not* the response I was looking for." Pointing the gun at Reisa's leg, he fired.

Reisa cried out, the bullet tearing through his leg, sending him crumpling to the ground.

"No!" Virgil screamed, trying to break free from Earl Bentley and Martin. "*Reisa! Reisa!*"

Reisa lay on the ground, unconscious.

Fallon walked back down the hill, facing the group. "Listen to me!" he yelled, pacing up and down the line. "I warned you, all of you ... do *not* fuck with me!" He pointed to Reisa, his body on the ground, still. "That man is going to bleed to death tonight because he was a fool! Unless you want the same to happen to you, I suggest you do exactly as I say. Now, *move!*"

Virgil shuffled along the path, looking down at his fallen friend. "Oh God, I'm sorry Reisa," he said. "I'm so sorry!"

#

"We have shots fired Jonathan!" Mark Oyama said into his cell phone, trying to mute the anxiety in his voice. "Where the hell are you guys?"

"Shot's fired – Roger that," Pike acknowledged over the thrumming of the helicopter blades. "ETA six minutes. Can you confirm if any of your operatives are down, Mark?"

"Unknown at this time," Oyama replied. "We don't have a clear visual on the subjects."

"Are you in a position to engage?"

"Not without creating a hostage situation."

"Then you've got to hold firm, my friend. We'll hit the ground running as soon as we're there."

"If you're not too late," Mark replied.

Pike turned to the pilot. "Get us the hell out to those coordinates!" he yelled.

"I'm doing my best, Commander," the pilot replied.

"Then do better, dammit!"

Abruptly, the engine revved, and the nose of the chopper dipped down, picking up speed.

"Sir," the pilot yelled. "Time to target is three minutes."

"Copy that," Pike confirmed. To his men he yelled, "Lock on. Stand by for my go signal."

NIGHT CRIES

Fastening their safety harnesses, the four members of the tactical team stood two aside on the landing rails of the helicopter.

"Two minutes to target, sir!"

"Roger that!" Pike yelled. "Get me a heat lock on the objective."

The Bell LongRanger swooped sharply over the peak of the mountain, beginning its descent to the Brethren compound.

A narrow red laser beam struck the ground, measuring the distance below. "Clear to deploy in 300 feet," the pilot yelled. "220 … 100 … 45 … Teams are good to go, sir!"

"Copy that," Pike replied. "Insertion teams … *GO! GO! GO!*"

Releasing their rappelling ropes, watching them fall into the darkness below, the tactical team zipped down their lines, landing on the ground, quickly spreading out, weapons covering the perimeter of the compound as the helicopter touched down. Pike jumped to the ground through the open door.

"Oyama, do you have your eyes on?"

"Roger that," Mark replied, watching the helicopter land. "Hostiles and friendlies have entered the woods. Have your team advance to our location."

"Copy that. On our way."

#

"Wait here Joseph, and keep an eye on them," Fallon said, training his weapon on the front door of the cabin. "I wasn't expecting Stone, and we sure as hell don't need any more surprises. I'll check it out. Wait for my all clear, then bring them."

"Maybe we should just keep moving, Reggie," Krebeck replied.

"And go where?" Fallon said angrily. "Fuck it! We do this now, then we're done with it. The two of us can manage fine on our own, but if we take them with us we're as good as dead."

"What do you want to do?"

"Lock them in the cabin."

"Then what?"

"Burn it. Like Kampala. No witnesses."

#

"There's a cabin beyond the ridge," Karen radioed to Mark. "That's probably where Krebeck and Fallon are taking them."

"Are they mobile?"

"Negative. Fallon has separated himself from the group, checking out the cabin. Krebeck's guarding the others."

"What about Martin and Claire? Are they okay?"

"I think so."

"And Amanda Prescott?"

"She's with Claire. Wait a minute, Mark … Fallon's on his way back. He's moving them into the cabin. If I can just get a little closer I can take him down."

"Negative!" Mark replied. "CIA tactical is moving in as we speak. Hold your position and stand ready. All teams confirm."

"Copy that," Karen replied.

"Affirmative," Dan responded. "Cynthia and I are in position."

"Good," Mark replied. "When this goes down, I want your focus on getting to Martin, Claire and Amanda, and extracting them to a safe zone."

"Roger that," Dan said. "Ready when you are."

Mark turned to Pike. "Are your men in position?"

"Yeah."

"They understand Krebeck and Fallon are the objectives?" Mark continued. "I don't want my operatives or any civilians caught in the line of fire."

NIGHT CRIES

"Don't worry. They're clear on the targets. Quick and clean - that's how we operate."

"These bastards have gotten away before. Remember?"

"Not this time."

"Good enough," Mark said. "Then let's do it. From here on in it's your op Jonathan. Good luck."

Pike placed his hand on the microphone collar around his neck. "This is alpha team leader. We have a GO order. We are clear to engage. I repeat – *we are clear to engage.*"

#

"Everybody in," Fallon yelled. "Keep moving!"

Krebeck ushered the group through the door of the small cabin. Martin and Earl helped Virgil into a chair in the corner of the room, his teeth chattering, violent spasms involuntarily racking his body. A blanket lay crumpled on the floor between the chair and the wall. Amanda wrapped it around Virgil to warm him as Claire removed his blood soaked compress, examining the wound. Turning to Martin she said, "This man has lost a lot of blood. He's going into shock. We need to get him to a hospital right away. His leg is badly infected."

"You're the doctor," Krebeck said, watching Fallon lift a kerosene lamp down from its hook on the wall of the tiny cabin. "Deal with it."

"I'm a psychiatrist, not a physician," Claire responded bitterly. "I'm sure you're aware of the difference."

Fallon stood at the open door, looking out into the dark forest. He turned around in time to see Earl Bentley running at Krebeck.

"Look out, Joseph! Behind you!"

Turning too late, the old trucker tackled Krebeck, knocking him to the ground. Before he could subdue the writhing man, Bentley slumped to the ground, rendered helpless by an unseen, crushing blow.

"Get up, old man!" Fallon said, training his gun on his forehead. Slowly, Bentley rose to his feet, massaging the fiery pain emanating from the back of his neck.

"Damned if I'm gonna just watch you walk out and leave us here," Bentley said. "I know what you're planning to doing with that lamp. You're gonna burn us down."

Krebeck moaned as Fallon helped him to his feet and out the cabin door. "Anyone moves an inch," Fallon said, "and I'll kill you where you stand!"

Setting down the lamp, Fallon picked up a broken branch from the ground. "Get the door Joseph."

Fallon wedged the thick branch under the narrow gap at its base as Krebeck closed the door.

"It won't hold for long," Fallon said. He smashed the kerosene lamp against the door. "Stand back." Aiming for the metal door handle, he fired. The spark from the ricochet of the bullet ignited the fluid, engulfing the door in flames. Within seconds, the front of the cabin had become an inferno.

"Come on, Joseph. Let's get the hell out of here!"

Yelling from the forest. Voices echoing from all directions.

"Federal agents! ... Throw down your weapons!"

"Damn it!" Fallon cried. "I warned you this would happen! Didn't I?"

He placed his gun behind Krebeck's head and pulled the trigger. Krebeck's body shuddered as he slumped to his knees, arms hanging limply at his sides, blood streaming down his face and chest, spilling over his thighs, pooling at his sides. Lifting Krebeck's lifeless body off the ground, Fallon dragged it across the path, heaving it against the cabin. He watched the body slide down the flaming wall, falling

NIGHT CRIES

on its side, blocking the door, staring in death at its executioner, the fire slowly swallowing it, legs first, then hands, arms, chest and head.

"Fuck you Joseph," Fallon said, spitting at the fire-ravaged corpse.

Behind him, footfalls. Crashing through the branch-strewn forest floor.

His pursuers were closing in.

He ran past the blazing cabin, through the fog of billowing black smoke, and down the mountain path.

#

"Keep you hands where I can see them!" Mark yelled, approaching the motionless figure laying on the trail ahead of him.

The body stirred, then moaned.

Oyama crept closer, training his gun at the center of the man's body. He lay on his side, his shallow breath pluming across the damp ground.

"Please ... *help me.*"

"Who are you? Give me a name!" Mark demanded, rolling the man on his back, searching him for a weapon.

"Reisa ... Reisa Stone. I've been ... shot ... F-Fallon ... sh-shot me."

"Where have you been shot?" Mark said.

"My ... leg."

Warm blood oozed from a stain on the man's pants. Mark tore open his jeans. Reisa cried out as Mark turned him on his side, checking the back of his leg. The exit wound appeared clean.

"You're lucky," Mark said, gently placing his leg on the ground. "It's a through and through. The bullet came straight out after it went in. You're going to be all right. As soon as I can get you medical attention, I will."

"Got to ... get ... to the cabin," Stone said, trying to move, to get to his feet.

"Sorry pal," Mark replied, holding Reisa down. "You're not going anywhere in this condition. Lay still and try to stay calm. I'll be back soon. You're going to get all the help you need."

Stone grabbed Oyama's leg as he tried to leave. "My friends wife and daughter ... they're in ... *there*." He pointed to the cabin.

Mark looked up toward the crest of the hill. The tiny house had become a funeral pyre.

"Oh Jesus, *no!* Martin! ... Claire!"

Clambering hand over foot, Mark ran up the hill to the cabin. Hands of fire climbed the shallow pitch of the roof, clutching out angrily at the night sky. Glass from the tiny windows hissed and whined before exploding from the heat.

From inside the cabin, screams.

#

Crackling windows blew out around them. Whistling flames, feeding on air, quickly sucked the oxygen from the tiny room, filling it with smoke. Claire and Amanda huddled together at the back of the room with Virgil, hands covering their mouths, choking on the noxious fumes of burning wood and roof tar.

"It's no use," Earl yelled, pulling his scalded palm back from the door. "The fire's roasted the handle to the frame. The damn thing's fused together!"

"We better think of something fast or we're all going to die," Martin yelled above the roar of the fire. "This place won't last much longer!"

"*Martin! ... Claire! ... can you hear me?*"

The voice, Mark's voice, came from outside the walls of the cabin.

NIGHT CRIES

"Mark!" Martin yelled. "Yes, we can hear you. We can't get out." Martin looked across at Claire and Amanda, huddled beside Virgil, slumped in the chair, head forward, unconscious. "We're trapped, and we have a civilian down."

"Alright," Mark yelled above the raging flames. "Can you get to the back of the cabin?"

"Yeah! ... oh, *shit!*" Martin cried. The roof sighed, and fiery timbers fell into the middle of the room, knocking Earl Bentley to the ground. "If you've got a plan to get us out of here," Martin yelled, "now would be a good time to use it!"

An unknown voice called out. "Get as far away from the door as you can! Let me know when you're clear!"

Martin and Earl dragged Virgil from his chair as Claire and Amanda moved to the back of the cabin.

"Ready!" Martin yelled.

"Cover your faces!" Pike yelled into the cabin. "When you hear the blast, run like hell!"

Pike lobbed a concussion grenade at the base of the cabin door. Planks of ember-laden wood exploded, leaving a hole in the front of the cabin where the door once stood. Inside the room, a second fire-stoked beam fell behind them.

"*Clear!*" Pike screamed, running into the cabin. "Everyone out ... *now!*" He snatched Virgil from between the two men, throwing him over his shoulder. "I've got your friend," he yelled. "Now get the hell out of here!"

Martin and Earl helped Amanda and Claire out of the burning building, into the welcoming arms of Karen, Dan and Cynthia.

Pike lay Virgil on the ground. He began to sputter and cough. Slowly, he came around.

"Sky ... Blessing ..." Virgil said in dry, whispering tones. "Where is ... my family?"

"Easy," Pike said. "Take a few deep breaths. Get your strength back before you try to talk."

Virgil pushed his hand aside. "No! I've got to find them! They were supposed to be in the cabin. They must be with Fallon!"

"That's a negative sir," Pike's team leader replied, kneeling beside the two men. "Team two has been tracking the subject. He's alone and on foot. They can't get a clear shot. The fire made sub-light vision impossible. Our glasses are useless."

"There's only one place he could go," Virgil whispered. "One place you'd never think to look for him."

"Where's that?" Martin said.

Virgil pointed. "Off the main trail, along the side of the mountain. There's a cave."

"How do we find the entrance?"

"Look for The Twins."

"*The Twins?*"

"Two granite pillars, about four feet high and a foot wide. They stick up out of the ground a few feet in front of the entrance. Find the Twins, you find the cave."

"That has to be where he's headed," Martin said to Pike. "Take it easy Virgil. Don't worry. We'll find your family."

"Be careful," Virgil said. "The ledge in front of the entrance is narrow. One wrong step and …"

"I'll be fine. You just rest up." Martin stood, turning to Mark. "I'm going after him."

"The hell you are!" Mark replied. "Pike's men will track the bastard down."

"Fallon's mine, Mark. The son of a bitch murdered my wife and kidnapped my daughter!"

"I can't let you go after him Martin."

NIGHT CRIES

"You don't have a choice!" Oyama's words fell behind Martin as he ran down the trail to the break in the path.

Mark yelled to Dan. "Follow him, and don't let him out of your sight! *Not for a goddamn second!*"

14

THE VAN IN the laneway ...
  Melanie, crying on the kitchen floor...
  Mysterious chanting ... then the coming of darkness...
  'Mellie! Where are you?... Oh God, no! Melanie!'...
  The voice on the end of the line: "I'm very sorry Mr. Belgrade. The identification is positive. The dental records are indeed those of your wife, Anne ..."

Spectral images and disembodied voices fueled Martin as he raced along the mountain path, dodging overhanging branches and bone-snapping rocks. In the distance, a pair of stone pillars jutted from the ground like ancient tribal markers.

The Twins.

The sound of running through the treeline above him. Dry twigs and branches cracking underfoot. Suddenly, silence.

Creeping past the stone slabs and along the narrow ridge, Martin reached the mouth of the cave and stepped inside.

Out of the darkness came the unseen blow, striking him hard in the chest, reeling him backward from the force of the impact. Losing his

NIGHT CRIES

footing on the broken ledge he slid over the edge of the cliff, clutching desperately at the outcroppings of tree roots and deadwood, his entangled arm violently ending his descent. Swinging back and forth he stared helplessly down at the mountain floor as loose particles of sand and gravel streamed over the ledge. He looked away, avoiding the assault on his face and eyes. Finally, he looked up. Fallon stood above him.

"No way you're getting off this mountain Fallon," Martin yelled. The pain ripping through his shoulder was unbearable, but he refused to allow Fallon to see the extent of his injuries on his face or hear it in his voice. "Too many people want to see you pay for what you've done. Especially me."

"Forgive me if I fail to give a shit," Fallon called down. "But from my elevated perspective, I'd say my chances are actually pretty fucking good."

"I'm warning you," Martin said, struggling for a foothold on the cliff face. "Give it up. As much as I'd like to put a bullet in your head myself, the Agency has other plans for you."

Fallon sat down at the edge of the cliff, comfortably crossing his legs.

"Guess they're going to have to find me first though, aren't they? Too bad they don't know the tunnels inside these caves like I do. They go off in a dozen different directions you know. It's one of the reasons Joseph and I decided to call this little piece of heaven home. So we could get out in a hurry, in case someone like you came snooping around. By the time they even find this cave I'll be history." He stood. "Oh well, gotta go. Time's a wasting, and as they say, there's no rest for the wicked. I've got to admit though, I really wish we could have spent more time together. I rather enjoy our little conversations, though they're always much too short. Come to think about it, last time I saw you there really wasn't much time to chat either, was there?"

"Go to hell, Fallon."

"Oh, come now Martin. No need to be so bitter. There's no reason we can't leave things on a high note. Besides, we can both honestly say some of our fondest memories are ones we share together, don't we?"

"Meaning?"

"Why, fucking your wife, of course."

Martin struggled with his good arm to reach the ledge of the cliff. "You're a dead man Fallon!" he yelled.

"Maybe one day Belgrade, but not today. See you around."

From behind, a low growl. Thick … guttural.

"Goddamn wolves," Fallon said, chambering a round in his gun. He turned to face the animal, and was surprised to see a golden retriever crouched in front of him, jowl quivering, teeth bared, eyes aglow in the white light of the moon.

"What the hell?"

Martin recognized the growl. "Maggy!" he yelled. "*Action!*"

Instantly, Maggy responded to the command as years of training had taught her.

Gun …

Danger …

Protect …

Action! …

Maggy leaped forward as Fallon raised his gun to shoot. Too late, the retriever struck him hard in the chest with her powerful front legs, chasing him down, forcing him backward, sinking her teeth first into his arm and then his leg, forcing him to drop his weapon. As though sensing the nearness to the edge of the cliff, Maggy pressed ahead in her attack. Fallon fell back, arms flailing helplessly in the open air as he toppled off the cliff, screaming as he fell past Martin, landing on the rocks below. Peering over the ledge, Maggy whined.

"It's okay girl," Martin said, stretching his good arm up towards the ledge. "Maggy ... *Retrieve.*"

Reaching down, Maggy fixed her teeth into the sleeve of Martin's jacket, digging her paws into the ground, backing up until Martin had cleared the edge of the cliff and rolled onto the ledge. Breathless, he lay on his back as Maggy cleaned the dirt off his face with her wet tongue.

"Thanks fur face," Martin said. At the sound of her master's voice Maggy whined excitedly, licking faster still.

"Okay, okay," Martin laughed. "I agree. Let's get out of here."

Raines met Martin on the trail beside the Twins. His face was cut and bleeding badly.

"You okay?" Martin asked.

"Yeah, I think so." He pointed in the direction of the ridge. "Bastards have the woods booby-trapped. I was up there, following you. Next thing I knew I was flat on my back. Must have tripped a wire. Damn branch nearly took my head off. Sorry Martin. Guess I screwed up."

"Forget about it. What about Claire and Amanda? Are they alright?"

"A little shook up I suppose, but generally none the worse for wear."

"And Krebeck?"

"Dead. Fallon killed him."

"Proof there *is* a God. The son of a bitch got what he deserved."

"No argument here."

"What about the others in the compound ... Krebeck's followers. Any reason to be concerned about them?"

"Doesn't look like it," Raines replied. "Judging by their response to the cabin fire they didn't have a clue what was going on. They all seem pretty shook up."

"What about Virgil's wife and daughter?"

"Who?"

"The man I helped out of the cabin who'd passed out from the smoke. He told me they were supposed to be in the cabin, but they weren't."

"I haven't seen them Martin."

"Then we better move. I promised Virgil I'd find them, and I'm not about to let him down. Radio Cynthia and Karen. Tell them to keep their eyes open and comb the woods. Let's hope they didn't meet up with one of your booby-traps."

"I'm on it."

#

Running along the path in the direction of the glowing embers that had once been the cabin, Martin and Dan met Karen and Cynthia on the trail.

"What have you got?" Martin said.

"Nothing south of the cabin," Cynthia replied.

"The woods are clean," Karen added. "We've checked everywhere."

"Then check them again. They've got to be out there somewhere. Find them. Set up a grid and search the area."

In the distance, the *thup-thup-thup* of the helicopter engine began to whine as its rotors sliced through the night air. Through the treeline a strobe light flashed on its underbelly.

"Sound's like the assault team's moving out," Martin said.

NIGHT CRIES

"Local cops and paramedics are on their way, but Mark insisted Mr. Stone be airlifted to hospital," Dan replied. "Poor bastard's lost a lot of blood. Keeps drifting in and out of consciousness."

"Is he going to make it?"

"Yeah, he should be fine."

"Good," Martin called back, running along the path towards the clearing. "I need to get to that chopper before it takes off. Bring Virgil's wife and daughter to the compound when you find them."

"You got it," Raines said.

#

Claire rushed to Martin as he and Maggy ran towards the helicopter.

"Are you alright?" she said, throwing her arms around him.

"Yeah, I guess so."

"Did you find Fallon?"

"More like Fallon found *me*."

"And?"

"Dead," Martin replied. "But if it weren't for Maggy, I'd be the one laying at the foot of the mountain. She saved my life."

Kneeling down, Claire kissed the retriever on her forehead. "Thank you girl," she said. Maggy chuffed and rolled onto her back, legs lolling, a bellyrub all the reward she desired.

Oyama ran towards Martin, ducking his head below the churning blades of the helicopter.

"Pike's men are recovering Fallon's body. You hurt?"

"No, I'm fine."

"Good. Raines just called in. They found the woman and the girl in the woods. They're safe and sound. They're bringing them back as we speak."

"That's great news, Mark. Virgil will be glad to hear they're okay."

"Yeah," Mark smiled." It's kind of nice when the good guys win, isn't it?"

"Damn right."

"Well, I better help Pike wrap this thing up. I'll tell him to get statements from you later. Take Claire and Amanda and get the hell out of here. You could probably use some rest, and a hot meal."

"Thanks. We'll do just that."

"Ain't nobody leavin' until I've had the chance to say goodbye," Earl Bentley called out, walking over to Martin and Claire. "What'd I tell ya little lady? Never mess with the code."

"I know," Claire smiled. *"Never leave a lady in distress."* She gave the old man a hug and kissed him on the cheek. "I don't know what else to say, except thank you. You put your life on the line for us Earl. That's more than anyone could ever ask for."

"Wasn't nothin," Bentley replied, "but if the wife ever found out she'd probably kill me herself." Martin and Claire laughed. "Speaking of my wife," Bentley continued, "she's probably wondering just where the hell I've gotten to. Guess I better be on my way too."

"You sure you can find your way out?" Martin asked.

Bentley glared at Martin and winked at Claire. "Mile marker 14.5. Through the woods on your left. Follow the broken branches and markers. Didn't you learn anything I taught ya tonight junior?"

"You have no idea," Martin called out, watching the old man walk into the woods. "Thanks Earl. You can back me up any day."

Martin turned to Claire and kissed her. "Come on," he said. "Let's get out of here. I think we've seen enough of this place to last a lifetime."

"I couldn't agree more," Claire replied over the roar of the helicopter, watching it lift into the air.

NIGHT CRIES

#

Martin knocked on the door to Claire's room. She opened it quietly.

"Sleep okay?"

"Pretty good, I guess." *No bad dreams*, she thought to herself. *For the first time in years, no nightmares.*

Martin glanced inside the room. "How about Amanda?"

"Not so good, I'm afraid. She tossed and turned all night, but I guess that's to be expected after what she's been through."

Martin was wearing his jacket and jeans. At the floor by his feet lay an overnight bag. Claire glanced at the clock. It was nine a.m.

"Where are you going?"

"The airport. I'll be back in a few days."

"What's going on?"

"I've booked a flight to Uganda. I'm going to look for Melanie."

Claire stepped out of the room, quietly closing the door behind her. "Let me come with you," she said.

"Don't be silly Claire," Martin replied. "You've just found your sister after being apart for years. You don't want to come with me."

"Yes Martin, I do. If it weren't for you I would never have found Amanda. Now it's my turn to repay the favor. To help you find your daughter. Besides, Justin and Cynthia told me she'd have to stay here for a while for observation and treatment."

"Yes. Like I said, they'll want to take her through a de-programming process."

"My point exactly. She's in safe hands. And besides, you don't have to say it for me to know how much you need me right now."

"I won't argue that," Martin agreed. "Alright. The plane leaves at noon. Think you can be ready to leave in an hour?"

"Forty-five minutes."

"Even better."

#

As Claire sat on the edge of the bed, Amanda stirred, conscious of her presence. Gingerly, she stroked an errant strand of hair from her sisters dampened brow.

"Good morning, sleepyhead."

Amanda sat up, surveying the room. "Where am I?" she said. "What am I doing here?"

"It's okay," Claire replied. "No need to be concerned. You're among friends. You're safe now."

"What about the others ... Virgil, Sky, Blessing ...?"

"They're fine. The authorities told me they'd be well cared for."

"I want to see them Claire," Amanda demanded. "I want to see for myself that they're alright."

"I'm sorry, honey. That's just not possible right now."

"Why not?" Amanda pressed.

Claire sighed. "The police have a great many questions to ask, for which only you and your friends have answers."

"Such as?"

"Learning more about Joseph Krebeck for a start," Claire replied, "and what went on at the compound where we found you."

"*Prophet*," Amanda corrected her. "His name is *Prophet*. You're not allowed to call him Joseph. *No one is!*"

"No honey, it's not. His name is Joseph Krebeck, and he's been on the run from the police for a very long time."

"You're lying."

"I wish I was Amanda, but I'm not. There's a lot you probably won't want to hear about Joseph Krebeck in the coming days, but I can assure you it's all true. You know I'd never intentionally set out to hurt you."

"But you have! You took me away from my home, from the very people who loved me!"

"No sweetie, Krebeck took you away from us."

"Liar!"

"Amanda, please."

"You lie! *YOU LIE!*" Amanda screamed, striking Claire in the chest with her fists.

Claire grabbed her crying sister, pulling her tight, gently rocking her in her arms as she sobbed.

"I'm so sorry, Amanda. You're going to be all right. Everything's going to be all right. Just give it time, sweetie … give it time. Now lay back and rest. I have to leave you for a while, but you'll be in good hands. *I promise*. I'll be back as soon as I possibly can."

Amanda turned away, curling her bedclothes around her neck and staring out the bedroom window.

Standing up, Claire walked to the door. Turning back, she held her quivering voice in check.

"I know this is difficult for you Amanda, I really do. But soon enough you'll understand. I'm never going to let anyone hurt you again as long as I live. *Never*. You have my word on that. I love you Amanda. I love you very much."

Closing the door behind her, she heard her sister begin to cry. Then, in hardly a whisper, "I love you, too."

* * *

GARY COPELAND

KAMPALA, UGANDA

Sitting in the tiny reception room of the Sacred Light Mission, Martin and Claire awaited the arrival of the director. Adorning the cracked concrete walls framed photographs of the hundreds of children who had come through their doors over the years were neatly arranged. In the center of the wall, a large, gold-framed photograph had been mounted. The picture was of a former child of the mission, Areebe Tumba, seated in his office at the United Nations, the flags of Uganda and the UN behind him. Martin read the inscription: *For the Sisters and children of Sacred Light Mission. Beyond these walls destiny awaits. Seize it with the knowledge that life's truest rewards come not from what you receive from the world, but from what you are prepared to give to it.*

Martin turned as the director entered the room.

"Mr. Tumba grew up in this orphanage," she said, noticing Martins interest in the picture. "I am very proud of him. He came from nothing. Destitute. Abandoned as a child. Against all odds he became a leader, a statesman, a great man, and a symbol to all my children that one's dreams can come true if you possess the desire and the will." She extended her hand. "My name is Akimbo Ubweete. Welcome to Sacred Light Mission, Mr. Belgrade."

"Thank you for seeing me on such short notice, Ms. Ubweete," Martin replied. "May I present my close friend, Dr. Claire Prescott."

The women shook hands.

The director motioned to an adjoining doorway. "Please, come into my office. Tell me how I can help you."

Martin opened his wallet, removing a crumpled, worn picture. "I'd like to know if you remember this girl. It was taken five years ago. She'd be almost eight now. Her name is Melanie. She's my daughter."

NIGHT CRIES

The director studied the picture. "She does look familiar."

Martin felt his heartbeat quicken. "So she *is* here ... May I see her please?"

The director shook her head. "I'm sorry Mr. Belgrade. I said I remembered her. This girl is no longer at Sacred Light."

"Do you know where I can find her?" Martin asked.

"Yes, but I'm afraid I can't provide you with that information."

"Why not?" Martin replied.

"Because Melanie, as you call her, has been placed in foster care. And as you can appreciate, those records are confidential. I remember her because she was with us for such a short a period of time. Six, seven months - not very much longer. You see, most of the children we receive are teens. Melanie was the exception. She was *very* young. Few families wish to accept young adults. But for a three year old there was interest almost immediately."

"I understand your position Ms. Ubweete," Martin said, "but you must understand mine. Melanie was not abandoned. She was kidnapped. She was taken from me against my will and brought to your country by her mother, without my consent. The only reason she wound up in this orphanage is because her mother's murderer delivered her to you."

Martin removed a worn envelope from his jacket pocket, and deposited the contents on the director's desk.

"These are copies of her birth certificate, hospital records, a picture with me when she was just a newborn, family photographs, her second birthday party --"

"Mr. Belgrade, please," the director interrupted, placing her hand over his. "I have no reason not to believe your story. I know you wouldn't have come all this way to see me without a justifiable reason. But as I said, I cannot help you. Certain policies have been followed. Procedures put in place. And there is Melanie's foster family to consider."

"Foster family?" Martin replied incredulously. "Melanie doesn't need a foster family! I am Melanie's family! With all due respect Ms. Ubweete, I really don't give a damn about your policies and procedures. Perhaps I didn't make myself clear. My daughter was stolen from me, and if you know where she, is I demand you tell me."

"I do not appreciate the tone you are taking with me Mr. Belgrade." The director rose from her desk. "I'm afraid I'm going to have to ask you to leave."

"Leave?" Martin replied. "You can't be serious. Tell me where I can find my daughter – now!"

"Will it be necessary for me to call the authorities?" Ms. Ubweete said sternly, placing her hand on her telephone.

Martin sat in stunned silence, realizing he had just offended the only person in the world who could undoubtedly help him find his daughter. He rose to his feet, wondering if his knees would be strong enough to keep him from collapsing.

"N-no," Martin replied. "We'll see ourselves out. But I'm telling you now – I will be back."

Claire took him by the arm as she rose from her chair. "Are you okay?"

"No," Martin replied, walking out of the director's office. "No Claire. As a matter of fact, I'm not okay."

Leaning against the stone wall outside the gates of the mission, Martin drew his hands to his face and slid down the cold wall to the ground, weeping. Claire knelt down, cradling him in her arms, eyes glistening, her voice weak. Passersby glanced down, uneasily stepping past them.

"You can't give up Martin. Not yet. We know Melanie is down here somewhere. We'll find her. I know we will."

NIGHT CRIES

"I'm just not sure how much more of this I can take Claire," Martin said, struggling through his tears. "My little girl is ... *gone*."

"You've got to be strong, Martin. Now more than ever. But if you can't, then let me be strong for you. Like you were for me." Claire helped him to his feet. "Let's go back to the hotel. We'll contact the American Embassy and explain our situation to them. There must be some way they can intervene on our behalf."

Martin drew a deep breath. "Yes ... the embassy ... I - I suppose it's worth a try," he agreed.

"Damn right it is," Claire said, hailing a taxi. "Besides, we've got nothing to lose."

The cab pulled away from the mission, honking its horn, weaving through the throngs of pedestrians and taxi vans into the busy midday traffic filling the street. Martin turned in his seat, looking back at the gates of the mission.

Akimbo Ubweete stood at the gate, watching the cab as it drove away. She lowered her hand, as though having tried to signal the driver without success. She turned away.

"Driver, stop!" Martin yelled. "Stop the cab! Now, dammit!"

"What is it Martin? What's wrong?" Claire asked urgently.

Martin threw open the door and jumped out, running down the middle of the street, dodging honking horns and parcel laden pedestrians until he reached the gates of the Sacred Light Mission.

"Ms. Ubweete!" Martin called out.

The mission director turned at the front steps, slowly looking back. "Yes, Mr. Belgrade?"

"There's something you want to tell me, isn't there? Something about Melanie."

Slowly, she walked back to the front gate.

"Yes, there is." She handed Martin a folded slip of paper. Opening it, Martin saw she had written an address.

"I looked up the girl's file as you were leaving. I don't know why, but I did. That's when I noticed the note."

"Note?" Martin asked.

"The one I had made to myself years ago ... about this." The director handed Martin a wallet-sized photograph identical to the photo he had shown her in their meeting. "It was in her pocket when we bathed her and provided her with a clean change of clothes. The man who delivered Melanie to us told us her mother had been killed in an LRA raid." She pointed to Martin in the picture. "He said nothing about her father. We assumed both parents had been killed, not just her mother, which was obviously a terrible error on our part. I explained to the sister who had been placed in charge of this file that we have a duty to God and state to exhaust every effort to locate surviving relatives prior to placing a child with a family. I don't know why, but it appears we did not do our due diligence in this case. If you are her legal guardian, and I believe you are, then you have every right to be reunited with your daughter. I'm very, very sorry Mr. Belgrade. If there's anything I can do to make this any easier for you, I will."

"I don't know what to say," Martin said, his voice trembling.

"I can come with you if you wish," the director said. "I can talk to the family. Besides, nothing can be done until the authorities have been advised of the situation."

"Can you call them for us? Ask them to help?"

"Of course, immediately," the director agreed. "Come inside. We'll make that call right away."

NIGHT CRIES

The mission van was rusted out and barely roadworthy. Claire looked at the dirt road rushing past her through the gaping hole in the floorboards.

"I'm sure you're accustomed to better means of transportation than this, Dr. Prescott," the director said, glancing at Claire in the rear view mirror, "but I'm afraid we have to make due with what we have, and this is the best we can do."

"It's fine, Ms. Ubweete," Claire said unconvincingly. "Just ... fine."

The director smiled. "This is not America, Dr. Prescott. We are not as privileged as your people." She pointed to the hoards of street children seeking refuge from an afternoon shower under the galvanized awning of an abandoned building. "Unfortunately, as you can see, Kampala is a city of slums."

"These children ... they're homeless?" Martin asked.

"Yes. Too many to count, I'm afraid."

"But why so many? Doesn't your government have social programs to help them?"

"Our government does what it can, Mr. Belgrade," the director replied. "However, in a country ravaged by war and disease, progress is painfully slow, if at all noticeable. These children are on the street because they have no other choice. They've been orphaned - forced from their villages due to war or AIDS. It's a very sad situation, and an inhumane way to live. Do you see those garbage bags they are laying on?"

"Yes," Martin said.

"They're filled with cheap toys and cigarettes which they sell to tourists on the street during the day," the director explained. "At night they sleep together in packs, like wild dogs, just to keep safe."

"Surely there are other missions like yours who could care for them?" Claire asked.

"There are only so many people who are willing to help, Dr. Prescott. Sacred Heart alone relies on the support of nearly three hundred foster families. Some children simply can't be helped because families with healthy children refuse to provide foster care to those with AIDS, so they end up living and dying in the street, or joining the rebel forces in the north."

"You mean the LRA," Martin said.

"Yes."

"*LRA?*" Claire asked.

"The Lords Resistance Army," the director said. "They are responsible for the majority of the killing that happens in our country. They've forced the vast percentage of our people to abandon their homes and villages and flee for their lives. Those who remain are raped and slaughtered. The children are given one choice - join the resistance, or die."

The director turned to Martin. "If your daughter had not been brought to Sacred Heart when she was, Mr. Belgrade, I can assure you she would have been dead years ago."

Martin said nothing, watching the road unwind ahead of him, refusing to believe Reginald Fallon could have in some way contributed to saving his daughters life.

"It's just around the corner," the director said. "As you know, I took the liberty of calling the police and explaining your situation before we left. I was told a car would be dispatched to meet us there, just in case."

Martin felt his chest tighten. "In case of what?"

The director smiled faintly. "You have to appreciate this will not be easy for Melanie's foster parents."

"Of course," Martin said thoughtfully.

"They have been very good to her over the years Mr. Belgrade, treating her like their own daughter, keeping her safe from harm.

NIGHT CRIES

You've seen the other side of life here in Kampala. The street life. That could easily have been your daughter's reality." Ahead, the lights of a police car flashed at the end of a driveway.

The brakes of the van squealed to a slow stop as the director pulled in behind the police car. The officer stepped out, greeting them.

"I've been authorized to escort you back to your hotel and on to the American Embassy," the officer said to Martin. "Take your time. Just let me know when you wish to leave and you'll be safely on your way."

"Thank you," Martin replied.

Claire opened the side door to the van and stepped out. Walking over to Martin, she took his hand in hers.

"Are you ready for this?" Claire asked.

"I've never been more ready for anything in my entire life," Martin replied.

"Do you want me to wait here?"

"No," Martin replied, squeezing her hand. "Stay with me. I need you very much right now."

"You don't have to worry Martin," Claire said. She kissed him on the cheek. "I'm not going anywhere."

The door to the small bungalow opened, and a young girl stepped onto the dirt lawn, holding her mother and father's hands.

"Oh God, *Mellie!*" Martin said, stepping forward.

"Please, Mr. Belgrade. Wait," the director said, taking Martin by the arm. "Give me a moment to speak to her foster parents first. They always know this day might come, but when it does, it's never easy."

"Yes, " Martin replied. "Of course."

Accompanied by the police officer, the director walked to the front of the house and spoke to the couple. Seconds later the woman fell into her husband's arms, sobbing. The director motioned to Martin and Claire to join her at the front of the house. Melanie's foster parents stepped back inside their home, closing the door behind them.

"Melanie honey," the director said. "I have a surprise for you."

The little girl held on tightly to the director's hand. "A surprise?"

"Yes, a wonderful, happy surprise," she said, extending her hand to Martin.

Martin knelt down in front of his daughter, taking her tiny hand in his.

"Remember me, Mellie?" Martin said, choking back his tears. "It's me ... it's Daddy."

Melanie's eyes welled up. A single tear trickled down her face. Martin wiped it gently away.

"Daddy?" Melanie said.

"Yes baby?"

The little girl began to cry. "Mommie's dead."

"I know honey."

"Are you going to die on me too?"

"No Mellie," Martin replied, his voice breaking through his tears, hugging his daughter tightly. "Daddy's not going to die, baby. Not for a very, very long time."

The little girl paused.

"Daddy?"

"Yes sweetheart?"

"I want to go home now."

"Me too honey," Martin cried, picking his daughter up in his arms. "Me too."

ABOUT THE AUTHOR

Photograph by Fiona Brown

Gary Copeland resides in Pickering, Ontario Canada with his wife Fiona, and their dog, Casey.

NIGHT CRIES is his first published novel. He is currently at work on his next book.

He can be reached via the web at www.garycopeland.ca or directly at letters@garycopeland.ca